AF257018

I PROMISE YOU A HAPPY ENDING

Four tales of Happy-Ever-After gay romance.

GETTING TO BLOW YOU

Can one gay man defeat Alaska's hairpocalypse and win the sexy lumberjack?

The logging town of Sithole, Alaska, hasn't had a decent hairdresser in two years. The men look like shaggy yaks and the women…well, let's not get too personal…they're in desperate need of a makeover. The mayor has sent out a mayday call requesting a female hairdresser but when the new hair stylist arrives it's the outrageous rainbow tornado, Frankie Burfitt, escaping a cheating boyfriend. Neither side knew what they were getting into but, after some initial reluctance, the women of the town pack his salon, the timber men need a bit more persuasion, especially one particular swarthy lumberjack, Bud Guyder, who's caught Frankie's eye. Is the shy logger a little gay curious or just a tease?

"I thought this was the cutest snarkiest story I've ever read!!... a fun, sweet, light read."

BEAUTY AND THE LEASED

Wanted: Fake boyfriend. Paid Position.

Wealthy, clueless college jock himbo, Jerrod Spicer, will do anything to make his cheating boyfriend, Kyle, jealous even down to messing with the affection of nerdish Colm Bransfield, one of his biggest fans, all under the prying eye of bitchy gossip columnist, Cicely Trublood. Colm needs money for his college fees and Jerrod is prepared to pay handsomely, at least in cash, for Colm to pretend to be his rebound boyfriend. What could possibly go wrong?

"Written beautifully and the ending of this is the icing on the cake…Fantastic. Hot sexy scenes are smokin'."

ELEVATOR SHAFT

Every love affair has its ups and downs but this one comes with a stop button.

Micky is attempting to improve his young life while living on a run-down high-rise public housing estate but it's difficult when he has no qualifications and is studying part time to get his high school diploma. After he is stabbed during a homophobic attack he wants out even though he finds himself attracted to Trig, the leader of the gang that attacked him. Blond-haired Adonis, Trig, is an enigma until the day he traps Danny in the elevator of their building. Expecting the worst, Danny is surprised by the favor Trig asks.

"...not your mushy and starry eyed kind of love story, it is messy and has ups and downs.. And in the end, I was satisfied with every moment I read."

NICE WORK IF YOU CAN GET IT

For any sort of a future together they both have to come clean.

Vinnie is a loser in love and in life. Even with his good looks and hot body he's unable to keep a job for more than a few weeks and his love-life is in tatters. His friends see him as just another piece of ass and their idea of support is to try helping him into their beds. Only his arch nemesis, Zeb, won't indulge Vinnie's pity party. So why does Vinnie feel a strange attraction to the only man who won't indulge him – a man with secrets and a bad reputation?

"...one of those stories where you fall in love with the characters and you hope to see them again in a future story...I loved this book."

I Promise You A Happy Ending
ISBN 978-1-911478-42-3
Copyright©2019 Barry Lowe
Cover art and design by Dawné Dominique

Published by
Lydian Press 2019
Find us on the World Wide Web at
www.lydianpress.com

I PROMISE YOU A HAPPY ENDING

BARRY LOWE

Lydian Press

GETTING TO BLOW YOU

~

*T*hey say first impressions count. If that's the case, this spot obviously didn't care.

Welcome to Shithole, Alaska.

Of course the sign didn't say any such thing. It probably should have. We weren't exactly off to a good start. In fact, there was no sign, just an old tin shed with a weathered sign that spelled AI P T. No name of the town, no nothing. As for a Duty Free shop, well, at least they'd made an effort and there was an empty Coke machine, beside it a machine that had once dispensed comfort food, the remnants of which was a forlorn tube of Pringles wedged between the glass and the metal apparatus that used to hold the container of crisps in place. I noticed the Pringles had an expiry date that had come and gone five years before. The vending machine was the proud owner of a large dent where some poor soul, desperate for something to prevent starvation, had obviously attacked it to dislodge the Pringles.

Also missing from the AI P T With No Name, was my name. On a card. Attached to a welcoming committee of at least one who would transport me to my accommodation. On the backs of a team of donkeys if first appearances were anything to go by.

Not that I had a lot of baggage. At least not the kind that contains underwear and skin moisturizer. Did they even have a store where the essentials for modern life were readily available? I'm not so pampered I can't rough it for, say, an hour or two – three at the max – but there are some things that someone of my constitution cannot, and will not, live without. My heart sank as I looked about me. I'd been told everything would be supplied but I was beginning to have serious doubts.

As to the other type of baggage – the psychological – there was no escaping that. I had that tucked up in my memory and, not to be too dramatic, my heart had been shattered into a million tiny shards that still pierced my ventricles.

I'd been single for sixteen days twelve hours and a handful of minutes because my boyfriend, Fred, had shown our relationship was over when I arrived home to find him being right royally buggered by two sailors he'd picked up off the street. When I'd caught him at it, in our bedroom no less, he suggested I might like to avail myself of the divan for the night.

I was angry, I was upset, I was jealous. He could have asked me to join in, for Pete's sake. Not that we had an open relationship. But if you come home to find your boyfriend being double dipped the very least he could do was offer his mouth. Fred piled insult on top of cheating the next morning when he kissed the two seamen at the door telling them he'd see them that night for another round and to bring any mates along.

I suppose my face had a giant 'Why?' spread across it because he launched into a spiel that seemed to be too rehearsed to be spontaneous.

"Because sex with you, Frankie, is so boring I feel the only place appropriate for what we do is in a pine box six feet under the ground."

"I thought you liked the way I make love?" I whined.

"Yes, you're delightful at making love, but sometimes I wish you'd let yourself go and just have sex for a change. Pure animal fucking."

"That's not me," I said.

"So I discovered about the second week of our relationship."

"But it's taken you almost three years to tell me?" I was screaming now.

"No biggie, love. I picked up what I wanted on the side because you don't know how good it is on the ego when you're as old as I am to have someone as young and cute as you are on a leash."

He's fuckin' twenty-eight.

"I've been nothing more than an ego booster for all but two weeks of our entire affair?"

"That's right, lovey. You are one gorgeous piece of eye candy but you know what they say, too much candy is not good for you. I've gorged myself on you lovey…"

Like a fat bloated tick, I thought viciously.

"And not to put too fine a point on it, you are one gorgeous package, I'm the envy of all my friends, but that one delightful mouthful that makes up the package you keep tucked up so firmly in your skin-hugging revealing trousers, perhaps if you let it breathe every now and then. You know, let it loose on my ass, that sort of thing. You get my drift? Lovey, sometimes even the most promiscuous top likes to flip flop, especially with such a succulent cock as yours in the bed beside him. But…" He shrugged.

"You knew I was a bottom when we got together." I was so upset I forgot to add the word 'power' before bottom.

"What can I say? I thought you'd change. But you haven't. So now it's time to bid you adieu. If you wouldn't mind moving your belongings out in the next couple of days, I'd like you gone by the weekend. I have a big party lined up and you'd just be a distraction."

After that all I could do was jump at any opportunity to remove my miserable butt as far away from my very former boyfriend and his cheating ass, so when my boss, Mr. Redmond, proprietor of *Redmond's Radiant Hair Stylings* where I slaved as the Head Stylist with dreams of owning my very own salon, suggested I check the professional hairdresser's magazine under positions vacant, I grabbed the most recent copy that sat on the reading table already opened to thumb through it. No surprise there as Mr. Redmond – no first name had ever been mentioned – was Fred's best friend.

"There is one position that's so vacant they seem desperate and willing to offer the world to the right person," Mr. Redmond prompted a little too eagerly. It merely confirmed my suspicions that he was attempting to install Charlie, his latest boy toy, in my head stylist position among other more obvious positions he had in mind. Perhaps it was time to move on. The writing was on the wall and if I didn't jump ship voluntarily then I knew from experience, Mr. Redmond was quite capable of creating some sort of misdemeanor on my part to give me a nasty shove out the door. I'd seen him do it to other members of staff.

"What page?" I asked.

"Twenty-six," he said without having to think about it even though he was up to his rubber gloves in bleach which was doing nothing to help poor old Mrs. Broadwurst's alopecia problem but she would keep on insisting that she was a natural blonde while her hair kept falling out in clumps like weeds dug up in a garden.

Not only had he memorized the page number, he'd also taken the liberty of drawing a heavy black marker pen around the advertisement so there was no chance of missing it. Subtle.

"What do you think?" he asked without giving me time to even read the position vacant. Okay, the heading sounded interesting: *Hair Stylist wanted to manage Small Town Salon.* I'd be my own boss. And the salary was better than I was earning currently. Amongst the inclusions was a very generous relocation and accommodation package.

"It sounds too good to be true," I told him truthfully.

"Only one way to find out. Go phone them. Your next appointment isn't due for another fifteen minutes." Mr. Redmond really was pushing. But what the heck? The writing was on the wall through no fault of my own at *Redmond's Radiant Hair Stylings.* The advertised position was drool worthy, if I was honest, and I'd have the cash to leave town with the salary package that was far more than generous in comparison to the lousy wage I had in my current position. That and the working conditions made it sound more like a bribe. On the plus side, I'd have my own salon years earlier than I could ever have anticipated.

And, if they were really desperate, whoever 'they' were, I could probably squeeze a few more favorable extras out of them. I rang the number.

"And?" Mr. Redmond asked after I came back from the small room where we hair stylists took our break from the gossip and the smell of bleach that was enough to strip the hairs right out of your nostrils.

"It's an employment agency. Said if I want further details I'd need to come in for an interview. They're very secretive about the whole enterprise." That should have rung alarm bells.

"Listen, Frankie."

I hate it when people begin a sentence with those words.

If Mr. Redmond saw the concern in my face, he ignored it. "You're one of my favorite people. You're an incredible stylist. So creative, so…" he struggled to find the right word before he settled on "stylish. You deserve your own salon." He sounded as sincere as a used-car salesman trying to get rid of last year's stock before the new season's models arrived. It seems I was very much last year's model at *Redmond's Radiant Hair Stylings*. "We're not really busy today. Charlie can easily handle your bookings. Go and make that appointment for this afternoon. We'll cope without you for an hour or two."

I glanced at Charlie who couldn't hide his superior smirk to save his life, not to mention the clients in the chairs as well as those waiting their turn in the plush designer seats with their pod coffee lattes and macchiatos who couldn't look me in the eye as they listened to my very public humiliation. I thought I heard the raising of the guillotine blade in the back of my mind. I was being prepared for the chop.

***

Professional Hair Services had their offices in a smart redeveloped Victorian low rise that had been restored to its former glory on the outside but screamed nouveau wealth on the superstar architecturally enhanced interior. While the exterior was all heavy cleaned stonework which proclaimed its peerage with ostentatious sculptural embellishment, inside was all glass and chrome and light.

Their waiting area was glamorously uncomfortable with plastic chairs that gripped your buttocks in the same way maiden aunts would pinch young children's cheeks. There was a large counter at which an equally glamorous and equally plastic receptionist fielded calls and appointments. I handed her my CV.

"Please take a seat, I'll tell her you're here," she said, her lips barely moving.

There were a few women and a smaller number of men patiently waiting their turn while thumbing messages on their cell phones or else thumbing through a series of plastic folders with available positions.

I gathered from the one-sided phone conversations I overheard from the front counter, there was a high demand for temp hairdressers.

"Frankie," the perky receptionist called to me, "Ms. Harrigan will see you now. Office 9. It's marked on the door."

Standing, I took a deep breath for confidence and strode to the designated office, knocked assertively but not aggressively. "Enter," a voice called. Inside the luxuriously appointed suite, Ms. Harrigan came out from behind her desk ushering me to a cozy spot where two comfortable armchairs awaited along with a glass coffee table on which a welcoming platter of old-style British cream biscuits sat alongside a steaming pot of coffee as well as milk in a jug and a small porcelain sugar cube holder with accompanying silver tongs. Either this was one classy establishment or they really needed to fill the vacant position.

Ms. Harrigan was a woman in her fifties, impeccably groomed and coiffed as you would expect in an organization devoted to hairdresser employment, with a no-nonsense approach which I found endearing. "It's no secret in the industry, Frankie…May I call you Frankie?" she began. I nodded. I didn't care what she called me, it was unlikely I'd ever meet her again. "This position has been a difficult sell. Don't get me wrong, it's not a bad position, in fact, it's extremely generous for the right person, it's just that the right person has been difficult to find."

That did not augur well. It went downhill from there when she tried pop psychology on me. "Are you the right person for a challenge like this, do you think, Frankie?"

Oh, spare me, I thought.

She continued. "Your CV is very impressive. In fact, more impressive than our client is looking for. But, to be perfectly honest with you, they're desperate. And so are we. We've had this position on our books for months and, so far, no takers. You said on the phone you were seeking your own salon eventually and that you wanted to get away from the city for a while. Well, this job offers both those opportunities, is paying more money than it's worth, it will give you artistic freedom, and experience you are never likely to gain in this city which is already overstocked with hair stylists. The downside is that the contract is for a year with severe penalties if you break it and…" she took a very deep breath, "they haven't had a hairdresser in the town in more than two years so, as you can imagine, things are getting decidedly shaggy…that's because the town is Sithole, Alaska. A timber town near the border with Canada."

I'm afraid I stopped listening at that point, my brain was screaming while my cock was drooling at the prospect of all those hot timber men. I've seen the porn. Those bulging muscles, those hairy thighs, those huge pendulous packages. Hell, I signed on the dotted line quicker than a premature ejaculation.

That's what comes of thinking with your genitals rather than your brain.

It was with a combination of trepidation and excitement that I cleared out my few possessions from Fred's apartment while he watched to ensure that I took nothing that he laid claim to. When in doubt, I left it. After all, how many Lady Gaga CDs do you need in a lumber town? Most of it went into storage while I kept just enough to pack into one suitcase and a large carry-on satchel which included my laptop. I'd been told luggage weight was strict.

I'd already cruised the gay personals to see if there might be some sort of clandestine gay scene in the area or at least one or two like minded men, but it came up blank. An advert of my own saying I'd be in town and look me up had its allure but I suspected that, even without my name, it would lead to reprisals of a particularly homophobic sort as I'd probably be the only new arrival.

I had just over a week in which to get everything in order because I'd be gone for twelve months, or longer if I got snowed in for weeks at a time. I knew helicopters flew in for emergencies but they weren't likely to brave the elements to pick up a gay boy who was homesick for the bright lights and cruising opportunities of the big city. Besides, did it snow in timber country?

It's when I realized what I was leaving behind that I got that awful feeling in the pit of my stomach.

What the hell am I doing?

I was much too bruised emotionally to head out to the bars and saunas anytime soon so Sithole did seem like a valid alternative. I had wounds to lick, self-doubt to overcome, piercings to have done.

What?

Fred had always hated piercings and tattoos. I didn't fancy something inked on my skin that would sag with old age but a nice shiny bar through my nipple where it could only be seen by my most intimate friends, that would be liberating. But chicken is as chicken does and my courage deserted me just as I was about to walk into *The Piercing Urge*. Suddenly, I had the urge no more.

There was no one to see me off at the airport. The boss and any of the few well-wishers at the company got their farewells out of the way during business hours the previous day. No one wanted the added effort of actually traipsing to the airport for the laborious task of making small talk in the overpriced cafés dotting the departure lounge. Even my best (only?) friend, Tommy, didn't bother turning up, sending me off with an email that said, "I told you so." Indeed, he did. He warned me that Fred was an asshole and that I would live to regret the liaison. When Fred and I first got together he let it be known his friends were now my friends and my friends were…well, superfluous. Amazing what new love will swallow.

Tommy was the only one who stuck by me until Fred demanded I never see my best mate in all the world again. It was a surprising reversal because Fred had intimated he liked Tommy hanging around. He was lively, he was fun, he was hot as hell. I had ignored Fred's demands and kept seeing Tommy, albeit on an irregular and a surreptitious basis. What Tommy also now belatedly related to me was that there was a very good reason Fred kept him around in the early months of our relationship: Fred and Tommy were fucking.

"He came on to me about three weeks after you began living together," Tommy confessed. "Said you were boring in bed and what he needed was someone like me, a slut with a wild streak. Some days, while you were at work, we'd spend five or six hours just flip flopping until we were all shagged out. Then just as quickly he got tired of me. It was all over within six months or so. I figured you must have found out and put a stop to it. So you had no idea? Fuck mate, you sure are one dumb fuck."

There was more but I didn't bother reading it. I deleted it from my inbox after adding Tommy's email address to my spam filter, then went to my address book to delete every detail of my erstwhile mate.

As my plane took off, I waved to the city I no longer cared for, feeling good about starting over.

The long flight was uneventful apart from the spasmodic panic attacks I had when it sank in what I'd done. There was a solution to that – copious amounts of alcoholic beverages to drink. As a result I slept the latter part of the flight until, with three other passengers, I transferred to a small plane about as large as an outsize moth that was buffeted on our flight by every breeze and updraft until I was in danger of losing my deliciously spiced cardboard lunch. We'd probably have gone into a nose dive if anyone on board had farted.

There was little chance for conversation in the aircraft because of the noise and my stomach's insistence that if men were meant to fly they would have invented something better to do it in than planes that bobbed miles above the earth like a drunken goose. The others, three bulky bearded bears who I would have eagerly bedded either together or separately didn't look the friendly type, staring at me as if I had nine heads or was possibly gay. What did they expect, I'm everyone's clichéd idea of a male hairdresser? Yeah, I was wearing a plain blue button-up shirt and jeans. Okay, the jeans were tight enough that I could barely sit down without my testicles withdrawing into my body in case they were crushed, and I was wearing a stylish Icelandic sweater as opposed to the sea of check shirts and grungy fake fur-lined coats they were wearing that smelled like the animal was indeed real and had been skinned the previous day. Don't get me started on the facial hair which looked as if it hadn't seen a blade since the invention of the disposable razor, or the hair that had obviously been hacked by a mate whose only possession was a pair of scissors so blunt he might just as well have used a spoon. My wit was sharper.

Our destination, when we finally arrived, seemed little more than an overgrown paddock with a hut at one end. We passengers toted our own baggage to the tin shed which saw service as both the arrivals and departures lounge with no one in attendance, overseen by the flickering soda machine. My rainbow striped suitcase had attracted a few snickers just as it had raised eyebrows at the airport before departure, as well as a classy business card complete with phone number and a scribbled 'Call Me' from a dapper passer-by.

A mini-van awaited our disembarkation, the driver greeting the other three passengers while I hung back, stupidly expecting some sort of welcoming committee.

The driver was something else. Sure, he had the shaggy look like all the others but he wore it well. It couldn't disguise the fact that beneath that fur he was as handsome a man as I'd seen in many a year. If I'd seen him back in the city, even with Fred as my erstwhile hubby, this guy could have tempted me into infidelity on a grand scale. When I made no effort to board his vehicle he came over and in a voice so deep you could probably mine gold, said, "You waiting for something, mate?"

"A proposal of marriage. A reporter. A photographer. Perhaps a welcoming committee," I said with an air of superiority.

He turned to his passengers laughing and then repeated what I'd just said. The guffaws from the van echoed his.

"You sure you're in the right town. No offense, but you sorta look outa place round here."

"If this is Shithole, Alaska, then I'm in the right place. Oops," I said sarcastically, "No offence." This was not the way to find a new boyfriend. Not that I was looking exactly, but…

He laughed, not offended at all. "You're not the first to call it that. Won't be the last neither." Then an idea seemed to strike him and his face lit up. "Your name's not Francis, is it?"

"That's what it says in my passport."

"Holy shit! You're the new hairdresser. And you're not a woman."

"Nope. Not last time I looked." I squeezed my package theatrically for confirmation. "Still all there." Then I realized, "Ah, you were expecting…"

"Someone with tits," one of the guys in the minivan called out.

"Francis with an E not an I. I get it," I said. "But you can call me Frankie."

"Just what we need, another guy to fight over too few women," another passenger grumbled.

"I don't think you need worry—" the driver said, thought better of it, went a nice shade of pink, the remainder of his statement dead on arrival although we all knew what he was about to say. He covered by telling me, "Climb on board. I'll take you to meet Chuck."

"Chuck?"

"The mayor."

"Gonna run me out of town already?" I joked, fearing it might not be too far from the truth.

"Nah, that'll have to wait. No flight again for another week."

Maybe it was time to get back on the wheezy small aircraft that brought me to this dump and get the hell out of Shithole, Alaska. As if it had read my thoughts, Fate at that moment had the plane taxi across the paddock and cut off my only means of escape.

The driver stowed my bags and I climbed aboard the van still to the amusement of my fellow passengers although they shifted uncomfortably to give me a wide berth.

As the driver took his seat, closing the door, he looked me in the eye via his rear-vision mirror, shaking his head. "I don't think Chuck is ready for this."

No more was said as we headed off from the little patch of cleared open space crowded on all four sides by forests that looked ready to claim the airport if anyone so much as closed their eyes.

As a city boy, born and bred, I prefer my scenery on a postcard or a biscuit tin lid. In the forest there were far too many trees for comfort, standing soldier-like and threatening, and way too much green while the sky was an unnaturally bright blue. You never got a sky this color in the big city. What was with the air? It had no odor. Everyone knows you need to be able to chew air before it was worthy of the name. Was it really air if you couldn't smell rubber tires, gas, and exhaust fumes? I didn't think so.

It was a half hour ride to the town. I think it was big enough to call a town. Apart from rows of houses, the commercial center had a general store that seemed to triple as the post office and gas station, three bars that were prosperously done up, each proclaiming the price of their beer in an obvious attempt to attract custom from the others, a plain single story schoolhouse that also converted to a community meeting hall and a church if the front signage was anything to go by. A small bank and a few other nondescript buildings completed the main street.

Almost as an afterthought was a lonely brick building with all the windows thickly curtained, no signage giving out details of its use. It was easy to guess. This was the brothel.

The town was situated on a bend in a river that rushed past with such fury it seemed as if it thought as little of the town as I did and couldn't wait to leave it behind. The driver saw me looking at the torrent.

"Winter snow's melting, river is dangerous for a couple of weeks."

He'd deposited the other three passengers outside one of the bars before taking me on to the General Store. He patted the seat next to him. "Don't be a stranger, come and sit up here."

He's a real charmer, I thought.

"But I don't even know your name," I hedged

He turned in his seat and held out a paw. "Bud Guyder. And you're Francis…Frankie Burfitt." His hand shake was gentler than I expected even though his hand dwarfed mine. He was confident in his own strength and didn't need to go all alpha by crushing my fingers.

I clambered into the front of the van next to him. The smile on his face seemed to imply I amused him in some way.

I couldn't stand the suspense. "Okay, get it off that incredibly hot muscular chest of yours. What do you want to ask, as if it isn't obvious as the smirk on those lickable lips of yours."

I just love playing with fire. It usually means I'm nervous. Like right now.

He chuckled. "You really are something else, you know?"

"Something else good or something else bad?"

"Just different to what passes as usual around here."

My "Ah" had the weight of historical homophobia behind it.

"No, don't go getting the wrong idea. I just meant that the town is rather, well I guess the only word for it is boring. You look like you're gonna liven things up. If you decide to stay."

Before I had an opportunity to respond, the van pulled up outside the general store and he quickly hopped out to hasten around to my side. "Here we are." He was there to help me out. I brushed his hand aside.

"For fuck's sake, I'm gay, not helpless." So saying, I got my foot tangled in the seat belt and face planted in the dusty street right next to Bud's rather large feet (if his boot size was anything to go by).

Shoot me now.

I glanced up in time to see him attempt to hide his amusement at my predicament. Dragging me to my feet, he dusted off my clothes as best he could, attempting to dismiss my humiliation, "Don't feel clumsy, that happens to everybody the first time. It's the way they installed the seat belt. Been meaning to get it fixed."

He did appear contrite so I forgave him. Ever notice that the rapidity of forgiveness is in direct proportion to the other persons good looks? I was prepared to forgive Bud just about anything.

"Apology accepted," I said proudly.

"Apology?" Bud muttered.

"Whatever," I said, totally unprepared to get into an argument.

Leaving my bags in the van, he dragged me inside. The double doors of the shop were open and all sorts of tacky plastic merchandise spilled out onto the street marked with prices that were so exorbitant I doubted they would ever be sold. Looks as if I'd be doing a lot of ordering from Amazon and other websites during my stay if this was an example of local prices.

"I want you to meet Chuck Devereau, storekeeper, property owner, and mayor of Sithole, Alaska."

Chuck was bent over rummaging through a wooden barrel full of god knows what, cursing enough I expected the air to turn blue. I'm not proud of myself but when Chuck turned around I shrieked so loudly I expect I caused an avalanche somewhere to the north or at the very least was responsible for a few premature births among the moose population. "You look like a fucking floor mop," I blurted out. I can only excuse my bad manners on the shock of discovering that Chuck was a woman and that her hair looked remarkably like someone had used one of Andy Warhol's silver wigs to clean the floor or deep down in the lavatory bowl. "Did I just say that out loud?" I asked sheepishly.

Chuck had the good graces to laugh as if it was the funniest thing she'd heard. I liked her immediately.

The driver removed his finger from his ear. "Chuck Devereau this is our new hairdresser…"

She was pumping my hand as if she was trying to get water up from a deep well but it felt mighty welcoming. "I get it," she smiled, "Like that old grammar rule, I before E. Maybe I should have worn my spectacles when I read the email from that woman in the big city we got to find us a, what did she call it, a stylist. Fuck me dead, all we wanted was a barber."

"No way. You need a professional if that mess on your head is anything to go by. Looks like someone attacked you with garden shears."

She laughed again. "Not far off the mark. Think you can do something with it?"

Warily, I ran my hand through what passed as her hair, careful not to draw blood on the spikes that would have done justice to a desert cactus. "You got a church handy?"

"Yeah, you religious?" she asked.

"Nah, I think the most you can do with that atrocity on your head is pray for a miracle and hope god is up-to-date on the latest hair stylings. Then I'd go out and shoot that poor defenseless creature sitting on top of your head to put it out of its misery."

"I like him," she said to Bud. "He'll fit in just fine."

He looked somewhat skeptical at Chuck's statement. "Isn't he a tiny bit…"

Here it comes, I thought. Scratch the surface and a thick vein of homophobia shines through.

"Colorful? Stylish for a town like Shithole, Alaska? Or do you mean too gay?" I passed it off as flippantly as I could because, when angered, my fury is sharp as a laser.

Bud put his hands up, begging for mercy. "Hell, no. I didn't mean it like that. It's just…well, fuck me, but you're a pretty little thing and the men around here…"

"I can take care of myself. And did you just call me pretty?" I said preening.

Chuck put her arm around my shoulder, steering my attention away from the utterly embarrassed Bud, "I just bet you can. And you are rather gorgeous. If I was that way inclined myself, why I'd—"

"Oh," I squeaked.

"I'm a vagitarian," she said and went off into peals of laughter.

"Must be difficult around here," I ventured.

"I get to the city when the itch is too great. Just like the boys from the timber mill. And there's always Madame Mabel's."

I didn't have to ask.

Bud looked extremely uncomfortable.

Chuck to the rescue. "Go on, piss off, Bud. I'll take care of Francis—"

"Frankie," I interrupted.

"I'll take Frankie over to the shop. You get about your business. I'm sure you'll be able to help spread the gossip about our new stylist so that everyone can come take a gander and clog up Main Street."

Bud nodded to me as he headed out the door and a few minutes later I heard the van drive off. Chuck looked me over. "What are we gonna do with you, eh?"

I had no answer to that.

Fortunately, I didn't need one for Chuck had a customer walk through the door. I gathered from the greeting that the newcomer was none other than the notorious Mabel, she of titular well-patronized local sexual relief establishment. She turned out to be something of a local beauty. Not conventionally beautiful but she disguised her unprepossessing looks with a personality that bubbled liked imported French sparkling water. I think Chuck was more interested in chatting to Mabel than in introducing the two of us so after we swapped names cursorily I twiddled my thumbs while the two of them went into a huddle obviously discussing me. I wandered away to examine the shop's paltry collection of merchandise because I presumed I'd be shopping here. It also looked as if I'd starve. They seem to have run out of essentials such as macchiato coffee pods, avocado – smashed or otherwise – in fact just about every fresh fruit or vegetable, except potatoes, and don't get me started on moisturizers. No, a plastic pump tub of sorbolene cream the size of a rainwater barrel was not gonna hack it.

I heard my name mentioned a few times but ignored it even though I felt like screaming, *"I am in the same room, you know."*

Eventually the two of them ran out of puff and Mabel took her leave but not before giving me the once over with a knowing smirk. "If you're looking for any part-time work, call round and see me." She swept out of the store like royalty leaving me with my mouth agape.

"Did she just—"

"Why? Are you looking to work on the side?" Chuck asked.

"On my back, you mean?"

"You'd be surprised. Some of the boys in town have very particular tastes." She unhooked a bunch of keys from a nail banged into the wall behind the counter before ushering me outside closing, but not locking, the store behind her. As we trudged along Main Street, windows popped up or else people seemed to find something to do outside their homes until the pavements positively hummed with activity. And that activity seemed to have everything to do with my arrival. I was stared at openly, glared at less openly, and discussed in whispers, a few of the braver women bowling up to Chuck for an introduction. The one thing they all had in common, men and women, was that fashionable hair styling had passed them by and they'd been reduced to a haircut that involved an upturned bowl and a pair of pruning shears.

Once we'd run the gamut, leaving people to compare notes in our wake, Chuck led me to what was to become my salon. It was a prepossessing two-story structure from the outside, with my accommodation above the shop. Bud had left my bags near the entrance and, after Chuck unlocked the door, I dragged them inside. I must admit I was impressed.

The salon was kitted out to the highest standard. Color me pleased, very pleased. I couldn't help the enthusiasm with which I gushed over the layout and design of the salon. The paint job colors might need a bit of work – who paints anything white these days unless it's a hospital ward for the chromatically challenged? – I was thinking rainbow, and the product they used was old hat, the chairs were less comfortable for clients than I was used to, but, over-all, I was impressed and I told Chuck so.

She started breathing again, obviously having held her breath until I gave my opinion. "Glad you like it. Does that mean you'll stay?"

"Do I have a choice?" I was being a smart ass.

"Of course. We wouldn't hold you to the contract if you were unhappy."

"Can I make a few changes?" I already had plans in my head.

"Go for it. You'll put Sithole, Alaska, on the hair style map of the world."

Sure, I was good but I couldn't perform miracles.

"Come on, I'll show you your apartment." Chuck grabbed one of my suitcases and strode off toward a set of stairs at the back of the salon. I rushed to grab the second bag and catch up.

The accommodation was pleasant. It would never make it into even the redneck edition of *Sophisticated Home Decoration* but it was functional, just waiting for a few personal touches. There was a widescreen television although I'd been told there was no reception to speak of in the town but the compensation was a bookshelf of DVDs and a player. The downside was they appeared to be titles I wouldn't watch if they were the only movies in existence.

I'd brought a couple of my favorite movies, a few of them containing full male nudity and a certain amount of penetration so I wouldn't lack for stimulation of the visual kind. The physical kind was another matter altogether.

The living area was comfortable, the fading lounge not too lumpy, the easy chair a luxury I was looking forward to. The room opened out on to a wide balcony overlooking not only the front of the shop and the gas station across the street but also the river a few hundred yards away.

The kitchen was sparkling clean, the hotplate and oven fit for a home chef, all the implements for cooking more than enough to satisfy my non-existent skills. As a fashionable stylist I was a mediocre cook. I'd have to learn. And fast. The larder was well stocked, as was the refrigerator, for which I was grateful. So far, so good.

The bedroom with its adjacent bathroom was another pleasant surprise. The bed itself was queen-size and solid enough to be comfortable. I do like a mattress that's supportive not one of those feathery things that your body sinks into until you feel you're being suffocated. The bathroom was modern and had a bath as well as a shower recess. I'd be comfortable even if I wasn't exactly bursting to invite my more critical city friends to visit. No biggie, they would never travel more than ten miles from the nearest gay bar without oxygen.

I made my pleasure known to Chuck who beamed her satisfaction, informing me the rent was paid by the town as part of the package deal. It was sounding better by the minute.

"That's about it," Chuck said after we'd done an inventory. "You must be tired after your journey. I'll let you rest. Later, pop into the store and I'll take you to dinner. My shout. Help you get acclimatized. You know, hints on whose feathers not to ruffle, who to suck up to, who to suck…"

She laughed at the look on my face. "Later," she called as she disappeared down the stairs leaving me to marvel at my new life. The panic would have to wait until I was rested.

***

Chuck was as good as her word. I saw a lot of her in the first few days I was a resident of Sithole. Finding my feet was both difficult and easy. I had a lot to negotiate. The basics were the easy part, I was good at my job, but the set-up involved activities I'd never had to negotiate before. I was good with hair, I wasn't so good with timber, hammer, and nails. I was also good with scheduling appointments but I didn't have any as yet. Sure, a few women called in, sticky beaks mainly who told me they styled their own hair – and didn't it look it? – who informed me haughtily they'd never pay for something they could do themselves and that I'd be broke inside a month because there wasn't enough money for luxuries.

Chuck told me there was plenty of money in the town but little to spend it on which is why the regular trips to the nearest city were always full. I was confident I could make it work, but first I need to let people know I was open for business, or would be in a week or so.

Publicity, that's what I needed. Word of mouth was good but only when it was recommendations not when it was gossip about the new hairdresser's sexual proclivities which were zero at this time even though I'd received a few late night visits from horny lumberjacks, sexed up on bravado and alcohol, keen to explore their bisexuality. Chuck had warned me about such eventualities, so I told them politely, as well as regretfully because they were hot, to come back when they were sober. All I got out of the furtive visits was an interrupted night's sleep and a better insight to the underbelly of this Alaskan town.

I'd decided on an opening date. If I didn't make it soon, the townsfolk would find something new to occupy their time and their gossip. But first, I needed a few minor internal alterations to the salon. After one visit to the town's medical man, Dr. Makepeace, for stitches after I lost the fight with a chisel, and a black fingernail from a similar attack from a hammer, I decided I needed help.

"Not much call for a handyman around here, Frankie, most people do it themselves," Chuck commiserated as she packed the shelves with the latest delivery from the city, none of it appetizing to my taste. Before I moved to this outpost, I would have sworn peas came in pods or else frozen in bags but I'd now learned one of the crueler facts of life: peas came from a can. And not just peas. Carrots, potatoes, corn, spam, tuna, you name it. If only they'd perfected Boyfriend in a Can. I'd be first in line at the general store.

"Leave it with me, I'll see what I can do," Chuck said, sounding not at all hopeful or, indeed, helpful. She seemed irritated that I couldn't fend for myself. She'd already sampled my poor excuse at cooking. "How can anyone burn spaghetti that comes out of a can?" she'd asked, incredulity in every syllable. Fortunately, the diner in town does takeaway.

It was late one night, I was in the apartment attempting to design a flyer for the currently inauspicious opening of *Rainbow Hair Stylings* (I'd briefly toyed with the idea of calling it *Francis is a Sissy* but good taste got the better of me) when there was a knock at the door.

Groaning that it would be yet another drunken proposition and disrupt my fragile thought patterns I was in a grumpy mood when I opened the outside door to fire stairs that led up from the street – the one my eager but secretive nocturnal would-be lovers chose. I could smell the alcohol before it was fully open. Bit of a surprise, it was Bud. Much the worse for wear. "When do you want me?" he slurred. "I'm up for it. Won't cost you a cent."

And they say romance is dead.

Pulling myself up to my full height which was pretty feeble in comparison to this mountain of a man, I snorted my contempt. "I don't ever pay for it and if that's your seduction technique I'm surprised you ever get laid." With that I slammed the door in his face, storming back toward the kitchen table where I had my laptop set up. A scream of pain stopped me in my tracks. Wrenching the door open I was spattered with blood. It was pouring from Bud's nose. "Stay there," I ordered, quickly running to the bathroom to get a washer and a towel; I didn't fancy blood all over the floor.

Back at the scene of the bloodbath, I wiped as much from his face as I could and told him to hold the towel to his nose, guiding him in to sit at the table after I'd carefully moved my laptop out of harm's way.

"Put your head back, Nurse Frankie to the rescue." It must have sounded as if I knew what I was doing because he obeyed without objection. I rinsed the washer and wrapped a handful of ice cubes in its folds before placing it gently on the bridge of his poor battered nose. It was bruised but not broken. You'd never know that from the wail that Bud set up. "Why'd you do that? You a sadist or something?" He didn't sound quite as inebriated as I'd first thought.

I hope he wasn't expecting sympathy because what he got was, "If you aren't dexterous enough to stand back when you see a door closing in your face, it's not my fault."

"Fuck you. I was only trying to help." He got to his feet still holding the ice against his nose and staggered to the door, pulled it open in a temper, muttered "I knew you'd be trouble the first time I saw you," and slammed it behind him.

I could have run after him and demanded my wash cloth back but I guess it was a small price to pay for getting rid of his unwanted attention. It was no use going back to work so I shut up the laptop and crawled into bed wondering if I should cut my losses and run back to Mr. Redmond, with my tail between my legs, and beg for my job back. I'm not a quitter under normal circumstances but this new life was so alien I was having difficulty adapting.

Even more so the next morning when I was awakened from a surprisingly peaceful sleep by loud banging on the outside door to the apartment. Surely Bud hadn't returned to wreak revenge. My bleary eyes registered it was something o'clock on the digital clock on the bedside table but I couldn't make out the numbers clearly enough. It had to be morning because sun was peeking through the curtains. I grabbed an old robe that I'd brought with me, wrapping myself inside as if it were armor for the forthcoming battle.

I opened the door only to be brutally shoved aside as a bundle of energy pushed into my apartment. "What did you do to Bud?" Chuck asked.

"His nose collided with my door," I said unsuccessfully stifling a yawn. "It was an accident."

"Not the way he sees it. Says it was assault."

"Oh, come on. He turns up here pissed as a newt, suggests a quick fuck, and he thought I'd tumble into bed with him?" I was indignant Chuck was taking his side.

"He what?" she shrieked.

"Can you take it down a notch on the shriek-o-meter. I haven't had my coffee yet. You want one?" I went to the kitchen and powered up the machine for an espresso.

"What did he say when he turned up at your door?" she asked. "*Exactly* what did he say?"

"Apart from the fact he reeked of alcohol," I said indignantly. I then repeated as best I could remember, Bud's proposition.

I thought Chuck was about to burst. "Oh, fuck, do you have a lot of apologizing to do."

"Me? I'm not that desperate." The coffee hadn't kicked in yet and I was confused as to why she would take Bud's side.

"First, he wasn't drunk. Sure he'd had a drink or two but he'd been at an engagement party and one of the guests spilled her drink all over him. The celebration was all but over by then so he decided to go home and call in to see you on the way through."

"Okay, that explains the smell of alcohol but it doesn't excuse the fact he thought I'd fall into bed with him just because he was offering. And he mentioned I didn't have to pay him. Like I'd be the one paying him for sex." I made a sound with my lips to emphasize how preposterous that idea was. "Explain that away if you can."

Chuck sighed as if I wasn't fully comprehending what was going on. "Let me just say, Bud isn't like the other…uh…late-night gentlemen callers you've attracted. He was offering his services for the bit of carpentry you want done. He'd do it on his days off from the mill and he wasn't going to charge you a penny."

I closed my eyes as I realized the full import of what I'd done. "Yep, I'm screwed," I admitted. "And not in a good way. I assumed the worst and almost broke his nose into the bargain." I'd better buy some kneepads if I was gonna grovel that much. "Anything I can do to make it up to him?"

Chuck and I brainstormed a few ideas to win Bud over but they were all contingent on my abject apology – a free haircut and blow dry wasn't gonna be enough.

"You know what you gotta do," Chuck said sympathetically. "Do it sooner rather than later is my advice." With that, Chuck kissed me on the forehead and let herself out.

My head slumped on the table. It was gonna be a long day.

***

The mill itself was a good twenty minutes upstream at a section of the river ideal to maneuver logs that came from even farther up. It was a higgedly piggedly assortment of buildings that had grown up around the central saw mill. Logs were stacked high enough to dwarf me, machines hummed, there was an air of chaotic order about the place.

Chuck organized a lift for me with one of the workers who was in town for supplies. He looked at me as if I carried bubonic plague as I got into his truck. He was hairy enough to be a yeti and I guessed he was related to that breed because conversation eluded him and all I got from my attempts at friendly conversation were grunts.

When he dropped me off at the lumberyard site office, I jumped out of the truck and with a cheery wave said, "Thanks for the scintillating chat, it's given me much to think about." I'm not sure if he got the sarcasm because all I got was yet another grunt. I thought perhaps he was merely constipated or in dire need of a conversational laxative.

I went to the office to ask for Mel, the site foreman. He looked up from the paperwork that cluttered the desk, his filing system seemingly as ad hoc as his manners. When I introduced myself and held out my hand, all I got was a barrage of abuse. "Fucking Jesus Christ," he swore. "You're what's been sent up for the barbershop? A fuckin' pretty boy who isn't old enough to wipe his own ass? And now you want to take one of my best men off the job for fuck knows what reason."

He slammed a few things about his desk, swatted papers on the floor, stamped his feet, and bellowed to his receptionist to get Bud up to the office as soon as. That seemed to be the end of our business so I shuffled toward the door and back into the waiting area. "Bud'll be here shortly," the receptionist assured me. I was too nervous to sit. She cleared her throat ostentatiously, obviously wanting to attract my attention. I looked at her and she smiled. "You're the new hair stylist, aren't you?"

I was tempted to ask, "What gave it away?" but went with "Yep," instead. Succinct and to the point.

"When's the opening?"

Ah, a potential customer. "I'm getting some flyers done for the grand opening. I'll drop a few out to you to put up on the notice board if you like."

"Cool. Think you can do anything with my disaster?" She'd obviously tried DIY. And failed. Valiantly.

"Mind if I touch your hair?" I asked as I went over to where she was seated. She was more than happy to have me paying attention to her, running my fingers through her stringy locks. "You're very pretty," I said truthfully, "but the style does nothing for you. I'm sure we can come up with something to suit."

That broke the ice. Coral and I were getting along like buddies when Bud came running up to the office, out of breath from his haste.

His face fell when he saw me. "Oh, it's you."

Coral, obviously sensing how serious our discussion was going to be, grabbed a bundle of papers from the corner of her desk. "I have to run these contracts up to the main office. I'll leave you two alone. I won't be back for twenty minutes or so. That should give you enough time for whatever." Then she was gone.

I just hoped Mel wouldn't come out of his hidey hole and interrupt.

Bud just stared at me, daring me to speak first.

"I owe you an apology," I said.

"Yeah, you do."

I got down on my knees and groveled in the most outrageously theatrical over-the-top manner, much like an overweight opera diva after she's taken poison but still has enough energy left to flap about like a choking sea lion for so many interminable arias you just want to shoot her to put everyone out of their misery. "Please forgive me, I'm such a drama queen. I don't recognize help when it's being offered."

"Get up off the floor," he said sternly although I detected the hint of a smile hovering around the edge of his lips.

I sulked. "Not until you say you forgive me. Please say you do." I looked up at him, pleading with what I hoped were puppy dog eyes. I couldn't help wondering what it would be like being in a similar position with Bud standing naked before me.

As if he could read my mind, his face reddened and he told me to stop being stupid and get up.

He helped me to my feet. "Look," I said with all the sincerity I could muster, "It was an honest mistake. I've had a couple of guys from the mill turn up late at night, pissed off their faces, offering sex."

He nodded his head knowingly. "Probably Cal and Hunter."

"We didn't actually get as far as exchanging names. It wasn't that sort of visit."

He appeared saddened by the news. "Okay, I can see how you might have thought I was like them two, but there was no need to slam the door in my face and break my nose."

"It's not broken," I scoffed although I noticed it did look badly swollen. "Let me kiss it better."

He backed away so quickly he was in danger of falling.

"Okay, no kissing it better. I can take a hint." He moved forward a few paces but kept the distance between us wide enough that I wouldn't be able to reach him if I was stupid enough to try anything. "What can I do to make it up to you? I don't expect you'd want to help me out now but I can still try to make amends for my rather appalling presumption by offering you a free haircut which, I might add, you are in desperate need of. And," here I added the *piece de resistance* which Chuck suggested, "Free haircuts for the rest of the year that I'm in town."

"You'd do that?" He seemed surprised by my offer. "That's very generous."

"I'll take that as a 'yes.' Pop into the salon any day and we can make arrangements. I'll be painting for the next couple of days to get it ready for the grand opening."

"Okay."

We stood looking at each other, lost for anything further to say, until he mumbled about having to get back to work and left me standing alone but obviously forgiven.

Then I spent a good half hour pitching the salon to Coral after she returned from her errand, hoping she'd gossip to her girlfriends about me and the salon before my ride was ready to take me back to an afternoon of backbreaking painting. It had to be done if I was to open soon officially. Music helped lessen the tediousness of the task and I was throwing my body about totally unaware how late it was when I heard a sharp rap on the door to the salon.

Occasionally people had stopped by to gossip or ask about appointments or just be nosy about what I was up to. This would be no different so I was surprised to open the door to Bud carrying a large kit of tools and wearing old torn jeans and a T-shirt.

"Don't act so surprised," he said, pushing his way inside. "Now what is it you need doing?"

The small jobs were all very simple if you had the wherewithal and the skills but my DIY carpentry ability was on a par with Coral and hair styling.

Bud made notes in a little book he took out of his pocket, licking the end of a stubby pencil endearingly every few entries.

At the conclusion of my rather formidable list of carpentry extras, he put his notebook and pencil away and turning to me, said, "I can get started now if that's okay but some of the heavier jobs I'll need to bring extra tools and do a measure up. That okay with you?"

"More than okay. How much will all this add up to?" Money wasn't a problem as the town was paying for it but I didn't want to go overboard.

He deflected as he opened his toolbox. "You missed a bit over on that wall." He pointed to the offending paint job.

The criticism stung. "I was getting to that," I said, miffed.

"Yeah, right," he said with a superior smirk.

I dragged the ladder to the offending patch of paint. It really was a shit job but when it came to coloring, on hair I was van Gogh, on walls I was Jackson Pollock. But I'd show him.

After I'd finished a patch-up job that looked as if it would need another patch up to cover mine, I glanced over to where Bud was wrestling with the demolition of particularly odious lumpen wooden shelving straight out of Noah's guide to arkitecture which smelled like it had housed myriad flatulent bird life. I caught him turning away quickly avoiding my eye.

"All right, say it," I groaned.

He turned back to me. "Don't give up your day job, mate."

"I'd like to see you cut someone's hair and do a good job of it," I grumped. It wasn't much of a comeback.

"You paint about as well as I'd cut hair," he admitted. "You got something else you can do?"

"Lots of promotional material to put together, getting all my color charts and chemicals ready for the grand opening. All that sort of non-butch gay stuff." Sarcasm is not your friend when you're trying to impress and wanting to keep the handyman around.

He didn't take offense. "Then go do it and let me get on with what I do best."

Looking at the wall again I knew his suggestion was the right one even if my pride didn't want to admit to it.

"Just let me get the construction work out of the way and then I'll do the painting for you."

"Doesn't seem a fair exchange rate to me." I'd have to pay him for all his hard work.

"Okay," he said agreeably. "Make it two years of free haircuts and beard trims."

I couldn't resist. Call me provocative, call me insensitive, call me stupid but I responded with, "How about two years of haircuts, beard trims, and blow jobs?"

Yep. The coloring that crept up his cheeks was like a forest fire taking hold of a weatherboard cottage. Time to put him out of his misery. "Get your mind out of your genitals. I meant a blow dry with this. It's my magic wand." I waved the blow dryer about as if I were Harry Potter.

Sheepish suited him. Of course, I'd meant the double entendre to see his reaction but I didn't want to spook him so he didn't come back. I guess there was a hint in there as well if he wanted to take it.

Bud went back to his carpentry while I went to the reception desk and opened my laptop to see if I could wrestle the flyer about opening day into some semblance of creativity.

He coughed as if to attract my attention and, without turning to face me, asked. "Um, did you do that with the guys who turned up at your apartment, you know, late at night?"

"Do what?" I asked. Why should I make it easy?

"You know, blow job, that sort of thing."

"Sex, you mean?"

"Yeah." He'd stopped working to listen to my response. It must have been important to him.

"No, I didn't. And I wouldn't gossip about it even if I had. Sure, they were cute or gorgeous or hung…"

"How do you know if you didn't…"

"I've got eyes," I said, pleased I'd made him uncomfortable. Okay, so I can be a bitch. "I can see when a man's got plenty to be proud of packed in his pants. Take you, for example. Unless you tuck your sox down your jeans then I'd say you have been more than adequately blessed by the size-queen fairy."

He spluttered in embarrassment. "So why didn't you then?"

What was with all this interest in my sex life?

"For starters, they were pissed and probably couldn't get it up anyway. But mostly because I want a man who's proud to be seen with me not someone who will creep in my back door, so to speak, and seek his man-on-man satisfaction only when he's horny and drunk.

"You not into one-night stands?"

Was he suggesting?

"Not all gay men are into indiscriminate promiscuous sex, okay? But sometimes the itch gets too great and the only way to scratch it is to get a big fat dick up your ass."

"Is that what you like?"

"A big fat dick up my ass?" I was taunting him. "Definitely."

"What about love?" he asked almost shyly.

"Yeah, I *love* a big fat dick up my ass." I was being deliberately obtuse.

"You know what I mean," he replied.

It was time to stop taunting the poor guy who was obviously just plain curious and not bi-curious so I told him all about Fred.

"He sounds like a dick," was the only comment Bud made about my prior love arrangements.

We both went back to our tasks, the silence less heavy than it was before our little chat so when Bud turned up again the following afternoon after his shift at the mill, we fell into an easy rapport, swapping stories and having a laugh. I learned a little of his background: mom, dad, two sisters, who lived in Wisconsin and with whom he had little connection once he decided the family funeral business was not for him. Better the fresh air of the timber industry than oven baking the dead for a living. They'd taken it as a betrayal, he'd taken it as liberation once he'd made up his mind to flee the family nest. He hadn't regretted it for a moment although it made for a lonely life.

"What about marriage? Kids?" I asked. It seemed that was what every red-blooded American man pined for.

"Not for me. Too set in my ways now. Besides, who'd want a dried up old crock of shit like me?"

Whoa. Who'd have guessed he'd have problems of self-image?

I wasn't going to touch that but he jumped in with another question before I'd had a chance anyway. "Is that what you want? Marriage and kids?"

I sighed dreamily. "Yeah. Marriage would be nice. With the right guy, of course. Kids. Don't think I'm the fatherly type."

He surprised me with his response. "I think you'd be great with kids. You're so open and so out there. Colorful. Bright. Like a shiny new penny."

I bowed deeply from the waist, "Thank you, gallant sir. I appreciate the vote of confidence. But I need a husband first."

"Don't think you'll find one around here."

Sighing sadly, I had to agree.

"Will you go back south when the year is up here?" Bud asked.

"Probably. Not much to keep me. If there was a sudden influx of gay lumberjacks or a gay bar opened up and I could find me a good man…"

"You miss the big city?"

"Haven't had time to as yet. Not been here long enough. Ask me again in about six months."

"I will," he said.

Each new evening I spent with Bud passed in gentle conversation as the salon took the final shape. When the flyers and business cards I'd ordered online on an occasion I was able to get the internet to work, a few days out from the official opening, I decided enough was enough.

"Come on," I said when I heard Bud exclaim in satisfaction as he hammered in the final nail and stood back to admire his handiwork. "Let's get out of here and I'll buy you dinner."

Did that sound like a date?

Calling a meal in Sithole's only diner 'dinner' was a little like calling KFC 'fine dining', but it was the best I could do.

"I'm not exactly dressed for a fancy meal," he said and, after sniffing his armpits, decided, "I'm much too rank to be out in close proximity to food."

I had an even better idea to sort out the men from the chicken. "How about takeaway, my treat, and we eat it upstairs?"

"I'm not gonna smell any sweeter because it's just you."

I was oh-so-tempted to sidle up and sniff him.

"You can take a shower while we wait for the takeout to arrive. I have all the mod cons like soap, towels, hot water. What do you say?"

"Sounds like you just want to get me naked." He was smiling when he said it.

I wiggled my eyebrows suggestively. "Could be. I'd be absolutely defenseless if you tried anything."

He laughed loudly. "That's the stupidest thing I've heard anyone say in days. You defenseless? I'd rather take my chances with a bear than you. I bet you eat men for breakfast."

"And lunch, and dinner, but only if they ask nicely." It was too good an opening to miss.

He choked on his laugh when he realized the double meaning of what he'd said. "Sorry, I didn't mean it like that. I'm not like those other guys who turn up at your door for a quickie."

Now was the time to get the answer to my curiosity, "So you're not bi-curious?"

He looked offended that I would suggest such a thing.

"Okay," I said, "Dial back the shock horror a bit. You are talking to a bona fide one hundred per cent genuine homosexual screamer. Or hadn't you noticed?"

He looked even more shocked. "You're…you're gay?"

Now it was my turn to be surprised. "You didn't know?"

He couldn't keep up the ruse any longer and the rumble of laughter began in his belly like an approaching steam train until it guffawed out his mouth like a belch of steam.

"You bastard," I spat. "I really thought—"

"You should see your face," he squealed, slapping his thighs in delight that he put one over me.

So the man had a sense of humor. Mark one up for him.

"But, I'm not much company tonight. Maybe some other time. I'm a bit tired," he admitted.

I snapped my fingers for dramatic effect. Nothing says important information ahead as effectively as a gay man's finger snap. Right? And my snap is second only to those dangerous crabs that can take your toe off with a single crunch. No, not those crabs that burrow into your pubic area and itch like buggery.

I pointed to one of the salon chairs. "Here, take a seat and lean back and relax, I'll make you feel real good."

There was probably a better way to express it but I was going for suggestive. It worked. He appeared startled, wondering about my intentions. To his relief, I added, "I promise to keep my hands above the shoulders." He sat down, obviously weary on his feet and I gently pulled his head back into the slot on the plastic washing tray after wrapping a towel around his shoulders.

"You're so trusting," I teased. "I said I'd keep my hands above your shoulders but I didn't say anything about my mouth."

He shot up out of the seat like a startled moose in the headlights.

I couldn't keep the humor out of my voice. "That was a bit more dramatic than I expected. Come on, sit down. I was only playing with you. Metaphorically speaking." I hoped that was the right term because I wouldn't know a metaphor if it invited me home for supper and then had its way with me. Hm, are metaphors hung like horses? Note to self: Google it.

Although he looked far from convinced, he sat back down in the chair and leaned his head back. I tested the warm water from the hose until it was exactly the temperature I wanted and then began to wet his hair before massaging in the shampoo. My fingers did the trick as his little moans of pleasure revealed. My hands worked their magic caressing his scalp, separating the knotted strands of his far-too-unkempt black hair.

Lost in the tactile sensation of fondling Bud's head, I wondered what it would be like to have this bear of a man at my mercy. Pining for straight men was a no-no in my rule book although they could make a most satisfactory one-off romp while they explored their bi-curiousness. But Bud was definitely out of the picture. I wasn't about to attempt seduction of a straight lumberjack who'd gone beyond the call of friendliness to help me out. Then I heard his gentle snoring. I couldn't leave him in that position all night. I rinsed, conditioned, rinsed and prodded him awake.

"Come on, big guy, time for your makeover."

He was groggy and easily led – if only I was leading him upstairs to my bed – and settled easily into one of the styling chairs. In a sort of slumbering wakefulness, he was easy to manipulate after his initial terror as the scissors approached his precious hair but I soothed him with just the right sounds until he relaxed and I could attack the forest of follicles, the horrendous hazard of hairiness, the…my mind was running away with me. I began cutting and styling, moving his head about without resistance. I attacked his bushy beard with equal fervor until I was knee deep in an avalanche of alpha-keratin. Maybe that's an exaggeration but there was a momentous amount of hair around my feet. Bud's head was propped up against the back of the sole barber's chair in the salon, his eyes closed, his breathing slow and sonorous. Stepping back to admire my handiwork…

OMG, you're gorgeous.

Beards, in particular, and long hair occasionally, are used to cover up a multitude of sins – scars, pitted skin, the fact you're a werewolf – but Bud's was a crime against nature because it hid his almost criminally handsome face. This man was seriously hot. I had to fan myself to keep from fainting at the sheer gorgeousness of Bud Guyder.

Pulling myself together after the revelation of his beauty – the other sort of pulling would come later in the privacy of my own bedroom – I couldn't deny I'd be defiling that gorgeous man mentally in my bed.

The lack of activity around his head must have woken him because he snorted and opened his eyes. For a moment he stared at the stranger in the mirror in front of him probably attempting to recognize the face. Then he saw my reflection standing behind him, scissors poised to cut a few stray hairs I hadn't seen before. He lifted his arm to watch the movement reflected in front of him. Realization dawned.

"Is that me?" he asked, incredulity in every word.

"Sure is. You scrub up real nice." I wasn't going to stroke his ego – something else maybe.

He preened a little but then thought of a downside. "The guys will give me shit about this." Then he admired himself again, turning every which way to see his new look. It gave me an opportunity to feast on him as well.

"You'll be an old married man in no time."

Pick me, pick me.

"Nah. I'm no good at relationships."

The grit in his voice signified it was not a topic he wished to discuss further.

"You happy with your makeover?" I asked.

"You're a miracle worker. You make me feel…special."

He felt so special, in fact, he grabbed hold of my hand and dragged me from the salon, closing the door behind us, pulling me along Main Street much to the surprise of passers-by who either whistled or catcalled him as they registered his new look, until we reached Madame Mabel's. He barged straight in.

"Holy hell, Bud, what happened to you?" one of the girls called. "You fall into a prettifying machine?" She sidled up to him, slithering against his body like a randy cobra. Obviously the smell of his perspiration was an aphrodisiac. I wanted to smack her away. He was mine. I created him just like Frankenstein created his man, except mine was handsome.

"How come we never see you in here?" another girl asked running her fingers up the front of his T-shirt.

Although I was pleased to hear he wasn't a regular at Madame Mabel's I was, unbelievably, eaten up with jealousy. I needed a cold shower and a very stern talking to myself.

Just as I thought the girls, their term not mine, were going to fondle poor Bud to death, or orgasm, whichever came soonest, Mabel appeared to break up the love-in by clapping her hands. "Now ladies, a little decorum if you please."

Well, I was pleased even if the ladies weren't.

Mabel looked Bud over like he was a prize bull at an auction, signaling with her fingers that she wanted him to turn around. She murmured in appreciation.

Bud was impatient for a comment. "So, what do you think?"

She turned to me. "Are you responsible for this?"

"Partly," I replied truthfully.

She looked surprised. "And who or what is responsible for the other part?"

"Good bone structure, genetics, gorgeous sperm. What you see before you has always been there, I just allowed it to blossom."

"And what a bloom," she enthused. "In a town full of weeds." She looked at her girls when she uttered the word 'weeds.'

The judgment was harsh but not totally without foundation.

I knew a good opportunity when I heard one. "A bit of pruning and a bit of nutrient and I think you'll find these weeds are not really weeds at all but seedlings that have been starved for a bit of attention and are just waiting to bloom."

"Stretching the metaphor, Frankie," Mabel snorted. "But I get your drift." She paused for a moment, "How about?" I heard the shrewd businesswoman in her voice. "How about I send a couple of the girls over and you show me what you can do. If I like it, then I'll guarantee regular clientele."

That would not only help the economic bottom line, the transformation in Mabel's employees would be seen around town and would hopefully lead to further appointments. Although there was always the possibility it could backfire among the more sexually moralistic.

I had gone over to the few women who were lounging about listening in to the conversation. "May I?" I asked. Once granted permission I ran my fingers through stringy hair that had been fashioned inexpertly but not without flair. "Who does their hair now?"

"They mainly do what they can themselves but Colette helps," Mabel admitted.

"Would it be okay with you if Colette came over first, say, tomorrow?"

Mabel seemed surprised. "Is the salon open already?"

"Not yet, but it wouldn't hurt to get some examples of what I can do out and about before the official launch. What do you say?"

"I scrub your back, you scrub mine," Mabel said with a sparkle to her voice.

"Metaphorically speaking." I hoped that was the right use of the word. I'd have to invest in a dictionary.

Bud and I left Mabel to the first of her customers.

"Mabel runs a good clean establishment," Bud said as we walked back along Main Street. He didn't elaborate further.

***

True to her word, Mabel sent Colette over for transformation the next day. I'd been busy setting up for my first real hair job since I'd hit the hairpocalypse that was Sithole, Alaska. I was itching to get my fingers tangled in a new creation. Sure, promotion was important, the design of the salon pivotal, but the business was about hair and it's where my heart lies.

I knew it would be the women of the town who would be my first customers, the men may or may not follow later. Having seen the initial reaction to Bud's amazing furry caterpillar to butterfly conversion, I'd begun to worry that some of Bud's work buddies may not be quite as appreciative as the women were. I didn't want Bud to become the butt of crude jokes. But once Colette appeared at the door to the salon, shy but inquisitive, I had to concentrate and let the peripherals go.

She was pretty and she'd made an attempt to highlight the best of her features without the necessary skills to do so. But *A for effort*, I thought.

"Come in, Colette. Would you like a coffee, hot tea?"

She shook her head, staring about the salon as if she were a young child in a toy shop.

"I'll show you around," I encouraged, hoping it would melt her reticence.

She showed more than passing interest in the lay-out of the salon and, in particular, the workings of the particular machinery used to make women more beautiful. She was full of questions and as I treated her with respect, not talking down to her, encouraging her interest – for the moment I had the time – she opened up, chatting amiably as I coaxed out her hair and just as expertly teased out information about the personality of each of the women at Madame Mabel's. It was information that would prove invaluable later as I designed a style as individual as each of the women.

Colette left not only satisfied but enthusiastic about her new look. It was, she said, what she had been trying to do herself with limited skill. I hoped Mabel would be as ecstatic.

I spent the afternoon distributing flyers around town, put a larger poster on the community notice board, with Chuck's permission – I was a stickler for the formalities – and made a trip out to the mill with a very different flyer aimed at the men, and an invitation to Coral to come in for a free consult in exchange for her support.

While I was chatting, Mel stuck his head out the door to his office. "I wondered what all the chatter was," he sneered. "They haven't run you out of town yet? Surprised you've lasted as long as you have. Been a couple of weeks now, hasn't it? Why don't you go back to San Francisco where you belong? Don't you miss your gay bars, your saunas, your brunches, the porn lifestyle?"

I sighed. No use arguing with a man like Mel or even informing him I didn't actually come from San Francisco. I went with what I know: Sarcasm. "What's to miss? Every day in Sithole, Alaska, is like a live porn show. All those hot lumberjacks with tight muscular bodies, pert butts and genitally packed jeans. A wet dream. I love it here so much, I'm seriously considering turning one of those derelict building in Main Street into a guesthouse-slash-resort for the jaded men of San Francisco. And a Pride March. Maybe a nude gay resort out amongst the trees. They'd love the ambience here." I doubted Mel would have any idea what 'ambience' actually meant so I made it sound as suggestive as I could with the inflection in my voice.

Coral almost choked on the coffee she'd been drinking while listening to our antagonistic banter. "Get back to work," Mel yelled at her before storming back into his office slamming the door on his muttered curses interspersed with 'god-fearing country' and variations on the word 'fag'.

"He'll get over it," she said.

But he didn't. Seems I'd poked the wasps nest. When I got back to town, Mayor Chuck headed over as soon as my lift dropped me off. I could tell from the look on her face what this was all about.

"Mel didn't waste any time then?"

Chuck laughed. "A Pride March in Sithole, Alaska? Now that's something I'd like to see?" she smirked. "And a GLBTQ+ guesthouse? I like the way you think." She then adopted a deep gruff voice, "But as mayor of this town, I have to take into consideration the feelings of the older, long-established citizens and their concerns. No matter how Neanderthal." She couldn't keep it up. "Who am I kidding? Who gives a fuck what the Mels of this world think? He would have closed down Mabel's if he could have. Then where would we be? Up to our eyeballs in men so keyed up with no opportunity to drain their balls they'd get their jollies smacking each other about."

"What a colorful portrait you paint of the heterosexual male," I replied.

She shrugged. "Not really my area of expertise."

I thought of Bud. "Or mine. Am I in trouble?"

"About what? Stirring up that old bastard Mel? I'd give you some sort of community award if I could for rattling him so badly. Keep up the good work."

She slapped me on the back so hard I almost lost my footing.

***

I was kept busy with another two of Mabel's employees. She'd obviously been impressed enough with the result that she wandered over in the afternoon to thank me. I made us both coffee and we sat in the salon waiting area chairs and chatted.

"This isn't quite how I envisaged my life turning out either," she admitted after I'd explained how I came to end up in this small Alaskan township.

"Does anyone go to a college careers advisor to be told they're best suited to be a madam?" I joked.

"I was a successful businesswoman down south," she said. "Life mapped out ahead of me. Destined to be in the Forbes list of richest women. Perhaps a political career. The sky was the limit."

"What happened?"

Her face lit up. "Bruce happened. I fell in love. Totally inappropriate match. At least my family thought so. I was a privileged white girl with upwardly mobile middle-class parents who wanted the best for their child. Only problem was that their idea of what was best wasn't necessarily mine."

I sipped my coffee waiting for the rest of the story. It didn't feel right to interrupt with questions.

"Bruce was a logger, you see. What's worse, he wasn't prepared to change his profession for a life sitting on his ass in some stuffy office. We knew it wouldn't work so I went back to my city job and he flew back to some funny little town I'd never heard of. We'd only known each other a week, not enough time to build a life on. But I couldn't stop thinking about him. Found out he couldn't stop thinking about me. That sort of romantic shit. We were pragmatic. Sure, we were like teenagers in the first bloom of lurve but we weren't stupid. He flew down to see me whenever he could. Until the day we realized that what we felt was not going to go away.

"My parents galvanized my friends against Bruce but it had no effect. I flew up to this godforsaken pimple on the earth's butt to have a look. And I never left. Not even when…" She stopped to compose her thoughts. "I lost Bruce about six years after we married. Crushed between a couple of logs that shouldn't have been there. The payout from the company was enough to buy a home here. I was devastated and decided to take a few years to plan my future. Situations have a funny way of forcing your hand.

"Late one night, when I was at a really low point in my sorrow, a young woman banged on the front door begging for help. She'd been done over by a number of men in the town. Nothing ever proved against them, of course. They banded together. Claire, that was her name, was one of the women about town known to rent out their body for the right price. All very clandestine, of course, but if you didn't know what was going on you were obviously in Helen Keller territory. I helped her through her convalescence. Helped her back on her feet which meant I literally helped her back on her back. She liked the money she made. I wasn't a prude. I just thought she needed a safer environment in which to ply her trade. I went to Chuck for help. She wasn't mayor at that stage. She was on board with my plans, helped me rent a derelict building. I did up a room and rented it out to Claire for a modest amount. When the other street workers saw the change, they wanted in one by one. So with each new arrival, another room got a makeover. You can see the results. Mabel's. There was opposition, there always is, particularly from that piece of scum, Mel, who was one of the guys who'd worked over Claire although nothing could ever be proved. It was only after another young woman was so badly damaged in an attack that the town decided Mabel's was a safer bet and, on the plus side, would allow them to sweep the whole problem under the carpet and out of sight."

"What happened to Claire?" I asked.

"She fell for one of the loggers. He was as smitten with her. It wouldn't have worked if they'd remained here, so they packed up to make a new life elsewhere. We keep in touch on social media when the friggin' reception is good. She has a little girl now."

"You should write a book," I said simply.

***

The opening of the salon was low-key, people popping in for canapés and cheap wine, beer, or non-alcoholic punch which someone tried to spike with vodka before being escorted off the premises by an angry Chuck.

People mingled, people gossiped, people pored over the plastic folders of hair styles I offered, and people scoffed publicly at the 'ridiculous' prices I was charging although they could easily afford them – they'd do anything for a discount – but I stood my ground. Chuck launched *Rainbow Hair Stylings* with a speech so thick with sugary praise you could have frosted a cake with it. I responded in kind, as expected.

The appointments, however, were initially slow in eventuating. Seems many of the town's women didn't think they needed a hairdresser. They were so so wrong. Among the men only Bud bothered. He never needed an appointment, I was always glad to see him.

He even came to the opening party. With flowers. It was an incongruous look: Bud with a huge bunch of flowers he'd had flown in specially. Downside, they weren't for me personally. But they were for the salon. "Something to make the place look pretty," he said as he thrust the blooms into my hands looking rather embarrassed at his gesture.

"You didn't need the flowers to make the place look pretty, you do that every time you come in," I flirted.

Yep, he turned Wine Red by Schwarzkopf.

Coral turned up with a group of people, resplendent with the new coif I'd created for her. As a result, a few women took business cards I noticed with pride.

What I also noticed was the distance some of the townsfolk keep between themselves and the women who worked at Madame Mabel's. I suspected there would be a few who would hold off on using my salon based on the moral high ground that I provided services for 'fallen women.' As time went on I knew the glaring difference between professionally styled hair and amateur attempts would grow wider until most women would cave in and make appointments. The men would take a little longer.

I was pleased to push the stragglers out the door once the party wound down. Bud stayed behind and began to clean up the mess that inevitably follows a major social event.

"That went well," he said.

I yawned. "Leave that. I'll clean up in the morning."

"You won't have time. You'll have so many people lined up at the door wanting appointments your life won't be your own."

I had to admire his positivity. "You think?"

"You're an artist, Frankie. A goddam genius when it comes to hair. This town is lucky to have you. If they don't see that then they don't deserve you."

As it turned out he was half right about the crowd. There was a lot of window shopping, people who popped in to go through the glossy photos of my work or to gorge on magazine styles that I kept handy in the waiting area. But in a town that was used to going without, it was difficult to get people to sign up again. I relied on Mabel's girls, plus a few of the younger crowd around town who wanted to look stylish for their boyfriends or to attract a boyfriend, and the same boyfriends who wanted to look good for their girl. Otherwise, men were conspicuous by their absence. Bud, however, turned up once a week for a 'top up' as he called it, regular as clockwork.

He'd arrive about half an hour before closing when there was rarely a customer. I'd wash and condition his hair before trimming it to keep it neat. I'd heard a few of my women customers speak admiringly of how well Bud scrubbed up and what a catch he'd be but nobody seemed to have pinned him down as yet.

I never charged him and in return he'd ensure we went to the diner for a meal on him. I'd attempted half-heartedly to seduce him into coming upstairs for a meal and to watch a movie but he wasn't to be enticed. "Nah, Frankie," he'd say. "Can't have you slaving over a hot stove after you've been on your feet all day. Wouldn't be fair."

Whether that was just an excuse because he knew my cooking was as bad as my hair styling was fabulous, or because he thought I might try something, I never knew. Eventually I gave up asking and he seemed relieved.

Life settled into a regular pattern and I spent my social hours with Chuck or with Mabel, sometimes with Coral. The major development was that I'd attracted groupies. Sort of. Colette took to hanging around the salon during her 'off-call hours' after I'd asked her once to answer the phone when it rang and I couldn't respond because I was up to my eyeballs in Velvet Violet Creamtone Hair Color by Manic Panic. Normally I'd let it go to voicemail and call back but I'd discovered a few customers were miffed at the lack of a receptionist and refused to leave a message. "Could you get that please, Colette. I'll owe you. If it's a booking just check the diary to make sure it doesn't clash. Okay?"

She nodded. Her voice was so professional I wasn't the only one who looked up in surprise. She handled the call with such aplomb I got her to sit behind the counter and answer any other calls that came in. All up she took three bookings. Impressive. After she'd finished her turn in the chair I slipped her twenty bucks for the phone.

"Not necessary," she said, then asked shyly, "Rather than the money how would it be if I came and watched you sometimes, pick up a few tricks. I won't get in the way, I promise."

I checked with Mabel and as there was very little business during the day she consented to Colette coming over to the salon from time to time. That occasional visit soon turned into every day until she became unofficial receptionist and general dogsbody. I found myself relying on her more and more.

The other groupie was a teenager. A young guy who'd turned up to look the place over. He sat and watched, chatted to some of the women who were waiting their turn so I knew he wasn't casing the joint to break in later. Colette knew him. "He'll die in this town," she told me. "He's suffocating already, hungering for bigger things that he'll never find here. He's like you."

"The kid's gay?" I had terrible vision of being tarred and feathered by the town morality squad for turning the kid queer.

Colette laughed. "He's creative. I think he's too young to know what his dick's for yet."

"How old is he?" I asked.

"Fifteen, I think," she said.

"Show me a 15 year-old boy who doesn't know that his dick is for more than pissing and I'll show you a boy on a slab in the morgue."

His name was Bram and his mom had died when he was five. He now lived with his dad and an older sister. I kept him at arm's length because I knew the repercussions that could very easily arise if even the most innocuous gossip started.

He, too, eventually became part of the salon family. It began with him grabbing a broom and sweeping up after a customer one afternoon when he dropped in after school for a haircut. His visits became regular and then daily when we were open. He'd sit at the reception and juggle his homework and his sweeping duties with great skill. I began feeding him a small wage under the table. It was a bit better than pocket money but not so generous he'd rival Steve Bezos's wealth any time soon.

***

Business wasn't exactly booming but it kept me busy enough that I'd need to take on an assistant sooner rather than later. Men and boys in the town were now turning up with increasing frequency pressured by girlfriends, wives, and mothers who were tired of being seen with a walking-talking furball. Suddenly men could see their own faces. There had been a few surprises, not all of them pleasant. Poor old Ruth Badger had discovered the man beneath the shaggy hair and bushy beard she'd been shacked up with for the past seven years was not the husband who'd set off eight years before to make his fortune prospecting for gold, but was a total stranger who'd seen an opening and settled for it. After a shrug of her shoulders at the deception, and a follicle make-over by yours truly, she realized she got the better of the deal although she could never remember to call him by his real name rather than her missing husband's.

Colette's role in the business had increased to such an extent – answering the phone had morphed into washing hair, a bit of manicure, and a few basic chores that I trained her for – she was spending more and more time at the salon and less and less at Madame Mabel's. I was expecting an irate visit any day.

"A word, Frankie," a voice called one afternoon as I was getting supplies from Chuck's store. I had my back turned and scrunched up my face when I realized I was trapped, recognizing the voice as belonging to Colette's employer.

Ironing out my features, pasting on a smile, I turned to face Mabel. "My, don't you look radiant today?"

"Cut the crap, Frankie. I look radiant every day," she snapped. "It's about Colette."

"I guessed as much." I shuddered at the thought of losing her help. I'd be up rainbow creek without a disco ball.

Chuck couldn't help sticking her bib in. "What's going on with Colette?"

Before I had a chance to defend her, Mabel jumped in. "She spends all her time at Frankie's. And when she is *at home* her mind's not on the business it should be, she's too busy doing the other girls' hair and makeup. She's lost the spark of being a working girl." She turned to me. "What are you going to do about it, Frankie?"

"She an enormous help to me in the salon," I said. "She's a fast learner and picks things up quickly. I'd be lost without her. I know it's unreasonable she spends so much time at what has become a part-time job…"

"Then make it a full-time job," Chuck butted in. "Problem solved."

"I don't know if she wants to work for me full-time."

"I'm sure she does," Mabel said. "Just ask her. I think you'll find she's keen to learn from you."

I was shocked. "Are you trying to get rid of her?"

"Of course, I am," Mabel said in exasperation. "You don't think I want the girls to stay in the profession for life. Okay, you get to retire at a young age. Usually through death, disfigurement or just plain exhaustion. The industry gives you up, not the other way round. I'm in the business to give my girls a better life as far as I can. If Colette is showing talent, initiative, whatever, for god's sake give her a chance, Frankie."

It was relief all round. "I thought you'd be angry," I confessed.

"I couldn't be more pleased," Mabel said. She walked away beaming.

"I'll have to go over the books to see how much the business can afford," I said to Chuck. "But I'm pretty sure it will all work out. Eventually, though, if she shows real skill she'll have to get training. That'll cost money."

"Let's see how things pan out first, Frankie," Chuck said.

Mabel was as good as her word and the next day an agitated Colette turned up at the salon as I was opening the door. I let her in and headed to the little nook where I kept the necessaries for a good cup of coffee or hot tea and a small refrigerator for milk and other perishables we served to customers.

"Did Mabel discuss anything with you, Colette?"

She couldn't disguise the enthusiasm in her voice. "She said you might have a job for me and train me to be a qualified hairdresser."

Mabel had obviously embellished.

"Is that something you'd like?"

"Oooh, yes. Even before you came to town, I was trying to save up to buy the old salon because I thought no one would ever come here to open it again. I thought I'd have a chance myself. That's why I practiced on the girls at Mabel's."

"And then I turned up and shattered your dreams. You must hate me," I said.

"I suppose I did. At first. But you've been so kind. I realize now that I didn't have the talent to make it work. It would have been a disaster. But, because of you, I'm learning properly how to do things. I appreciate it, really I do, Frankie. Give me a chance. Please. I won't let you down."

And she didn't. Tentative at first, Colette soon caught on to the way I worked until she became engaged more and more in the everyday running of the salon. Occasionally, we asked for volunteers from among Mabel's girls so I could take my time after closing to show her how things were done professionally and give her the opportunity to practice her skills. She was such a quick study I knew she'd soon outgrow me. But, as Chuck said, we'd look into that when it happened.

It was late one afternoon, I had but one client, Mrs. Regina Stark, as imperious as her name suggests, when Bud turned up for his weekly appointment. Mrs. Stark had turned up unappointmented and demanding. She is a woman of some importance and influence in the town (and particularly in her own opinion) that, regardless of her attitude, it was politic that I oblige her. She pointed to a hairstyle in my catalogue and said, "That," as if any further discussion was over.

I was as polite as it's possible to be when clenching your teeth, "I think you'll find that style would not suit you at all. It's what young people…"

She jumped in, "Are you implying something here, Mr. Burfitt."

If the ruby slipper fits…

I didn't need to answer because she sailed right on. "I don't really care what you think. I know my hair better than you do. I'm the expert, not you."

I find the best answer for this sort of behavior – apart from dismemberment – is to nod politely and say, "As you wish," as if they are making the biggest mistake of their life. Hers was a huge blunder as the style she'd chosen was for late teens.

Bud chose that moment to enter. "Take a seat, I'll be with you in a moment."

"I can come back if you're busy," he said.

"No, please, take a seat." I hoped he could read the pleading in my eyes for him to stay. "You have an appointment, Mrs. Stark came in on the off chance, but I'm sure we can accommodate both of you. Mrs. Stark, if you would, please."

I ushered her to the washing seat, wrapping a towel around her shoulders, and had her slip her neck into the slot in the tray. I warmed the water, "Please tell me if this is too hot for you," I said as I tested the spray. It was lukewarm when I began to wet her hair. She sat bolt upright. "What are you trying to do, scald me?"

"I'm so sorry," I said humbly, "You must have ultra-sensitive skin. Please be seated again. I'll ensure it's at a more amenable temperature."

She harrumphed her displeasure but did lower herself back against the tray. Clearly she was the sort of customer who complained about everything.

Colette returned from an errand I had sent her on earlier and I nodded at Mrs. Stark in the chair. Colette rolled her eyes and I saw Bud attempt to suppress a smile.

Colette picked up the hose and gently wet Mrs. Stark's hair while I prepared Bud for his haircut and beard trim. "How's that, Mrs. Stark?" Colette asked, making small talk.

Mrs. Regina Stark, who had closed her eyes in relaxation prior to the changeover with Colette, rose from her seat like a whale breaching the surface of the sea. "Who are you?"

"Colette is my assistant, Mrs. Stark. She washes and conditions the client's hair," I informed her.

She turned on me. "I pay for the organ grinder not the monkey."

I wasn't sure which of the three of us gasped the loudest. That did not faze Regina Stark. She was in full flight now. "I will not have a whore touch my hair. Not even in rubber gloves. You never know what sort of terrible disease her sort has. Do I make myself clear?"

All eyes turned to me. I looked for a camera in case I'd been transported to a crappy realty TV show. Nope, it was real life.

With great politeness, I replied, "Perfectly clear." It took great effort to remain calm. "Let me make myself equally clear. Firstly, you will apologize to Colette for your slur." Regina Stark began to splutter at the obvious outrageousness of my suggestion. "Then you will sit down in the chair and Colette will wash and condition your hair. And, in future, you will make an appointment before you come in for a styling."

Regina Stark flung the towel from her shoulders and drawing herself up to her full height, bellowed, "I will do no such thing. I do not associate with whores let alone apologize to them or pay good money to them."

I wasn't going to allow this woman on her high horse so she could insult my staff and myself. "In that case, Mrs. Stark, we need not detain you further. Until you apologize you are not welcome in my salon."

"You don't know who you're dealing with," she snorted as she swept up her capacious handbag.

"Indeed, I do, Mrs. Stark," I responded, "Your reputation precedes you." She preened at that compliment. "I chose not to believe what people said about you being a stuck-up, obnoxious, arrogant, rude, opinionated relic of a bygone age. But now that I've met you, I see that everything I'd heard is absolutely true."

I turned my back on her, leaving her speechless momentarily because she used that old reliable threat, "I'll make sure your business suffers for this. I have influence in this town, my husband is a man of no little importance. We'll see who will arise triumphant from this little fracas." She spoiled her exit by tripping on the front step of the salon and almost face-planting on the pavement.

I turned my attention to Bud's haircut to be met by two open-mouthed individuals who then spontaneously broke into applause. I did the only thing I could, I bowed.

Colette was shaken by the experience so I sent her home, giving Mabel a call with an explanation of what had occurred so she'd know in advance what needed to be done, then turned my attention to Bud.

"Come here," he said, then pulled me into a bear-like hug until, I swear, I could hear his heart fit to burst out of his chest.

"She's had that coming for a long time but just about everyone in town is beholden to her or her husband and they're too scared to stand up to her. I couldn't be more proud that it was you who put her in her place, Frankie." And he hugged me extra tight.

Just what I needed, another enemy in town.

***

All Chuck said next time I ran into her was, "You know exactly the right people to needle in this town. Keep it up and we'll have a contract assassin fly in very soon to take you out. Keep it up, Frankie, some of us love you for it."

Mrs. Regina Stark had ensured the entire town, if not the entire state of Alaska, had heard of the abominable way in which she'd been treated by the upstart hairdresser ('He's a little that way', she's reported to have said whilst limping her wrist). Mabel told me later even Regina Stark's friends didn't believe her version of events although they stuck by her. Except when it came to their hair. They still patronized *Rainbow Hair Stylings*. Having decent hair, it seems, trumps friendship every time. Besides, a salon is the best place to pick up the latest gossip.

After that I saw a great deal more of Bud who seemed to adopt me as some sort of hero. He was like a puppy dog and I was his master. Quite an odd position for me.

Life was good. The dark cloud on the horizon was that I was developing feelings for Bud and I didn't know what I could do to short circuit what was destined to be a broken heart. I would never put him in the awkward position of knowing I had a crush on him but it would eventually become so painful to have him around that I'd have to leave the town I was beginning to fall in love with or tell him our friendship would have to stop.

Before that, though, I had a wedding to hairganize. It seems just about everyone in the town was going to popular young locals, Brenda and Sam's grand occasion and they would all need their hair styled, including the men, and there are only so many hours in the day.

I have only two hands. I'd be relying on Colette for a mammoth amount of help. Bram offered his services. He could take the phone bookings, sweep the floors, even do the washing and conditioning. Colette could be trusted on the simpler women's styles and any of the men's usual cuts. Between the three of us we thought we could manage to swing it so everyone got a turn. Everyone who wanted one, that is. A certain Mrs. Stark preferred to fly elsewhere with a few of her closest friends for a more 'superior' style than anyone could possibly receive in Sithole, Alaska.

Good luck with that, I thought immodestly. *She'll come back mutton dressed as tadpole.*

I had enough to think about without the extra stress of the indefatigably unsatisfied Regina Stark.

Bud was busy as well doing double duty as my (albeit platonic) puppy dog admirer, and as best man to the groom of the forthcoming nuptials. I was fortunate that Brenda, the far-from-blushing bride, knew exactly what she wanted and how much she wanted to spend. One of those sensible brides who thinks a deposit on a future home is far more important than ostentation at a wedding, she and the bridesmaids had chosen styles and gowns less frilly and frou-frou and more down-to-earth and less time consuming than the norm where people go all out to impress. Plus they had the added attraction that their hair wouldn't deteriorate as the alcohol flowed and the night turned into a dance party.

Colette was talented enough that she could concentrate on the lesser members of the bridal party while I managed the top table.

Bram volunteered to spend his spare time helping out, eager to be involved. It was easy to teach him to add ribbons and decorations to the women's hair – Colette became a patient guinea pig for his practice efforts – and he showed great flair for design wedded to amazing natural skill. I breathed easy knowing we could get through this.

***

It's a fact of life that you'll have diarrhea rather than constipation when the shit hits the fan, so there'll be plenty of it to be flung far and wide.

Life was peaceful. Life was calm. Life was on the good side of boring. I found I didn't miss my old life too much, well I did miss the sex, but the relaxed pace of Sithole, Alaska, seemed to agree with me. Chuck commented on how content I appeared. Bud thought I slotted right into my niche and had been welcomed by most of the town. "No one is ever accepted by everyone," Bud said when I pointed out there were a number of people such as Mel who went out of their way to harass or criticize. I couldn't be too harsh because Mel was Bud's boss. I know when to tread warily.

Well, I did, until the day the implacable homophobe took on the immovable sparkling rainbow hairdresser.

I was open late in the days before the big event. Brenda and Sam were both popular locals and the whole town was turning out for the open-air event after the more private wedding itself. The weather promised warm, the mill promised only a skeleton staff would be required and they would be paid appropriate shift allowance so most of the loggers could attend, and everything was moving like a well-oiled machine. Until the spanner in the works turned up.

Colette was helping me with color, Bram was sweeping up as well as making and serving refreshments to those who'd been waiting patiently for their turn. The atmosphere was celebratory and everyone knew we were working as fast as we could so there was little by way of complaint.

Except the one that turned up belligerent and pissed – with a gun.

I wouldn't know a pistol from a machine gun, all I knew was the street door to the salon was flung open with such force the opaque glass shattered, showering glass over one of the bridesmaid's waiting her turn. Blood was minimal, the shouting was not.

"What have you done to my son?" Mel screamed. "You've turned him into a fuckin' fag. I knew you were bad news the moment you set foot in Sithole."

His son? Bud was his son?

I turned to make sure everyone in the salon was okay when my eye caught it.

Oh, no.

Bram was cowering in the corner, trembling so violently that piss was running down his leg soaking his jeans. I didn't dare go to him because it would probably set Mel off even more. How had I not known Mel was Bram's dad? Why did no one tell me I was courting trouble with a capital T. Hell, every letter in the word was capitalized. Why didn't the glitter fairy knock me on the brain with his size-queen thick wand when Bram asked that I keep his time at the salon as secret as possible because he didn't want his dad to find out where he spent his spare time?

Yeah, like that would remain a secret for long.

"Why don't we go outside and discuss this? You're distressing people who are not involved," I suggested calmly but feeling much the same as poor Bram but without my sphincter and bladder giving out.

"Distressing?" He turned to the people in the salon. "This piece of scum is fuckin' my under-age son. How's that for distressing? Are you sure he hasn't fiddled with your family members as well."

I could see a number of clients were flustered by the accusation. I needed to put a cork in this quick smart.

"I have never touched your son. I don't even know if he's gay," I said reasonably.

"Yeah, that's what all you kiddie fiddlers say."

There was no arguing with him. I moved toward the door in order to get him outside although I had no idea what my actions would be then. I was lousy at sports at school, as well as physics and math as it happens, but a quick mental calculation convinced me there was no way I could outrun a bullet fired from close range even if I had a few seconds head start. Who am I kidding? I'm so unathletic I couldn't outrun a one-legged tortoise tied to the spot by a piece of string.

He backed off slowly probably believing I'd be a safer target outside. He wouldn't want to be shooting any of the long-time residents of the town if he hoped to plead insanity or extreme provocation at his forthcoming trial for murder.

So this is how life ends? Shot by a homophobe in the main street of town. Hell, I didn't have to come to Alaska for that, I could have stayed back home. Except, for all its faults, for all its lack of sophistication, this was home now. This was where my heart was. It had snuck up on me and the joy I had in helping people prepare for the special occasion had lodged itself inside me. They'd accepted me, welcomed me. I even had a wedding invite on my kitchen bench waiting for me to specify a Plus One.

If only I'd had the guts to tell Bud how I felt, maybe I could have got one last hug, felt his hard muscular body against…

Hold on a minute, am I getting an erection when I'm staring down the barrel of a gun wielded by a maniac who wants me dead for the fictional crime of seducing his son and turning him gay?

"Put the gun down, Mel," a voice commanded. Someone had obviously phoned Chuck and she had dragged the sheriff along with her. He was an old geezer who needed an oxygen tank to breathe and sat in the office doing paperwork while his deputies performed the legwork. The position was a sinecure. The old guy had asbestosis and it was the town's way of allowing him his dignity while he waited to die.

Here was me also waiting to die in far less dignified circumstances, my reputation in tatters.

It was young Bram, with more guts than I had, who came to my defense.

"Dad? Put the gun down. Frankie has never laid a finger on me. Okay?"

"No son of mine is hanging around with a fag. Get it?"

"Then I guess you won't be wanting me at home in the future," Bram said.

Of all the times in all the days in all the months, he had to do it now.

His dad wasn't so hot with math either. Putting two and two together seemed quite beyond him at the moment "What do you mean?"

"I'm gay, dad. Or in your terminology, a fag."

"What the fuck. If it wasn't this piece of shit hairdresser, who turned you?"

"Dad, I was born this way."

Mel moved the weapon to point it at Bram. "A dead son is better than a faggot son."

"Get behind me Bram," I said as I moved to stand between him and his old man.

Mel didn't take his eyes off me even when a new voice that made me ache cried out, "What the hell are you doing, Mel? Put the gun down."

"Do as he says, Mel," the old sheriff rasped.

"Why should I? Abraham was a good kid until he started working for the fag hairdresser. Turned him with his fancy clothes and talk about sex and drugs in the city. Abraham has been restless since the day little Frankie Fag arrived in town like some fag messiah. Well, not anymore."

"Frankie couldn't have seduced Abraham," Bud said.

"Why not?"

Bud took a deep breath, "Because he has a boyfriend."

"Fake news. No other fags in this town."

"What about me, Mel?" Chuck shouted.

"You're a lezzie, doesn't count. So who's the boyfriend then?" Mel demanded.

"I am." Bud said it with such confidence even I believed him.

"More fake news," Mel sneered.

Bud appealed directly to me. "I've been such a coward, Frankie. But I've grown to love you over the months that I got to know what a special person you are."

Given the situation, I had to laugh. "So you are bi-curious then?"

"Fuck, no," he shouted. "I'm gay, Frankie. Always was, always will be."

I couldn't work out if it was true or a ruse to distract Mel. Either way, it worked. Well, up to a point. Unfortunately, that point entered my body when Mel turned in shocked surprise at Bud's outburst and must have squeezed the trigger. I thought I saw a splash of blood. Then I died.

There were unicorns and sparkles and a rainbow bridge enticing me to cross over. It was so pretty. But most beautiful of all was Bud, the magnificent man who said he loved me. I never got to say it back. Was he dead, too? Why else was he at the rainbow bridge? It was now or never. "I love you, too, Bud. It's been months but I thought…"

"Shh, it doesn't matter. Sleep now." And his lips pressed against mine. There were no tongues, just the gentle pressure of lips against lips. If that's all I could get I'd be happy, satisfied I was allowed that much.

Then came the pain. I thought I must be in hell. Yes, that was it. Hell had white walls and the most godawful color reproduction of swans in a lake on the wall? Satan sure needs an interior decorator. And fast.

Aloud, I muttered, "I expected more red."

"He's awake," someone cried excitedly.

Suddenly there were faces leaning over me, smiling.

"Hurt," I said. "Pain."

A nice man shoved something in a plastic bag dangling beside the bed. It led to a tube that seemed to be stuck into my body somewhere. I began to feel good, really good. I could get used to this.

I was told later it was days before I was fully awake with all my faculties.

I imagined I heard Chuck and Coral and Bram and Colette and Mabel. But mostly I heard Bud. He'd hold my hand and just talk. His voice soothed me and I hope there was a smile on my face because he told me…

"I've been waiting all my life for someone like you. A man I could give my heart to. I love you, Frankie Burfitt. I love you more than I thought was humanly possible. I never expected it would happen to me. I hope you can hear me in there because I'll never have the courage to say these things to your face when you're conscious."

Inside my head I was screaming, *"I hear you. Say it again."*

Bud couldn't hear me. "I want us to make a life together. I know I'm not much. I'm a dull penny next to your shiny silver dollar, Frankie. I can't promise you wealth but I can promise I will care for you and I will do everything in my power to make you happy.

"I'm not a virgin, Frankie. I've had experiences. Lots. Well, not lots but enough. I'm a top, Frankie, is that okay? I can flip flop if that's the way you like it. You just have to be patient, that's all. I wish I knew if you can hear me in there, Frankie. I'm scared that when you wake up I'll find out I'm not your type at all."

I squeezed his hand as tight as I could through my medically induced haze.

"Frankie? You can hear me?"

I squeezed again.

Bud brushed the hair out of my eyes. I couldn't focus properly but I knew the handsomest man I'd ever seen was staring lovingly at me.

"I didn't mean to embarrass you, honest," he said modestly. "I was just getting shit off my chest. If you want, I'll just shut up, or leave you alone."

"Stay," I croaked.

"I'll stay with you forever if you want me to," he sobbed.

Dredging up all the strength I had just to utter a few words that I would never regret, I said, "I do."

BEAUTY AND THE LEASED

~

*H*e was the most handsome man I had ever seen, while I'm what you'd probably describe as plain or unprepossessing. No matter, it was me who made him scream like he wanted to bring the roof down. He wasn't faking it either.

"I left the cash in the usual spot," Jerrod said as he came back from the bathroom, his damp dark hair coyly hanging over his tanned face, now scrubbed clean of my sticky warm spunk. Given the opportunity, I could stare at this man all day. Unbelievable that I'd just had those perfect lips pressed to mine, that hard, muscular body bent beneath me as I ploughed his taut bubble butt. My body, still naked under the sheet, was…stocky. Yeah, that's another word for overweight. Just slightly. My muscles were hardly the stuff of anyone's wet dreams. My face is so ordinary that if I lost it, it would be weeks before anyone even noticed. No one would go searching Lost and Found to get it back.

I must be the luckiest guy in the world. Somewhere in my youth and childhood, as Julie Andrews sang, I must have done something good.

In case you're wondering if you read Jerrod's comment correctly, let me reveal that, yes, you did. Jerrod Spicer was paying *me* for sex. Not the other way round. There was no need for him to pay anyone; people were lining up to bed him: all ages, genders, nationalities, religious affiliations, political persuasions. In fact, just about anyone who was still breathing, although I'm sure had zombies existed they'd get hard for Jerrod as well.

Pity it was a commercial transaction. I never wanted it this way. Still didn't, but if it was the secret to getting Jerrod Spicer to bed, then so be it. Didn't mean I had to like it. See, I loved him. Had done all through college but he was so far above me in every department, no way would he ever reciprocate. In those days, he didn't even notice me. I wasn't a jock, or even a particularly bright scholar, just one of those inconsequential mid-range students who walk the campus invisible to all except their closest friends, and I had few enough of those.

I'd been fucking Jerrod, jock extraordinaire, most popular guy in college, the student most likely to become president, for weeks now. Dreams don't get any better than that.

It didn't start out as a sexual arrangement – far from it. That happened by accident. I have Jerrod's previous boyfriend, Kyle, to thank for moving our relationship up a notch. He'd be spewing if he realized that through one stupid action he'd inadvertently accomplished for me what I had a snowball's chance in hell of accomplishing on my own.

But you want to know how it all happened. From the beginning. Deep breath. Well, I'd been a member of the (unofficial and gay) Jerrod Spicer Fan Club since I'd first arrived at college and noticed him across a crowded campus. He was so handsome, so fit, so charismatic that I stopped dead in my tracks forcing other students to walk around me while I gawked at his 'perfectness'. I was smitten. I knew in my heart he was meant for me – okay, too much Disney in childhood fucks with your head. I also discovered he was from town royalty: grandson of the acknowledged matriarch of the town. Shit! Not only was he gorgeous, talented, sporty, and droolworthy, he was also wealthy and privileged. That was a lethal combination. The surprise was that Jerrod was down-to-earth, friendly, and not so far up his own fundament that he didn't have time to acknowledge his fans.

During football practice, we all-male admirers would slip into the darkened stands to watch Jerrod run through his paces with the other members of the team. There were usually about a dozen footie tragics besides us, mainly campus newspaper sports reporters or opposition team spies, as well as a smattering of cheer leaders and players' girlfriends. I happily admit I had absolutely no interest in the game, its rules, or its outcomes. I was there to watch my idol, my cock straining to escape the confines of my jeans as I soaked up the image of Jerrod in tight shorts, wishing it was me in the pack with all those ripped guys, hugging my arm around Jerrod's muscular shoulder.

Damn! I almost blew in my briefs just thinking about it.

If I saved my admiration for one man out on the grass, I focused my hatred for another of the players: Kyle Jenner. If Jerrod was the most beautiful man in the entire university, then Kyle ran a very close second. They both played for the same team, both achieved high marks scholastically, although in different fields of study, and they were an item. One was out and proud, the other was sort of out and less than proud, but they were doin' it – to each other.

I could have put my dislike of Kyle to one side if the lovers had wanted me to be the meat in the sandwich. Never gonna happen! Besides, Kyle was Grade A. A standing for asshole. Whereas Jerrod was open and friendly, Kyle was secretive and taciturn and, rumor had it, playing around on the side unbeknown to Jerrod.

Unbeknown no longer, it seemed. We Jerrodophiles seated in the bleachers were witness to the break-up. Even the campus newspaper gossip reporter was there to watch the fireworks. Cicely Trublood (not her real name), kept her identity secret, lodging her stories anonymously in order to minimize the possibility of legal threats and/or physical violence. Her items were always scrupulously true even if not always in the public-need-to-know category, and always sufficiently salacious that it was the first page to which readers turned when they picked up the stuffy student newspaper. Although she didn't always name names, most people could easily guess the identities of the targeted subjects of the gossip.

I was one of the few who knew Trublood's true identity. That was because I'd accidentally slept with *him* one night when we were both so inebriated neither of us remembered anything about the escapade. Except that Mason Fletcher, the cute nerdy fellow student I'd picked up had, in a moment of testosterone envy at my incessant chatter about my love for Jerrod Spicer, announced that he was none other than the notorious Cicely Trublood who had outed that very same football hero, and Kyle, his equally closeted squeeze. I had to swear as an atheist on a battered copy of Christopher Hitchens's *god is not Great* (sic) that, on pain of death, I would not reveal his secret. As Mason/Cicely had been at that very moment brandishing a large kitchen knife, drunkenly thrusting it in my direction to emphasize the importance of secrecy, I readily agreed. I was just grateful I didn't have to sign a contract to that effect sealed in my own blood.

Cicely's outing of the two jocks was a mixed blessing. Neither had gone the usual route of denying the accusations and, in fact, Jerrod had called a meeting of the team and college coaches to confess all, saying he would resign from the team if they felt it was in their best interests – it wasn't, and they voted so – and then gave a frank and full frontal interview and photograph – his most private body parts discreetly covered by a football – to the same newspaper that had outed him. If anything, he attracted even more fans and admirers. Nothing enhances your fuckability more than being involved in a gay sex scandal (of the right sort).

Kyle had to be dragged out a few weeks later, complaining bitterly about 'invasion of privacy' the whole time. His announcement was greeted with less interest than the story about the number of iPads stolen from vehicles in the science wing car park. I guess he was worried about all the college students, and others, who would come out of the woodwork in order to get their share of the publicity glare, claiming an intimacy with him he'd prefer be kept secret.

Cicely had already dumped on Kyle in his column, interviewing a number of college undergrads who were obviously pissed off with the Rugby star for sharing his charms too liberally. The fan club realized that the two players did not have an agreed 'open' relationship when, the afternoon after the infidelity gossip item appeared, there was a ruckus on the oval as the team practiced. How fortuitous that Cicely had his mobile phone camera primed and ready. His shot of Jerrod landing the blow on Kyle's jaw was splashed on the front page of the city's major daily newspaper with a Mason Fletcher byline, quoting extensively from his own report from the college newspaper written as Cicely.

Jerrod was suspended for two matches and sent off for rage counseling, refused permission to join his team-mates until he'd been given a clean bill of psychological health. That was rubber stamped because the team needed his sporting prowess to win their games and only a few diehard team-mates liked Kyle.

That lover's tiff is how I got to know him a little better. It began innocently enough. During his suspension, he sat with members of his fan club while watching practice. He was so enamored of the game that if he couldn't participate in warming up and honing his skills, he'd at least watch.

While some of his devotees had bailed out of the appreciation society because of Jerrod's use of violence, others were more forgiving. The latter group included me. I abhorred resorting to fists but I consoled myself with the knowledge Jerrod had been sorely provoked. Besides, I'd forgive the man almost anything. I had it bad.

Most of the guys seated in the stands were impatient to make an impression on Jerrod, eager to wrangle him into their rebound beds if they could without putting in the mileage. Their pick-up conversation with him petered out very quickly and, when they realized their attempts to impress were as feeble as their chances, they moved on. I sat away from the sycophantic throng of admirers, listening to the unsuccessful attempts at seduction, not because I didn't want to take my own chance but because I was such a dipshit I'd bungle it even worse than the other followers. My social chat was less than small – it was miniscule.

I guess, in the end, that was my salvation.

Jerrod, obviously fed up with the incessant puerile conversational come-ons moved to a bench not far from me, nodding an acknowledgement as he sat down. I nodded back, adding, "Sorry about your break-up," before turning back to the team's practice run, sending evil thoughts to Kyle who kept looking up into the stands because he knew Jerrod would be watching. He was showing off, attempting to engender jealousy in his former boyfriend by playing up to other hot guys on the team, and even a few of the female cheer leaders working their butts off rehearsing a new routine.

I kept my eyes straight ahead, my tongue paralyzed with shyness, even though I was desperate to see how Jerrod was taking it. Not well if the grunts, groans and curses were anything to go by. It didn't get any better after football practice was over as Kyle called up into the stand as he exited to the dressing rooms, "I can see you there Jerrod. I'll be waiting for you outside. You can't fool me. I know you still want me."

I heard Jerrod take a deep breath as if to reply, but he must have thought better of it, because he merely muttered 'shit.'

"Anything I can do to help?" I asked.

He swore a few more times as he paced among the benches, totally ignoring me. I could see I was of little use so I mumbled, "Well, see ya," and walked off. I hadn't gone far when I heard Jerrod call.

"Hey."

I turned to face him.

"You really want to help me?"

Fuck, yeah. Use me. Use me, please.

"Any way I can."

"Listen, I'll pay you for your time," he said. "This is a purely commercial transaction so don't go getting any ideas. Okay?"

"O–kay," I said hesitantly, wondering what the fuck he had in mind.

"I'm also paying you to keep your mouth shut tight. Understand?"

I understood perfectly that I was little more than goods and chattels to someone like Jerrod to whom money was no object. Yes, I flinched at his callous disregard for me as a human being but my puppy infatuation over-rode my self-esteem and the idea of cash in hand detoured my good sense. I was such a sucker.

He lowered his voice. "Long story short, Kyle is an asshole. I don't know what I ever saw in him. I guess I turned a blind eye to the fact he was cheating on me. So, I'm stupid when it comes to love—"

"Just like everybody in the whole wide world," I interrupted in a futile attempt to make him feel a little less foolish.

Jerrod was obviously pissed off at my attempt to level the playing field to include him with the general populace. "I am not like everybody else," he snapped, putting me firmly back in my place. At that point the alarm bells should have been ringing, but my brain had switched off the soundtrack.

When I should have been walking away, I merely leaned closer to listen to Jerrod's instructions.

"Just follow my lead," he said with more than a hint of exasperation to his voice. "You think you can do that?"

I nodded.

He looked me up and down as if examining me like a biology specimen, his face souring with what he saw. He looked around, obviously hoping for a better choice than me.

He sighed deeply. We were the only people still in the bleachers. "I guess you'll have to do. Come on."

Grabbing my arm, he dragged me toward the exit. "You will not under any circumstances make a move without my say so. You will keep your mouth shut at all times unless spoken to. You will never, I reiterate, never, contradict me. None of this is real. All I need is someone to ride shotgun."

Kyle was waiting at the bottom of the stairs, a smug grin writ large on his handsome kisser. It made me just want to smack him.

"What's your name?" Jerrod whispered at the last moment.

"Colm."

"Colin?"

"C.O.L.M."

Jerrod looked at me as if I had two heads.

"Who's the lapdog?" Kyle sneered as we got closer.

I bristled. Jerrod put his hand on my arm to calm me before making introductions. There was no attempt on either side to shake hands. Social niceties over, Kyle all but elbowed me aside to take his perceived rightful place beside his former lover.

"What's say we head back to your place for a little…" He finished the sentence by slapping Jerrod on the butt. Hard.

Jerrod took my arm, insinuating me between himself and Kyle.

"You betrayed me, Kyle. You think you can just go on as before. No, mate. Things have changed."

"Don't be such a girl," Kyle moaned.

Jerrod bristled.

"Wrong thing to say, mate," I smiled, ignoring Jerrod's instructions not to speak. "Next time, try saying sorry."

I steered Jerrod toward the car park as Kyle vented his anger via an explosion of expletives that would have got him arrested if the area hadn't been so deserted.

"Deep breaths," I whispered as Jerrod hyperventilated. "That's it. Calm now. Breathe. In. Out. In. Out."

By the time we reached his car, a silver Lexus, the most expensive vehicle on the lot, he was almost himself again. He beeped the central locking and opened the driver's door. I stood watching, wondering what he expected of me now. "For fuck's sake, get in the car," he hissed. "I'll drive you home."

I guess it was fortunate I couldn't afford my own wheels and had traveled to the sports ground on public transport. Buckling myself into the passenger's seat, Jerrod said, "He's probably still watching us. Now, where the fuck do you live? It better not be too far out of my way."

Nice. It's always a pleasure to discover your hero has a potty mouth and a short fuse. Still, I could forgive Jerrod anything, especially as he was driving me home. I had no delusions it was anything more than it was: I'd been hired to help him escape his cheating boyfriend.

Jerrod took off with a screech of tires, obviously still upset. The car cost more than my four years of tuition and smelled like I always believed luxury would smell if it had a scent, the leather seats so inviting I begged forgiveness of what poor creature had involuntarily donated its skin for my comfort. I hummed my satisfaction.

I couldn't just relax and let the silence envelope us. No way. If he'd so much as turned on the radio it might have stopped me and my big mouth. But he didn't.

"You still love him, huh?" I ventured.

"I'm paying you to keep your mouth shut," he snapped.

I shrugged. "I guess I just like to talk. I've always had a fear of silence."

He slammed his open palm against the steering wheel. "Just my fuckin' luck. Is there anything else can go wrong today?"

"I don't like to be the harbinger of bad news," I replied with, I hoped, just the right amount of levity, "but I think Kyle's following us." I'd been watching for him in the rear vision mirror since I'd noticed him pull out of the car park not long after we left.

"Shit! Shit! Shit!"

"Okay. Answer me one thing. Are you trying to make him jealous?"

"I'm not normally a bad person, but Kyle is such a bastard."

"You do still love him, don't you?"

"Yeah, I guess. I'm not sure what love is, but he gets my dick hard. I think about him all the time. It kills me when I know he's with someone else."

I could have told him he deserved better but that wouldn't have helped the current situation.

"If you wanted to make him jealous then, perhaps, you should have chosen someone a bit better looking than me. Another jock, maybe."

"Nah. It'll be a blow to his ego that I chose to go off with someone so much ug…plainer than he is."

If I'd had a fragile ego myself, I would have been devastated by that statement. I let it go, remembering I was merely a paid companion.

Mistaking my silence for sulking at his comment, Jerrod attempted to placate me. "I'm sorry. That was insensitive."

"But right on the button," I added. "I know I'm not in your league, or Kyle's. Never was, never will be." Time to twist the knife to get a little of my own back. "But then, I won't have to look in the mirror and watch my looks deteriorate, my hair thin, my muscles turn to blubber with the ravages of time like you and Kyle will, wondering what happened to the good looking young man you still feel inside."

Jerrod turned to examine me closely, as if seeing me for the first time. "Ouch. But I deserved that."

I wasn't about to pull my punches. "Yes, you did."

"You're not just the unprepossessing little nerd I took you to be. You've got spirit."

This guy was as good looking as Michelangelo's David but he was also as cold as marble with about as much sensitivity as a Brussels sprout. He might have said more but we pulled up in front of the dilapidated frat house for the chronically uncool that I called home. There was an awkward moment as Jerrod extracted his wallet and peeled off a fifty, thrusting it into my hand. "That should cover any inconvenience and any unintentional slight on my part."

It did more to put me in my place than anything else he'd said or done that evening. I was sorely tempted not to take the money, but then I remembered how much fifty bucks meant to me and how little it meant to him. Had he treated me more like a human being and less like a convenience for his use, it may have been a different matter.

I opened the door and got out of the car, pocketing the cash as I did so. I made a mental note not to get up close and personal with anyone in future whom I admired: they would only disappoint. I also mentally tore my membership of the Jerrod Spicer Fan Club into a million pieces. No big deal, I only attended the rugby matches for the eye candy. The internet had a much better range of hot men and they were usually naked and sometimes even in action. Besides, I didn't have to shower for them. The net was also a source of the folder of Jerrod pics, gleaned from newspapers and magazines, I had on my laptop. I would have to consider deleting it.

Jerrod was about to take off when a familiar car roared into the street pulling up a little way behind. The ostentatious power and overt aggression of the vehicle and the way it was driven were Kyle's trademark. I'd been about to cross the street which would have given the game away. Instead, I diverted to Jerrod's side of the car praying he'd seen Kyle's stealthy approach and would not start his engine just yet. I also hoped he was perceptive enough that he'd power down the window before I got there. Nothing says true romance more than having to tap on your boyfriend's car window to get a goodnight kiss.

He was on the ball, so I leaned inside the car to the hissed instruction, "No tongues." What was it with Jerrod? He couldn't ask nicely? Maybe the rich think their bucketloads of cash give them the right to order people around like servants. Well, fuck you, Mr. Jerrod Spicer. I was seething inside so that our goodnight kiss for the benefit of our stalker was more akin to two men bonking heads together than genuine affection.

"Ow, watch what you're doing," he complained, keeping his voice as low as possible.

I was about to give him a piece of my extremely pissed off mind when he wrapped his hand around the back of my head to pull me in for the kiss. It may have been fun except his lips were clamped shut so tightly that dynamite would not have prised them apart. Sure he moved his head as if he were giving me enough tongue to satisfy demand at a butcher's for a month or more, while the reality was his mouth was as hard as the grimace on his face.

I was relieved when he let me go; my lips were definitely going to be bruised in the morning. I managed to whisper unkindly, "Thanks for the fifty pieces of silver" before striding toward the frat house, forgetting my acting for the moment.

Jerrod must have realized that I was a less than convincing boyfriend, opening the car door to call after me. "Colin, wait up."

Colin? For fuck's sake!

His hand on my shoulder stopped me in my tracks. However, he wasn't prepared for the look of thunder on my face. "It's Colm, asswipe, not Colin. I thought you might have at least tried to remember that."

Before I could vent any more of my spleen, he dragged me close and pressed his lips to mine, much more gently this time. Still no tongue but it no longer felt as if I was rubbing my face against one of the stone heads on Rapa Nui.

I melted into the kiss, actually returning a bit of heat, until Jerrod spoke with his mouth against mine. "Is he still looking?"

Peering over his shoulder I saw Kyle smoking, leaning against his car, becoming more and more agitated as the kiss seemed to linger. Finally, he threw the cigarette on the roadway grinding it with his shoe, probably visualizing my head under his heel. With one last glance in our direction, he hopped in his car and roared off, shouting 'Faggots' as he sped past us.

Jerrod quickly broke away from me once the sound of Kyle's car faded in the distance. "You're a lifesaver," he said, withdrawing another fifty from his wallet. "This is just between you and me, right?"

Could his assholeness get any bigger? I took the cash and turned on my heels. "Any time."

I heard his car drive off, with, I suspect, any memory of me dumped at the side of the road as surely as I was.

Once back in my room, depressed as buggery over the way the night had played out, I called up one of the porn movies I'd saved. It had nothing at all to do with football and starred no one who looked even remotely like my former hero. My orgasm was all a bit mechanical but I wanted relief in the shortest possible time. Then, I'd sleep soundly.

My head was in a better space the next morning, as was my bank balance now that I had an extra hundred dollars in exchange for an hour or so of humiliation and put-downs. Easy money. Whore? Moi? I preferred to call myself a Male Companion. All I had to do was wrap my ego in cotton wool. If the situation wasn't so pathetic I'd be laughing. I also had a better understanding of that old cliché about a hero with feet of clay. Still, it was difficult to keep the smile off my face. I hadn't exactly swapped spit with Jerrod but he'd been in my face, closer than I'd ever had any right to expect.

I'd learned a valuable lesson and I'd earned a hundred bucks, I was smiling. I wouldn't have to live on pot noodles all week. So heroes were thoughtless assholes? Who'da thunk it, eh?

I was remarkably chipper the next morning considering Jerrod Spicer's tumble from the Temple of Adulation into the Pit of Puerility. Odd as it was, I felt like we'd split up even though we'd never been in a relationship, unless you count the less than an hour I'd spent as a human shield against Kyle's weapons of mass seduction. I was liberated from my totally useless life of wallowing in the unattainable. Time to get real. What I needed in my life was less fluffy fantasy, pleasant as it was, and more earthy pursuits.

Word must have got around among Jerrod's admirers that I'd been seen getting into his car as, over the next few days, I was approached by a number of students with whom I was on a nodding acquaintance asking me what he was really like. I tried the truth with the first two or three until I noticed the looks of anger that signified their displeasure at having their idol's reputation blackened. How did they think I felt? After that I merely muttered a few platitudes and the enquirers scuttled away happy with the few crumbs of information I'd given them, secure in their comfortable fantasies more or less determined to win where I had failed. None of them knew the truth that I had been paid handsomely for my time.

I didn't go back to watch the college games. I'd had my fill of football. I heard rumors about Jerrod and Kyle, most of it about their public snarking. What did I care? It had nothing to do with me. Or so I thought. It was Cicely who revealed otherwise.

"I heard your name mentioned a few times at their last public slanging match. That is if you're going by the name Colin these days."

I sighed. Jerrod would never get my name right.

"You know he was looking everywhere for you after the game. Wanted to rub your affair in Kyle's face big time."

"What affair?"

"Jerrod Spicer is a mess. Doesn't know what he wants. Thinks it's Kyle but those two bring out the worst in each other," Mason said.

I'd always thought Mason had an ulterior motive when it came to his gossip columns, and that secret agenda was splitting up the two jocks so he could try his darndest to console Kyle. I called him on it. "This couldn't have anything to do with you having the hots for Kyle Jenner, could it?"

He didn't deny it. Okay, he didn't confirm it either. "Honey, my main concern is you. And Jerrod Spicer."

"There is no me and Jerrod Spicer. No amount of your gossip is going to prove otherwise."

"You going to the game on Saturday?"

"Nope. I picked up an extra shift at the Burgertorium."

Big mistake as it turned out. I found out only later – from my gossip source, Cicely – that Kyle upped the ante in the jealousy stakes, pawing one of the cheerleaders at every opportunity before, during, and after the game, much to Jerrod's distress.

Of course, not being aware of the escalation in the Jealousy War, I was totally unprepared for a confrontation on the front lawn of the geek frat house where I had my rather minimalist accommodation. No, it wasn't Kyle lying in wait as you would expect, but Jerrod. One of my frat brothers who worked that same shift at the Burgertorium had given me a ride back. I was not even out of my seat – in fact, I hadn't released the seat belt – before Jerrod wrenched open the car door and began screaming. "Where the fuck have you been?" I wish I could say he was like some jealous harridan, but he wasn't. I didn't know, at that stage, what was fueling his anger.

As I pushed past him to get out of the car, I replied as calmly as I could under the circumstances because a number of frat boys had brought beers and fold-up chairs out onto the front lawn to watch one of their own go head-to-head with the Campus Jock Queer. "I was at work, what does it look like?" I was still wearing the hideously embarrassing Burgertorium uniform with the talking burger logo. "What does it smell like?"

Didn't matter that I'd tried to leaven the fraught situation with a little humor, Jerrod merely sidestepped it and continued our high volume argument, although can it really be an argument if only one side is involved. "You know what it's like being left high and dry by my boyfriend at the football game?"

Boyfriend? Was he talking about me?

I scanned the growing numbers on the lawn to discover, to my horror, Cicely Trublood with cell phone aimed in our direction. This would make a nice scoop for the gutter journalist, particularly as we were standing on the kerb. I smiled at the joke.

I'd just made matters worse. "This is no smirking matter!" Jerrod was purple in the face he was so angry.

"Perhaps you'd like to tone it down a notch or two," I whispered. "People are watching."

"I don't care who's watching," he screamed. "I will not be treated this way. It's why I broke up with Kyle. I never expected you to treat me the same way."

I kept my voice low. "Treat you what way? You paid me to pretend to be your boyfriend for one night."

"Look what it got me," he shrieked. "Heartbreak again and again. Why can't anyone love me for me?"

I can be so thick sometimes. This was all playacting for the public. Word had got out about our 'relationship' and he was publicly ending it with me before I became an embarrassing albatross.

It was my turn to be irate. "You're embarrassed by me, aren't you?"

"What do you think?" he sneered.

This time I raised my voice. "I think you're the most conceited, puffed up, selfish little shit I've ever had the misfortune to mistakenly think I was in love with. You think money can buy you anything at all. I've got news for you, mister. You may be good-looking but you're fucking ugly inside."

With that I strode across the road and into the frat house to a smattering of applause from the front lawn and, I hoped, an open-mouthed Jerrod watching me walk away. He had to get the last word in. "I will not be just another notch on your belt."

I felt so Bette Davis. For effect, I slammed the front door, leaning against it panting that I was brave enough to say what I did. I was furious. How dare Jerrod think he could use me that way. My fault, too, I guess, that I allowed myself to be dazzled by his charm and his cash into the deceit. Oh, well, that was my fifteen minutes of fame.

Ms. Trublood ensured my fifteen minutes became a half hour, then a full hour, then…the campus newspaper was full of Jerrod's confrontation with me, plus the movie footage Cicely had taken appeared on the online edition, Facebook, and YouTube. I got over a thousand likes plus some comments about standing up to 'bullies who think they're God's gift.' And, yeah, a couple of invitations to go on a date. All very flattering but I knew all the interest would dry up as quickly as last night's cum patch.

Cicely tried seduction, alcohol, and the promise of untold wealth to get me to spill the beans. I was tempted, not by the glitzy baubles of notoriety but because I was so pissed that Jerrod was such a selfish twat. I'm prepared to give him a little leeway because it must be such a burden to be born with all the right DNA for looks, sporting prowess, intellectual ability, and a quick track to a powerful career in politics, medicine or international finance. You got the sarcasm, right?

My blood stopped boiling at the way Jerrod treated me about a week after the 'incident' by which time it had been supplanted as university news by the astounding discovery of pornography in the campus library. It turned out to be a large-format prestigious art book of wall paintings from Pompeii. A conservative university group had 'stumbled' across the volume which had been on the library shelves for well over a decade and demanded its removal because of the moral harm it could cause if anyone opened the book inadvertently. Ah, the world was back on its axis.

Jerrod's popularity trajectory didn't even blip.

Obviously the guys on the team thought love was as much a game as football because about two weeks later I heard Jerrod and Kyle were back together. According to Cicely Trublood, and let's face it she knew more about what went on around the campus than even the people involved, Kyle had begged forgiveness and Jerrod had been played for the sucker he was. They were an item again. If I wasn't still smarting over the patronizing manner in which I'd been treated I would have laid bets on the survivability of their relationship. Cicely was keeping a book.

If I'd put money on two weeks I would have been a wealthy man. Most people had opted for a much longer term. It's amazing how many want to see two good-looking jocks in love.

The reignited spark of romance had kept the duet at the peak of their game and the team was ranked top in the state; they were invincible. Jerrod and Kyle were seen everywhere together, not a breath of scandal or infidelity was attached to Kyle's name. Perhaps he had turned over a new leaf, although if he'd been my boyfriend he would have needed to turn over a whole encyclopedia of pages, electronic or paper. It was beyond me why Jerrod kept going back to him. I guess love does that to the suckers who get ensnared in its tentacles.

It was around the third week of the two jocks' reunion that I heard a knock at my door early in the evening. It was a Saturday and, as usual, I had no date, no prospects, in fact, no life. I'd been reading in bed and felt no compunction in answering my dorm door in baggy boxers and an old sweat stained T-shirt. It was unlikely any of the guys in the frat would be shocked or disgusted by my attire and I wasn't expecting any hot studs calling on my services. I was only half right.

Mason stood at the door, bouncing up and down in excitement. Before I'd had an opportunity to ask what he wanted, he shoved past me into my room, and pulled out the only comfortable chair after removing a soiled jockstrap that I'd managed to steal many months prior when I'd been really passionate about Jerrod and had sneaked into the dressing rooms pretending to be a reporter for a non-existent sporting newspaper and stolen his jockstrap and scarpered.

Mason lifted it to his nose and sniffed deeply. "Still the slight scent of Jerrod Spicer. You're a man after my own heart, Colm. Any time you want to come along to my room, I'll show you my extensive collection, all stolen of course, of male jock accoutrements for a sniff and tell."

Tempting as that offer was, I cut straight to the chase. "What brings you here at this time on a Saturday?"

"I have heard such delicious scandal through my contacts." He paused as if wishing for me to beg him to go on. I was too impatient to play this game.

"Spit it out," I said irritably. "Especially if it concerns me."

"Not everything is about you, honey. Most of it is about our lovebirds, Jerrod and Kyle."

"I couldn't care less," I grumped.

"Come off it. You're just a bit brittle because of the way Jerrod used you and dumped you. But you were well compensated for the jock's patronizing behavior."

"How the hell did you–?"

"Cicely Trublood knows everything, honey. And what she doesn't know, she makes up. What she makes up she puts out there in the hope that someone will give themselves away. In your case – snap!"

"I suppose I will now be the laughing stock of the entire campus when your next column appears?"

"By no means, honey," he said. "I have much bigger trout to gut and debone. I thought you might like to be there for the first thrust of the fish knife." If Mason's words didn't suggest an event of earth-shattering proportions, his evil smile certainly did. "And it involves two people who are near and dear to your heart."

That clinched it. It was no hardship to attend the game as I'd missed watching Jerrod in action – hot, sweaty football action – and Cicely was very convivial company. Cicely/Mason was a raconteur of the highest order and I'd seen him, as himself, keep a party full of macho jocks enthralled and laughing fit to burst when all they'd wanted to do initially was beat him to a pulp. Most people thought he was wasting his time getting a degree because he was already more intelligent than most of his professors and could have been banking his skills as a stand-up comedian, a talk-show host or a sitcom writer. I knew why he stayed, pimping his skills to the uni newspaper: he was looking for a boyfriend among those very same jocks he pilloried in his gossip column.

He was a very different personality when he was Cicely although he was not in any way transgender. Cicely was the persona he adopted when in gossip journalist mode, as if he was channeling the old Hollywood gossip queens such as Hedda Hopper. "It helps me to focus when I'm Cicely," he told me once. His tongue took on a razor edge, his concentration was a laser beam as he honed in on his hapless victims. 'Victims' is perhaps too strong a word as he had a certain morality to what he did. He had no patience with bullshit or corruption, whether it was of the personal, political, or institutional kind. I admired him for that and even though I felt he went too far at times, I couldn't fault his zeal to unmask hypocrisy.

Armed with our hot dogs and sodas, Cicely (for tonight he was in full Cicely mode) and I crammed ourselves among the lower echelons in the bleachers. We wanted front-row seats for what I was told would be the fireworks of the season although he was reticent about revealing their nature.

The cheer leaders were working their pom-poms on the field with the same energy and skill that, rumor had it, they worked their pussy muscles off the field. Call me psychic, but there was an unmistakable tension in the air. Or maybe that was just me. I was strangely agitated when the home team burst onto the field in a blaze of adulation and hysterical cheering and when I saw Jerrod acknowledge his stadium of fans by waving and blowing kisses, well, it did something in my crotch area. I adjusted myself as unobtrusively as possible but Cicely smirked. "Still like him, eh?"

I didn't deign his observation, as accurate as it was, with a reply. I'd been lying to myself for weeks but the touch of Jerrod's lips against mine had left me confused and hopelessly devoted even as I attempted to cast him from my mind. He was nothing to me. Untrue. He was my fantasy. I was nothing to him. Very true. He hadn't even bothered to acknowledge my existence on the few occasions we'd passed on the campus after our 'breakup,' he was too busy with his real friends. Kyle, however, always smirked in that superior way that made me want to knock his teeth in any time we were in close proximity. Yeah, right, like I had the strength or the courage to do that.

The game went well although the score meant nothing to me really, I was more taken with staring at Jerrod's ass. He was undoubtedly a top but that didn't stop me fantasizing how I'd like to snuggle my nose between his cheeks, lick his tight little hole, ram my cock into his…

Cicely nudged me out of my erotic reverie. I hadn't noticed people around us were headed to the exits and the rest rooms. The game was over. "Here comes the shit storm."

We had perfect seats for what was about to unfold. The team was straggling off the field toward the tunnel to their dressing rooms when Bethany, the head cheer leader broke ranks and catapulted herself into Kyle's arms. Startled at first, his face turned to abject horror as Bethany waved her hand, wiggling her fingers, in the face of his exhausted team mates. I had no idea what was going on but I knew whatever it was it was not good.

Bethany was climbing Kyle's body even as he attempted to disengage her. The local TV cameras were moving in for the kill. This was better than a soap opera. Then I noticed that Jerrod looked stricken, like his world had collapsed, like he wanted to curl up in a ball and die.

I looked up at the mammoth screen that was now broadcasting the kerfuffle on the field and got a close-up on Bethany's hand. A ring sparkled on her engagement finger.

"Let me translate," Cicely said with a satisfaction that I felt was unbecoming. "Kyle. Homophobic parents. Ultimatum. Hurried engagement to gorgeous head cheer leader. Boyfriend not invited. Not even notified of change in relationship status. Succinct enough for you?"

My head hurt. Jerrod would be devastated to hear the news this way, I could see it. The crowd was in uproar with chants of Kyle's and Bethany's name as if they were royalty. Jerrod stood to the side, lost and alone. It would be a matter of time before one of the TV channels picked up on him and went in for the kill.

Cicely elbowed me. "Go get him, Tiger."

That was all I needed. Deaf to the cheers and raucous catcalls around me I was down over the fence in a flash before security could catch me. I got to Jerrod before the camera crew and barreled into him, knocking him on his ass. Flinging myself on top of him, I pasted my lips to his and hugged him tight. Coming up for breath, I whispered, "It's gonna be okay, I promise. But right now the cameras are circling, so close your eyes and pucker up. Kiss like you've never kissed before or they won't believe it." He seemed stunned momentarily. "Colin?" This was neither the time nor the place to correct him. I cared that he couldn't remember my damn name but not enough to storm off. I was there to prevent his utter humiliation.

He wrapped his arms around me where we lay and I could do little else but relax into him as his lips brushed mine. Hard to concentrate on your kiss when someone is trying to shove a TV camera up your nostril – I'm ready for my close-up, Mr. DeMille, but not that close. A sob escaped from Jerrod but no one but me could have heard it. I smoothed his hair down over his forehead covering his eyes so the moisture in the corners wouldn't be seen. We went in for a second kiss. He relaxed this time.

Jerrod opened his lips and I slid right in, our tongues wrestling for dominance. It was sweet, just the way I'd always imagined it would be. Whoa, I was getting carried away. At least a lower portion of my body was. "Jerrod! Jerrod?" the pack of newspaper hounds were trying to prise us apart as a groan went up from sections of the crowd because our kiss was showing in glorious color on the huge screen.

What did we do now? I really hadn't thought this through at all. But maybe I'd given Jerrod time to pull himself together and he'd come up with a simple solution to the problem. Maybe he didn't see it as a problem.

The questions started again, the journalists a cacophony of screeching parrots that did my head in although it gave me time to look over to where

Kyle was surrounded by his well-wishing team-mates and cheer leaders, Bethany flashing the ring like she'd just won an Oscar. That award certainly should have been Kyle's since he'd obviously been playacting his relationship with Jerrod. I wanted to wipe that bloody smirk from his face as he glanced over at our little huddle.

The media scrum was spooking Jerrod who looked ready to flee. "What have you got to say about the situation, Jerrod?" one particularly nasty piece of scum asked. "I thought you and Kyle were going steady." She looked down her nose at me, obviously found me wanting, then indicating our linked hands, asked, "Who the hell is this?"

What could either of us say? We both began garbled sentences at once and then stopped as if to allow the other to embroider some fiction. This wasn't going to end well. Jerrod's face was etched with exhaustion. He nodded and I drew a deep breath to give my mind some feeble chance of coming up with a plausible explanation.

Before I could utter a word, I heard "Let me through please. Move out of the way. I represent Jerrod Spicer and his boyfriend, Colm Bransfield."

Jerrod looked at me and I gave a confused shrug. I had as little idea of what was going on as anyone.

"And who would you be?" the nasty female journalist sneered.

Mason puffed up his chest in an approximation of importance. Very approximate, I thought, but now was not the time to mention it. I had to admire Mason's style if not his technique. There was a touch of Cicely in his behavior but he'd put a leash on her for the moment.

"Mason Fletcher of Fletcher Management."

"Never heard of you or your management company," Little Ms. Nasty jeered.

It didn't faze Mason at all. "Perhaps you need to get out more," he responded, to gales of laughter from her confederates, pointedly turning his back on her to address the media pack. "I've been authorized to give a brief statement on behalf of my clients but, let's not forget, today is about the beautiful *secret and rather sudden* engagement of Kyle Jenner to Bethany Townshend." His emphasis did not go unnoticed. So saying he turned to them, all sweetness and light, to draw attention to Bethany's disheveled state and Kyle's embarrassed (I would have said unhappy if I didn't know better) face that was smeared with Bethany's bright purple lipstick from their celebratory kisses.

"Not really your color, Kyle. Try something that matches your personality," Mason called. He was definitely channeling Cicely at that moment.

"Black," I heard Jerrod mutter.

Kyle's response was a look so murderous it would have turned Medusa herself to stone.

"Now, where was I?" He cleared his throat. "Mr. Spicer and Mr. Bransfield have been going steady for almost six weeks now."

There was a murmur from the crowd and a group of journalists sensing a hotter story than the perennial *Jock Gets Engaged to Cheerleader*, peeled away from the other couple to attend our engagement story, fictitious though it was. I squeezed Jerrod's hand as I felt him getting more and more nervous.

"As you all know Jerrod and Kyle have had an on-again off-again relationship for quite a while. Basically, at heart, even though Kyle readily admits his bisexuality…" Mason paused as if expecting someone to cry 'bullshit', but I bit my tongue. "Well, Kyle is much more comfortable with his heterosexual side so it's not surprising that he would eventually get engaged to someone more to his taste. And Bethany Townshend is quite a morsel. What's not to like? Her dad's money and conservative political affiliations make her the ideal candidate for matrimony with the handsome heir to the blue blood Jenner estate." Mason raised an eyebrow to see if anyone would dare to suggest it was a marriage of convenience because the Jenner's had been hit hard by the global financial meltdown. No one uttered a word, much too frightened of a libel suit.

Mason was laying it on thick now. "Jerrod, of course, was heartbroken when he and Kyle finally split up but for the sake of their fans they kept up a pretense of a relationship no matter what the personal cost. It was during this period that Jerrod met Colm." He spelt out my name for the pack of journalists. Jerrod looked at me strangely before leaning in to whisper, "I thought your name was Colin." I restrained myself – just – from hitting him.

There was another four or five minutes of Mason's fairytale about the romance between Jerrod and myself before he wrapped it up. "Thank you, ladies and gents. I may also add that Ms. Cicely Trublood, whom I am also proud to represent, has all the inside dish in tomorrow morning's edition of the *Daily Tatler*. Thank you all for your time."

There were a few shouted questions but Mason began shepherding us toward the car park. Kyle had hung around obviously to smooth over the rift between Jerrod and himself caused by his unexpected engagement. "Not now, Kyle," Mason said belligerently, shoving him aside as we walked rapidly away.

"I thought he was going to hit you," I said to Mason.

"He wouldn't dare. Not with all the photographers and TV cameras still hanging around."

"Um, guys," Jerrod said meekly attempting to put the brakes on our departure. "I have to go collect my gear."

"All done. It's in my car," Mason said.

"WTF?"

"I have to be on top of all contingencies considering the small fortune you pay me to be your manager."

"I pay you fuck all," Jerrod responded, about to lose his cool. "And who asked you to butt in anyway?" He turned on me. "Is this your idea?"

"How about we discuss this in private without the benefit of the sports and social press getting a whiff of fairy dust about the bullshit I just peddled. Oh, and glad to see how grateful you are that Colm and I just saved your sorry ass."

Jerrod huffed but kept walking until we reached Mason's car. "You two hop in the back. People are still watching so it wouldn't look good to sit apart." I obeyed automatically because I was still too shell shocked from all that had happened. Jerrod grizzled but did as instructed. As the car pulled out of the parking lot, I caught a glimpse of Kyle glaring. A far-from-happy Kyle.

"Okay, you've done your saving-the-jock routine and I thank you. I'll ring home and get someone to come pick up my car. I have no intention of going back there tonight." Jerrod was being obnoxious. "Let's get one thing straight here…" He unclasped my hand with more vigor than necessary as if he was trying to dislodge his cum after jerking off.

Mason interrupted, snorting. "I don't think anyone around here at present even comes close to being straight. And I include the lovely Kyle in that. Engaged? What a joke."

"It's his family. They've forced him into it." Jerrod was in denial.

"Justify it any way you want, sweetheart, but Kyle is no good for you." Mason was taking no prisoners.

"Let me guess, Colin here is what's good for me? Right?"

My irritation was such that they could probably hear me grinding my teeth in China.

"You could probably do a lot worse."

Jerrod was quiet for a few moments. "Hey, this is not a shakedown, is it?"

I was perplexed. "Shakedown?"

"You know, blackmail. That sort of shit."

I couldn't work out whether Jerrod went out of his way to be obnoxious or whether it came naturally. Mason spoke for both of us. "You are the most unlikely blackmail victim I've ever met. You have no secrets. Your whole life is out there."

Not the brightest bulb. "Oh, yeah. I guess you're right. Hey, you're not gonna sell me into white slavery?"

I let the ball through to Cicely for the return on that one. "Not much call for brain-dead himbos at the moment."

I could hear the cogs in Jerrod's brain attempting to work out whether he'd just been insulted. "Hey!" *Houston, we have contact.*

The remainder of the journey was silent, Jerrod moving over to the window to stare blankly into the darkness outside while I fumed a body length away. I lost track of time and was just about to doze off when Mason slowed the car. "Showtime, folks, so get snuggling."

"Wha…?" Jerrod had obviously fallen asleep. We were both somewhat groggy and exhausted. "Wha… showtime?"

"We are on approach to your house, Jerrod. There will be photographers and journalists and TV cameras. Time for you and Colm to start playing snuggle bunnies…"

I was beginning to resent this intrusion into my life. "Really, Mason? Snuggle bunnies?"

Mason tone got decidedly waspish. "Look, I'm not doing this for my own health. Short story long. We are about to save Jerrod a lot of abject humiliation brought about by Kyle, that lying, cheating, sniveling…"

"Okay, I get the picture," Jerrod snapped.

"If you do what I tell you, you'll come out of this smelling of roses. You'll be the wronged party. Kyle will be the bastard. Jerrod, I thought you'd want revenge. And I think you can parlay this into lots of personal promotion that will be a boost in the ass for your career."

Jerrod muttered. "Hmm." He was interested.

I wasn't as easily seduced. "What's in it for me?"

Mason winked in his rear vision mirror. "You get to play house with Mr. Hot and Funky tonight." The implication was that I'd get to touch and kiss even if nothing further. But, more importantly, I had free access to make said Jock god fall in love with me.

Jerrod panicked. "You can't move in with me. My gran would kill me. She thinks it's a phase and I'll grow out of it."

Mason slammed on the breaks. Fortunately, the road was deserted. "Okay, Jerrod. Time to make a commitment. You and Colm. I'll spell that again for you. C.O.L.M…"

Mason and I said it together before Jerrod could even open his mouth. "I thought your name was Colin?" We high fived to Jerrod's consternation.

Mason started up the car. "It's a lot to take in. Humor me for the moment. Hold hands. A quick virginal kiss goodnight at the house. Have a look at the news in the morning. The press will be on your side. Make good use of it. You, too, Colm." He winked at me.

Jerrod was hesitant. "O-kay."

"Buckle up, boys. We're home."

I moved to grab Jerrod's hand but he responded by yanking me forcefully against his chest. He'd turned side on so he could cradle me in his arms as he rested against the door. "Revenge will be fuckin' sweet," he said, smiling for the first time that night.

By the time we'd run the gamut and finally made it to the front door of Jerrod's home – well, that's underselling what was a mansion – we had been questioned and photographed and generally pummeled by the press. Jerrod and I posed on the front porch giving each other a chaste goodnight kiss, after which Mason escorted me back to the car and with a final Camille-like wave, as if my heart were broken to part for even a minute, we took off down the driveway.

My last view of the mansion was not of Jerrod letting himself inside the hefty front door but of a figure staring from a glass panel to one side of the entrance. She stood bolt upright as if her spine was the strongest steel, her countenance stern and judgmental. I shuddered.

THE BURGERTORIUM kept me occupied for the rest of the week although there was startlingly little fallout from my rescue of the humiliated Jerrod Spicer. I hadn't seen or heard from him since Mason had dropped him off at his home. Perhaps he was mortified by the totally fictitious story of our 'true meeting of souls' that had appeared under Cicely's byline the following morning. I'd had a good laugh although deep down I regretted there wasn't even one word of truth to the fable. Oh, well, it would blow over in a very short time when Jerrod and I never appeared in public together or did any of the other things out-and-proud boyfriends were supposed to do.

Back to everyday reality. Cars backed up for yonks, most of the customers polite and understanding, some grizzlers, while a small minority decided to big-note themselves in front of their friends by belittling the staff. I was on the front line, at the server's window, so I knew I was gonna cop shit. I just didn't know what sort of shit was headed my way.

Name calling I can cope with, even the occasional threat of bodily harm can be laughed off because the guys never get out of their cars, but the homophobic abuse gets tiresome. Occasionally, very occasionally fortunately, someone will brandish a weapon at the window. We have a special button to press on such occasions which focuses the security camera on the offending vehicle and patches immediately to the cops. I'd never experienced one of those calls in all the time I'd been in the job. I didn't that night either although I did have the worst problem ever in my experience.

Late in the evening a familiar car pulled in and the window rolled down. I'd already begun my spiel, "Good evening. Thank you for stopping by the Burgertorium."

Fuck. It was Kyle with a car full of his football mates. I had already heard there'd been wild celebrations over his pending nuptials. As a result they were a little exuberant by the time they stopped at my server window.

I was about to rattle off their order before handing the paper bags over to them when Kyle's voice broke my concentration.

"Well, look who it is," he sneered. "Colin, isn't it?"

I didn't bother to correct him

"Where's your new boyfriend? Does he know you're a working girl?" he asked before turning to the others in the car. "Hey, guys, this is Jerrod's new boyfriend." He did that irritating air quote thing with his fingers, and his audience laughed.

There was no point continuing the conversation, so I began reeling off their order but Kyle wasn't going to let it be. He rattled off a string of abuse including a multitude of references to the F-word: faggot. I merely finished off the inventory and held out the burgers and French fries.

"Is it safe to eat here, what with a faggot handling the food?" he asked.

It was a rhetorical question so I didn't bother answering him. He kept up a string of abuse along a similar vein until even his buddies in the car were embarrassed, their laughter choking in the throats.

"I'm not eating food a faggot's touched," he proclaimed.

"Must make it very difficult for you to make your own meals then," I responded with a polite smile pasted on my face.

There was nervous laughter from one or two of the guys in the car, before someone said, "Come on, Kyle, grab the bags and let's get going. We're hungry."

Kyle was apoplectic with rage. I knew because he was as red as the ketchup on our burgers, his face contorted into a life-threatening snarl. He grabbed the bags and drinks from me, taking off in a squeal of tires followed by my "Please call again soon."

"What's with that guy?" Jerry, my assistant, asked.

I shrugged. No way was I going to get into a discussion about Jerrod and Kyle. "His team must have lost today."

It was late by the time we'd served the last stragglers on their way home, tidied up the premises, put out the garbage for collection, and locked up. Exhaustion seeped into my bones. All I wanted was to go home, take a quick shower to wash off the smell of deep fried fat that gets into all your clothes as well as your hair and your skin, and flop into bed for eight hours. I needed it for both my mind and my body's recuperation.

As I stood at the stop waiting for a bus that was already twenty minutes late, dreading the long journey home, willing myself to remain awake because the drivers were notorious for leaving passengers behind if you didn't signal correctly, a car stopped in front of me. The interior was dark so the driver could have been a serial killer…or Kyle. Same difference really. I blinked. No one I knew could afford a car like that. The passenger window powered down. "Need a lift?" Jerrod. How many cars did he own?

I'm not proud. I ambled over as Jerrod opened the door for me. "I'm a bit rank," I warned, fearing my grease-spattered clothes or the smell might permeate his luxurious leather seats.

His response was brusque. "Get in."

No argument from me. I clicked my seat belt in place and Jerrod took off. I glanced at him, his profile making my heart beat faster. He really was a gorgeous man. I had to mind slap myself to stop drooling over the unattainable.

"Missed you at the game today," he said.

I did note the lack of a personal pronoun to his sentence, so I knew it wasn't that he missed me, he meant rather that I wasn't there.

I thought it politic not to mention I had no intention of giving up extra shifts at work to just be relationship candy at his games. "I did an extra shift at work."

He looked at the hideous Burgertorium uniform unable to conceal the smirk on his face.

"What?" I said grumpily.

"You look kinda cute in that outfit."

"No one has ever mistaken me for cute, especially not when I'm wearing this rubbish," I responded.

It was true, no one had ever called me 'cute' before, not even in the throes of lackluster passion which is the only sort I ever seemed to attract.

"You are, you know. If you just updated your fashion sense a bit and styled your hair—"

I'm afraid I snorted. *Me? Cute? Me? Afford fashion and a stylist? In your dreams.*

"You don't believe me?"

"Not everyone on campus has an unlimited source of income," I retorted. "Especially not me."

"That's what I wanted to talk to you about."

"Hey, you missed my turn-off." I knew he'd only been to my frat house once so I cut him some slack although I was eager to get to bed.

"I'm not taking you home."

"If you're selling *me* into white slavery I think the buyer will want his money back."

Jerrod laughed. "Okay, you're not male model material, but you've got something."

"Don't tell me I have inner beauty unless you're gonna pay some surgeon to cut me open and re-attach it to the outside."

"Nah, I wouldn't feed you that bullshit. Beauty has a lot to do with confidence and the way you present yourself to the world. Now, you're cute, so if you played that up, you could grab yourself a real hunk for a boyfriend."

"You know how patronizing that sounds?"

"I guess it does. Sorry."

"Now, what was it you really wanted to talk to me about?"

"Don't get the wrong idea…"

He paused, so I guessed he expected a response. "I won't."

"How would you like a job as my boyfriend, full-time." So I couldn't mistake his intention, he emphasized the word 'job.'

"It has its appeal," I lied. "But I have to earn a living. I don't have parents to rely on who can send me money." I meant it to sting a little and from the surprised look on Jerrod's face it had.

"Ouch. I thought if I emphasized the word you'd realize this was a paid position."

"Oh, I did. It's just I can't afford to lose my job at the Burgertorium in exchange for a couple of bucks when you feel the need to parade me about for whatever reason you may have. I need a guaranteed permanent income to pay for a few luxuries such as books and, oh, food."

Even though he must have picked up on my sarcasm, Jerrod managed a smile. "You mean you don't get to eat all you want at the burger joint?"

"I prefer my arteries unclogged. Besides, when you see how the food is prepared it rather turns you off eating it."

He held his hands up in surrender. "I'll keep that in mind."

"Why?"

"Why what?"

"Why do you want to hire my services again?"

"Is that a trick question?"

"Of course not."

"What does it matter why I want to hire you? This is purely a business transaction; nothing more, nothing less. The reasons are totally beside the point."

"Provided it's not some sick game to humiliate me."

"I can assure you that it isn't."

He looked sincere but I never was a good judge of character. Still, I hesitated.

"If the idea of being seen with the hottest jock on campus which, incidentally, should not only do wonders for your own self-esteem but will increase your cache as a desirable date a thousandfold..."

He paused just long enough for me to show my gratitude that out of all the available males he had deigned to bestow his largesse on poor, humble moi. Instead, I just rolled my eyes at his ego. He saw me.

"Hmm. In that case, I'm sure we can come to a mutually satisfying arrangement. What is it you want?"

I wanted to suggest he shove his cock in my mouth or my ass as a suitable deposit but I suspected Jerrod would be offended by my effrontery. As a result, I merely suggested the rather mundane alternative, "I want a guaranteed semester. I don't care whether you keep up the charade for that length of time, but I want to be paid for a semester." When there was no indication of his baulking at that demand, I thought why the hell not, and added, "In advance."

His smirk rather indicated that this had been his intention all along and that I was an easy mark although he was gracious enough to say, "You're a tough negotiator. But, I agree. Give me until the end of the week to get the cash together – I assume you want cash in hand?" I nodded. "Then how about we make our first date next Saturday? At the game?"

I agreed. I had no intention of giving up my meager income at the Burgertorium but I could cut back on the extra shifts. Bridge burning was not part of my cautious nature.

Jerrod asked for my cell phone into which he programmed his number, much to my surprise. "In case there's some sort of emergency, in case you get delayed or something prevents you from keeping a date." I was about to tell him how considerate that was when he went and spoiled it by adding, "I don't want to be standing about like a loser if you're not gonna show."

That's when I should have walked away.

I didn't need to use his number and I didn't leave him standing about like a loser, I turned up on demand at the requested times. That's how my life slipped into the Twilight Zone where I was photographed with the best looking jock at the university.

It's difficult when you spend so much time with a person not to get to know them better. Although we'd begun our 'relationship' as strangers we'd been forced to talk to each when we found ourselves thrown together in a casual setting. Then things got serious. There was talk of 'dinners' – very public dinners. I didn't mind although it was demeaning to me that Jerrod would pay every time. The first such event was for the press. They'd been forewarned we'd be celebrating – I think it was our third month together or some such rubbish – and Jerrod had come to rely on Mason to organize the social media presence for the two of us. He'd made it sound as if we were a match made in heaven. I'd been nervous, getting prepared as best I could in my room, trashing my wardrobe in an attempt to find something to wear. Anything. My entire collection consisted of shorts, jeans, T-shirts, a few ratty polo necks, and shoes that had lost their shine during the Roosevelt administration.

I did my best but was uncertain enough that I walked down the hall in my finery to knock on Mason's door. He'd be honest and not varnish the truth, although I was feeling vulnerable enough that I hoped he might leaven any criticism with a little polish. There was nothing I could do to improve my wardrobe at this late stage even if I'd had the cash.

Mason was wrapped in a flashy red Asian robe, a large green dragon embroidered into the silky material. He ran his eyes from my face to my shoes and back again and I could tell it was an incredible effort not to reveal his true feelings. He clucked like a mother hen as he ushered me into his room. "Oh, love, I'm so so sorry. I hadn't heard."

I never tired of Mason's room. When he and I had moved in on the same floor on the same day we'd both inherited accommodation that he classed architecturally as Derelict Modern. "Even junkies would refuse to die in here," he'd shouted loudly to all the new frat inhabitants. Whereas the rest of us were happy to paper over the depressing surroundings with a cheap poster Blu Tacked to the wall and perhaps a throw rug sent by a well-meaning but colorblind relative to cover the bed, Mason had converted his shabby room into something that resembled a Persian bazaar.

He seemed rather more concerned than I expected when he told me to sit in one of the precious armchairs that he had re-covered in gaily cheerful fabric. "I'm so sorry," he commiserated. "No one told me."

Puzzled, I asked, "Told you what?"

"That there'd been a death in your family." I thought he was joking until he continued seriously. "Must be someone of real importance in your life to dress so depressingly."

If I looked that forlorn there was no way I would pass muster at a classy restaurant. I sank into the armchair and sighed. Perhaps I could use the excuse of a death in the family as a reason to bail out of my date with Jerrod.

Mason draped a consoling arm across my shoulders as he sat beside me. I shrugged him off. "Don't be an ass, Mason. This is my outfit for my date with Jerrod."

"OMG," he shrieked. "He's taking you to Denny's for dinner. I've sent the photographers to Gorau Glas." He made a show of grabbing his phone. When I didn't react, he really looked at me. "Is this all you've got? Really?" The question was asked kindly.

I nodded.

He went into full chirpy Cicely/Mason mode. "Okay." The problem became a mere blip on the radar of life. Flinging open his expansive antique wardrobe that had required three hot removal men and a crane to squeeze it into his accommodation, he rifled through his extensive wardrobe. "We're about the same height although you're more on the bearish side. So…um…I think I was around your size before that ill-fated castor oil and pickled soya cheese diet…let me see…" He kept up a steady stream of fractured monologue as he disappeared into the guts of the wardrobe and began to fling items of clothing onto his bed, conspicuous by the absence of a colorblind relatives' wool weaving efforts.

Once he'd completed the cull, he emerged triumphant, instructing me to stand as he held items against my body. His monologue began again as he dismissed several items as 'too fat', 'too bland', 'too slutty', until "Voila! That's it." He thrust the garment into my arms. "Go change in the bathroom." I was too shell shocked to move. I felt like Dorothy *during* the tornado.

He shoved me and I stumbled into the bathroom and closed the door. It was my first chance to actually look at myself through his eyes. Yes, he was right. I couldn't go out dressed as I was. I looked like a particularly unhappy undertaker. He'd handed me a dark maroon suit. It was gorgeous. Almost in a daze I changed out of my old clothes and wrapped myself in his cast offs. I looked at myself in his full-length mirror. It certainly was an improvement.

"You ready?" he called. "Get out here so I can take a look." I went out for my forensic examination a little sheepishly. "Look at you," he smiled. Then he set to work. Okay, it's not perfect but with a bit of a tuck here and a lift here…" He got to work with pins and a serious sewing kit. "Would have been better if we'd had time to get you to a tailor to tuck and trim but…not bad. Just don't do anything too strenuous. And next time give me a bit of advance notice, will ya?"

We went through the process all over again for the shirt, the tie (who knew how difficult it was to match the correct tie with the shirt and suit?), and the shoes. The footwear threatened to kill the effect. "Hm, your feet are bigger than mine and there's no way I can squeeze your clodhoppers into my dainty shoes. Unless we go the Cinderella's Ugly Sisters route and cut a little off here and a bit off there. Do you really need your toes?" he asked.

"I've grown quite attached to them," I joked.

"Just a minute." He bubbled with excitement. "I think I have a solution." He dragged a chair to the wardrobe and searched on top, dislodging a ton of dust and an old cardboard box. With no regard for air quality he jumped down from the chair, blowing dust off the old box, making me wheeze.

He pulled open the flaps to rummage through the contents, holding up a pair of fine, albeit large, stilettos. "I'm not wearing those," I snapped. "I'd rather go in flip flops."

Mason ignored me. More shoes tumbled out.

"What are all these things?" I asked.

"Some are from theatre shows I was involved in and some…ah, here they are. I knew I had them." He turned to me holding aloft a pair of exquisite leather shoes so shiny once he'd brushed the dust off with the hem of his robe I could see my face in them. "Try those for size."

"Where did you get them?" I asked.

"A gentleman caller who was so far in the closet he left his shoes, his undies, and any dignity he still had when he climbed out my window after someone knocked on my door whilst we were in the throes of, I have to admit, somewhat lackluster passion even though the rumor that foot size matches cock size in his case was very true."

I tried them on after I spit slicked them with my handkerchief making them shine even brighter. "They're a little big."

Mason insisted I walk about in them so he could see. "Better too big than too small," he muttered.

"Is that your life's motto?" I asked.

He took no offense. "I have it monogrammed on my underwear." He fetched a pair of thick woolen socks. "Try these."

And, in Mason's word, voila! The shoes now fitted almost perfectly. I was ready. I had to twirl about so he could examine me from all sides before he gave his tick of approval. "You scrub up well. Now go get him."

I sighed. There was no getting to be got. This was a purely commercial transaction. I'd get a decent meal and Jerrod would get his revenge.

My date was right on time when he pulled up at the curb outside the frat house. He didn't even bother looking at me as I got into his sports car. He mumbled a greeting and I mumbled a reply. He looked particularly handsome that night and my heart sank that there was no way I could keep up with this man. He smelled as good as he looked. Jerrod Spicer exuded confidence, I sweated poor self-esteem and defeat.

At the restaurant we were bombarded with paparazzi. Cameras flashed as Jerrod stepped from the car, handing the keys to a bus boy, before he came around to open my door, looking at me closely for the first time that night. "Wow. You look almost good enough to be seen with me."

Ouch.

The meal itself was delicious, the likes of which I would never have been able to afford in three of four lifetimes, but the conversation flowed like bitumen. Neither of us had much small talk although we both attempted to paste smiles on our faces to fool the buzz of gossip at many of the other tables. Jerrod even reached over to clasp my hand in his but I flinched at the touch because it was so unexpected. He looked puzzled as if my reaction meant I didn't like him. The hand holding lasted just the requisite amount of time for surrounding tables to take note.

Exhausted by the time he dropped me back at the frat house, there was no chance of my inviting him in. He would have refused at any rate. And there was no chance of my being invited back to his place. "Grandmother wouldn't approve," he told me. "She's scary."

A quick peck for show in case anyone was watching although Jerrod had ascertained there were no photographers about so he wasn't about to put much effort into his good night. With a wave, he gunned his car and he was off. I went to bed feeling abused emotionally.

There were a few more dispiriting evenings like that one, not helped by Jerrod's quizzical eyebrow raising when I wore the maroon suit more than once. Mason had been very generous with his wardrobe but even he did not have a genie's cave of sartorial treasures.

After a particularly miserable evening in which everything seemed to go wrong: the wine was 'off,' the waiter was incompetent, the food was below par, the ambience was awry, my tie was 'off-putting,' my conversation boring, I'd had enough. "Next time, I'm taking you out," I said as I slammed the door of his car.

He gave a skeptical snort as he drove off.

But I was true to my word. I had to fight for it but Jerrod relented in the end. "I'm paying you to do what I say," he snapped when I told him I'd had my fill of boring nights at expensive supper clubs. "Boring?"

"Maybe it's the company," I sneered.

He smiled like a crocodile might when it knows it has you. "Okay. Your treat next time." He didn't think I heard him when he muttered, "This should be good for a laugh."

He was right about one thing – we did a lot of laughing. I'd confided in Mason that I'd made a fool of myself by demanding the next date be my choice and the fact I had nothing by way of ready cash to impress a wealthy spoiled brat. His suggestion was pure genius, not that I'd believed that at first.

"Where?" Jerrod looked at me with total incomprehension.

"Come on, you'll enjoy it," I cajoled although I wondered whether I'd made a terrible mistake. I also couldn't help putting the boot in now that the shoe was on the other foot. "You call what you're wearing dressing down?"

Casual, I'd told him. So he turns up in expensive designer jeans that hug his crotch and ass as if they've been sculpted to his body. His casual shirt showed that when it came to pecs and biceps, Jerrod Spicer was second to none. He was magnificent. He looked ready to take off to a photo shoot.

"There's nowhere to park," he moaned. His litany of complaints was getting on my nerves.

"Fine," I yelled. "Don't come with me then. I've put up with a lot of shitty restaurant dates, bored out of my tiny mind, waiting to have a good time with a comatose dinner partner who's using me for hell knows what ends and you won't lower yourself to go somewhere that I think could be fun. It's so far below Mr. High and Bloody Mighty Jerrod Spicer. Someone might actually see him smiling when he's out on a date with me."

"What if we're seen by someone important and it gets back to my grandmother?"

My mouth dropped open. "You should have thought of that before you started dating poverty stricken little me." I wanted to scream but I kept my temper under control. "And just FYI, Jerrod. Those clothes you were so keen to disparage after I wore them more than once. They're not mine. I had to beg, borrow, thank god I didn't have to steal, just to look presentable on our so-called dates. But did you ever think of that or did you just assume I had an unlimited budget for wardrobe. If it hadn't been for Mason's kindness I would have absolutely disgraced you."

"You're not...you know...with Mason?"

I groaned. This time I let all my frustrations out. "Are you even listening to what I'm saying?"

"Yeah, but I have a position to uphold." My face registered my disgust. "Okay, that didn't come out right. You know what I mean though."

"No, I don't Jerrod. We've been photographed and spread all over the social pages. It's not like people don't know about my existence. Your grandmother must be wise to our so-called dating unless she's a total recluse."

"Of course she knows," he retorted. "She was the first one I told."

That made me pause. "Told her what?"

"About our ruse. I didn't want her or any of her friends thinking it was serious."

I ignored his overwhelming dismissal of me in what he'd just said because I needed essential information. "You told your grandmother that this whole set-up is fake?"

He smiled as he nodded his head, proud of what he'd done.

"So she would have told all her society friends that Jerrod was just having a bit of a lark to make Kyle jealous."

"Uh huh."

"That same Kyle whose mother is one of your granny's best friends."

"Yeah." The look of satisfaction slowly gave way to sheer horror. "Oh, fuck."

"Jerrod, you have the common sense of diabetic cockroach at a sugar factory."

In an effort to salvage the situation we went straight to Mason's room. I felt like dragging Jerrod by the ear like a naughty child.

Mason looked startled when he opened the door. He was immaculately groomed and wearing sweet bugger all. He also kept looking at his watch. "I can give you fifteen minutes." Was he expecting a date?

I explained as succinctly as possible our dilemma. Mason's sigh was an echo of my own. "What the hell do you want, Jerrod? You want to make Kyle jealous? You want him back? What is it you're after? Because quite frankly, you seem to have no idea what you're doing."

Jerrod shrugged. "I don't know what I want. Kyle keeps ringing me, begging me to be his fuck buddy on the side. Yeah, I'd love to be back with Kyle but I'm not gonna be some secret fuck that he hides away from his girlfriend."

"Girlfriend, soon to be his wife," I added.

"Not if I can help it," Mason mumbled.

"I don't think the guy has a faithful bone in his body," Jerrod said.

Mason was cruel. "He might have for the right guy."

"Then I'm not the right guy for him." It looked as if that was the first time the thought had entered Jerrod's mind.

"Now, children leave it to me. You just go out on your date and your fairy godmother will fix it all up for you. No need to worry." With that he pushed us out of his room and closed the door firmly behind us.

"You think he knows what he's doing?" Jerrod asked. He looked like a little boy lost.

I replied more confidently than I felt. "I'm sure he does." I really would have liked to see who his visitor was. Something was up and I didn't like it. I felt, however, it was my duty to cheer up the confused jock who was paying me for companionship.

Without giving him a chance to bail out or complain I bundled him on the train and we headed for the amusement park where we would spend a leisurely few hours at my expense. It all turned out better than I expected (damn Mason and his ideas). Jerrod was like a kid let loose in a toy shop. Hot dogs, chips, even cotton candy were like wonders to him. "Why haven't I been here before," he asked, his eyes shining with excitement. He was up for any experience and his enthusiasm was infectious.

We rode the ghost train and he gave an uncharacteristic shriek at something that scared him unexpectedly. He was wobbly on his feet as we got out of the tiny car in which we'd been wedged together enough that I could feel the heat from his body. I grabbed his arm to help him negotiate the steps down from the ride. "Did you see that ghoul jump out. I almost shit myself."

I put on a patently fake he-man voice. "No ghoul is gonna get my man while I'm around. They'd have to kill me first." I probably sounded more like Minnie Mouse but Jerrod looked at me strangely.

"Wow, no one's ever laid their life on the line like that for me before."

I would have pointed out to him we were talking here about beings that had no basis in reality but I didn't want to erase the look of wonder in his eyes.

Jerrod desperately wanted to try the Devil's Drop, "The Best Coaster Ride West of the Pecos" it proclaimed in large flowering lettering above the entrance. In much smaller lettering underneath was a sign recommending the ride as unsafe for pregnant women, people who suffered from vertigo, bad backs, obesity and a list of ailments that must have disqualified half the people we saw buying tickets.

"Let's try that," Jerrod enthused.

I hesitated. "I don't know."

"Don't be a scaredy cat," he teased. "It'll be fun. I'll let you hold my hand if you get really frightened." This from the man who jumped and screamed at the electrically manipulated ghoul of the ghost train.

I'm not too proud to admit that the idea of the Devil's Drop did make my stomach queasy. The ride begins with a multi-story straight drop before the coaster levels out and takes a seriously chuck-inducing series of twists, turns, bends and loops before heading down a number of hellish high dips in quick succession, coming to a halt underground in 'hell.' I'd heard rumors that the carriages were hosed down after each ride to swill out the vomit from terrified patrons.

We'd tried most of the other rides that were even remotely suitable for adults – I drew the line at riding the carousel – which left only the Devil's Drop remaining of the 'big boy' rides we hadn't tried. Jerrod cajoled me into giving it a go. I admit my heart was thumping as I paid for our tickets and waited in line for the next available coaster.

"You know, I'm having a really great time," Jerrod admitted.

"Me, too."

"We should do this again. Maybe not this exactly but something like it."

"Okay. That would be nice." I quickly scanned my brain: the zoo, art gallery, beach…As my mind ran through all the alternatives the line snaked forward and before I could psych myself, Jerrod and I were fastened side by side in a metal death trap. As the coaster was winched up the incline to Devil's Peak (as the publicity called it) I just had time enough to send out a prayer or two, closing my eyes to the nausea that was threatening to empty my stomach. Jerrod was remarkably quiet considering the amount of yahooing going on around us from more seasoned riders.

"I think I may have been too ambitious," he whispered as we reached the top. We hung suspended for what seemed an eternity, Jerrod squeezed his eyes shut, grabbing hold of my hand. Then the bottom dropped out of my stomach and we were hurtling toward the earth and imminent doom at a pace I thought unimaginable. Before I could make contact with my stomach again we were buffeted from side to side, upside down, our bodies pushed and shoved in every direction until, after one final gut wrenching descent, we plunged into the tunnel. That was obviously when Jerrod's stomach finally gave up and he emptied the contents over the side.

I patted his back gently. "Get it all out." Jerrod had gone a sickly green.

Handing him my handkerchief because he was going to wipe his mouth on the back of his hand, I helped him out of the seat while others who'd been on our ride smirked or nodded sympathetically at his predicament.

Once I'd maneuvered him outside it was easy to find a kiosk selling water and he was able to rinse his mouth out and wash my hankie. "Thanks," he groaned. We sat awhile just watching the passing parade. He was embarrassed but there was nothing I could say that would alleviate his humiliation. He swallowed a few mouthfuls of water, burped loudly, and seemed to regain his sense of humor. "Oh, man, I haven't been that sick since…" He thought about it. "Hell, I've never been that sick before."

I laughed. "I thought you were gonna puke your stomach lining right outa your mouth."

"You didn't think it was…um…gross or anything?" He seemed sheepish.

"Of course, it was gross. Puke is gross. But you took it to a whole new level. You're the king of megagross."

He beamed. "You think so?"

"I know so."

We high fived.

Wow. Bonding over puke. Who knew?

"Kyle would have given me shit like forever over something like that."

There was that name again. "I'm not Kyle," I said more sharply than I intended.

"No, you're not," he said quietly. "You're much nicer. I just never noticed before."

I was gobsmacked. "Jerrod Spicer, is that a compliment?"

He blushed sweetly. "Take it any way you want."

"Then it was definitely a compliment."

He looked at the pavement. "Yeah. It was."

Not wanting the moment to become awkward, I suggested we make our way back to campus as it was getting late.

"Hey, there's something I want to do," he said grabbing my hand and pulling me toward one of the less crowded attractions.

The guy in the booth saw us coming. "Five bucks gets you six shots, Knock over four of the little duckies, easy as pie, win the little lady a fluffy teddy. Knock over six and get your pick of anything on the walls."

I looked at the merchandise. It was all cheap shit that guys would try to win for the girl they were trying to get to put out later in the night.

"Ooh, look, pandas." Jerrod was the most enthusiastic I had ever seen him. "I love pandas." He'd already slapped his five dollars on the counter.

I would have warned him beforehand that it was well-known these games were rigged, but let him have his fun. His concentration was fierce but in the end he managed to knock over only three ducks. His disappointment broke my heart.

"Here," I said dropping my five dollars on the counter. "Let me try." At least my failure would leaven his.

The carny looked from Jerrod to me and shook his head knowingly. Do I really look that useless?

Bang. One duck down. That was enough to startle both of them. When I demolished the next five in a row, the cigarette dropped from the carny's mouth and Jerrod looked at me with wonder. "I'll take that panda," I said pointing at the one Jerrod seemed most keen on.

"Where did you learn to shoot like that?" Jerrod asked as we walked toward the exit. He was clutching the panda under one arm, people staring enviously as we passed them.

"Beginner's luck," I replied.

He didn't look convinced but let the subject drop. I had no intention of informing my jock pretend boyfriend there was something I was much better at than he was.

The date was over much too quickly as far as I was concerned. Jerrod sat closer to me on the train back, his face a goofy smile as he cradled his panda.

"You're drooling on the bear," I said.

"What will I call him?"

"You're going to name a stuffed toy?"

He was indignant. "Why not?"

"Well he's yours to do as you like." I just prayed he didn't call the panda Kyle. I'd have to seriously consider disemboweling the stuffed animal if he did.

"It's the nicest present anyone's ever given me."

I looked to see if he was being sarcastic but I couldn't discern it. He was serious. That melted my insides.

"Thank you." He kissed me on the cheek, looking slightly shocked at his own spontaneous behavior. Perhaps Jerrod Spicer was human after all.

By the time we arrived back at the frat house, he was eager to get away. A perfunctory "Thanks for the very unusual date" and he headed for his car. I watched him walk away. Beeping the security and opening the door to his car to get in, he paused. Then he turned and marched back toward me, a smile lighting up his face making him even more handsome. He'd not smiled much since Kyle had announced his engagement.

He wrapped his arms around me, hugging me to his body. "I had a really great day. You made me happy. I thought I'd forgotten how to be." With that he kissed me on the forehead and went back to his car whistling. I stood stunned until he was out of sight.

"Date went well then?" Mason was hanging out his upstairs window.

"I'll be right up." I had no intention of discussing my social life with the entire neighborhood listening.

When I got upstairs, Mason stood in his doorway, a fruity cocktail in his hand. "Come in and tell me all." He looked somewhat lived in since Jerrod and I had spoken to him earlier that evening and his usually neat room was in disarray, a used condom on the floor not quite hidden behind his trash bin – someone's aim was bad. My natural curiosity was sidelined by my overwhelming need to tell someone about my date with Jerrod. "Am I telling this to Mason or to Cicely?"

"Anything you tell Mason is automatically repeated to Cicely."

"In that case…" I turned toward the door but Mason pushed me back on his bed.

"Come on, spill. I won't use any of the information unless it's imperative I do so. That's the best deal you're gonna get."

It wasn't all that reassuring but I was going to burst. By the time I had finished embellishing my tale, Mason was rubbing his hands with glee, muttering, "Excellent. Excellent."

I didn't have a chance to ask about his visitor as he shut down the conversation and had me out the door as soon as I'd completed my story and before I could start getting all mushy about my pretend jock boyfriend. Probably just as well.

***

"WHAT DO YOU mean *we* have to go?" I was going purple in the face at the mere thought of it.

"Come on, you can't expect me to turn up at a frat bash in honor of our relationship on my own. How would that look?"

"Maybe it would look like the fake relationship that it is." I don't know why I was taking my anger out on Jerrod. Except that accepting the invitation was just about the worst idea I'd ever heard in the entire history of not just western civilization but the world.

"The guys on the team just want to be friendly so they're throwing a little party to celebrate you and me," he explained again patiently.

"Jerrod, there is no you and me," I said quite reasonably.

"You know that and I know that, they don't."

"I wouldn't be so sure of that what with your loose lips letting on to granny who probably then passed the information on at her bridge club so you can bet your balls Kyle knows too."

"My grandmother doesn't play bridge."

I was adamant. "It smells like a set-up to me."

He put his arm around my shoulder. "I won't let them hurt you if that's what you're thinking. The guys are cool with gay people."

"I've heard about the jock parties you guys have."

"Yeah, they can get a bit out of hand but this one won't be like that."

He was doing everything to reassure me but I wasn't buying it. I am a sucker for cute men pouting, however. I put my hands up in surrender. "All right. All right. I'll compromise. I'll ask Mason what he thinks and if he okays it then we're going. Deal?"

"Deal."

I knew Mason would nix the idea.

Just goes to show how wrong I could be. "What a fabulous idea," he beamed. "Things are working out nicely." For a moment I almost believed that Mason had something to do with the invitation but that was impossible, right? Besides, I couldn't see what he'd get out of it. Hell, I couldn't see what *I* would get out of it apart from ritual humiliation.

Still, it was a few weeks off yet. We had another date organized by yours truly before that. I'd gone all out to make it special, praying to whatever gods were available to watch over an inconsequential nerd like me that it would all work out for the best. I just wanted to make Jerrod smile. That was payment enough.

"Why won't you tell me where we're going? I don't like surprises."

"You'll like this one." I was supremely confident.

I couldn't keep the destination secret for long, however, and as we approached the entrance I saw his recognition. "The zoo? We're going to the zoo?"

I wasn't sure whether his tone was consternation or excitement. It didn't matter because I was on a mission. "Come on or we'll be late."

"Late? For what?"

I could scarcely conceal my grin. "You'll see."

We took a roundabout route because I wanted our destination to be as big a surprise as I could possibly make it. Jerrod was still in the dark when I knocked on the door marked STAFF ONLY. A cute twink opened up, his face beaming when he saw me. "Colm. Long time no see, man." I hugged him and I could feel him looking over my shoulder sizing up Jerrod. Then the penny dropped.

"OMG!" he shrieked. "You're Jerrod Spicer. You're like my favorite jock of all times. I have your posters all over my bedroom wall."

I turned to Jerrod. "You'll have to forgive Rhys, he's a star fucker."

Jerrod snorted. "Reece? Isn't that a girl's name. You know, like Reece Witherspoon?"

If Rhys's hackles had been visible I would have bet they would have risen like the dead in a zombie apocalypse. He seethed. "Listen, tall, dark and brainless…"

"Hey, watch who you call brainless. Tall and dark are okay though. Sorry I didn't mean to cause offence."

"Jerrod is not so good with names," I snickered.

Rhys calmed down. "Okay. No more name calling." Turning to Jerrod, he said. "Get your clothes off."

"What?"

"You can change behind that row of lockers." Rhys shoved a set of khaki shorts and shirt at him. And get out of those expensive shoes, you'll ruin them. I'll see if I can find some boots."

"What the fuck is going on?" Jerrod whispered.

"Just trust me on this one, okay?" I pleaded.

"You, I trust," he said, "It's Ms. Witherspoon I'm not so sure about. I think he's coming on to me."

"Just go with it. It will be so worth it."

Grizzling as he changed outfits, I kept my eyes averted even though I'd seen more of Jerrod in the flesh than he was revealing at that moment.

"So who is this Rhys guy?"

"He's a friend from college. He works here at the zoo to pay off his student loans and to earn credit toward his degree in animal science."

"Cool."

"He's doing me an immense favor letting us in here so chill with the insults please."

"Here, try these for size." Rhys returned with a pair of soiled boots that he thrust at Jerrod who screwed up his nose.

"You'll thank me later," he said.

I wasn't so sure about that.

Jerrod stood up. "A bit tight but they'll do."

"Come with me," Rhys instructed.

Jerrod looked concerned when I stayed put. "You're not coming?"

"This is your treat, go and enjoy it."

Rhys led him through a large metal door. I just had time to hear Jerrod gasp, "Oh my god. Oh my god," before the door closed securely behind him. I let myself out the staff door and wandered around to the front of the enclosure which was crowded with people waiting patiently for the advertised Feeding Time for the Pandas. Jerrod wouldn't be able to pet the animals but he'd be able to get up closer and more personal than the people behind the barrier. I could just see him at the back slopping out the pens while the pandas lazed in the shade of large overhanging rocks.

It must have seemed like forever to him back there but it was only about ten minutes before he and Rhys emerged with bamboo. The pandas got off their asses and headed for their feed and Jerrod's eyes widened in delight. Rhys was instructing him, and Jerrod, for once in his life, followed orders. One of the young pandas broke away from the others and went for the bamboo Jerrod was holding, wrapping its body around Jerrod's leg as it reached for its meal.

I had my phone ready for just such a moment and shot a few pics. They were as much for me as a memento for Jerrod. I couldn't have asked for better.

It was all over much too soon and I wandered back to the staff door giving Jerrod enough time to change. Rhys opened up and I handed him a hundred bucks toward his college fund. It was worth every penny.

Jerrod was bubbling over with excitement although he still smelled somewhat of his adventure.

"Fuck, that was awesome. Best. Surprise. Ever." He wrapped his arm around me like we were buddies. Best. Feeling. Ever.

I think Jerrod bored everyone shitless with his tale about feeding the pandas, he just couldn't stop raving. I'd suddenly moved up in his estimation to the extent he became very handsy at times. Nothing overtly sexual but manly hugs, arms resting behind my shoulders when we sat together, the sort of intimacy that good friends shared. I must have made an impact. Mark one up for Colm Bransfield.

Of course none of that helped when the fateful Night of the Jock Knives arrived.

It was all very sedate when we arrived although the back-slapping and glad-handling was tedious and appeared to me to be as sincere as Liberace's protestations of heterosexuality. Kyle was there with Bethany draped across him as if she were part and parcel of his wardrobe, fortunately they both kept their distance even though they snarled every time I caught their eye.

People were looking at me strangely. I was a fish out of water, to use that old cliché. But it was true, I was suffocating in the atmosphere that pervaded the party. I shouldn't be here. I was out of my element. These were not 'my people.' I'm not a snob or anything. What I mean is these people were tanned – not from a salon either, this was bona fide holiday-in-the-sun tanning – confident, smooth, wealthy, and staggeringly good looking. These were the people other folks looked up to. Which is perhaps why most of them were looking down their nose at me. I obviously wasn't good enough for their jock buddy and I heard a few whispered accusations to Jerrod. 'What are you doing with him when you can have Kyle?' That sort of shit.

If it was a set-up, I still couldn't see the point. It's not like Kyle could make a play for Jerrod while Bethany was his second skin. Until I could work out what they were up to I was tense.

Jerrod's buddies were plying him with liquor and one or two of them attempted the same thing with me although I was stone cold sober courtesy of the alcohol puddle forming in soil around the inebriated rubber plant where I poured my unwanted drinks.

At one stage Bethany disappeared with a gaggle of other cheerleaders to do whatever it is women do in the ladies restroom. That gave Kyle an opportunity to seek me out. I looked to Jerrod for help but he was being shielded from what was going on by a phalanx of his team mates.

"I don't know what Jerrod sees in an ugly little toad like you, Colin," Kyle hissed, placing one of his muscular arms alongside my head, propping himself up against the wall. "Look at you. No muscle tone. I bet you don't even exercise. I know you don't play any sport." He chucked me under the chin with two fingers, lifting my face ostensibly to examine me closely but I knew it was to look in my eyes as he attempted to belittle me. "You're such a homely little thing. Whereas, I'm drop dead handsome."

I couldn't let it pass. "Yes, isn't it amazing what surgeons can do these days if you have enough ready cash." I'd heard from Mason that Kyle had had his cheeks cosmetized as well as having his impressive pec implanted.

He recognized it for the insult it was. He drew his fist back and…

"There you are, Colin," a voice interrupted. "You disappeared when I went to get your drink. Here you are, love."

Jerrod handed me a plastic cup of some foul smelling and foul tasting liquid but I was grateful to have something to stop the shakes. If Kyle's fist had met my face it was me that was going to come off the worse for the interaction.

Jerrod took my arm, dragging me away from the bully. "Come on, honey, there's someone I'd like you to meet. Bye, Kyle. So good to catch up."

We left a fuming Kyle in our wake, as Jerrod hustled me away.

"That was close," I said, breathing easier once we were out of earshot. "Honestly, Jerrod, the man is beneath you. He will never treat you in the manner you deserve."

He smiled. "You mean like the way you treat me?"

I didn't respond. "We've done our duty to your friends, can we leave now?"

"Yeah, it's so boring. Not like the parties we used to have."

I raised an eyebrow. "What were those parties like then?"

Jerrod regretted he'd said anything and mumbled a few words in reply that certainly didn't answer my question. I was intrigued. Ready to pursue the interrogation further I opened my mouth to speak when there was the sound of a knife against glass to get everyone's attention. It was Kyle.

"Well dudes and dudettes, hope you're enjoying the party. I guess those of you who have been to some our more, um, exciting raves are wondering what the fuck. Simple, we had to play nice early in the evening for the more respectable members on the invitee list. But they have now departed the scene so you know what happens now."

A huge cheer went up and deep bass sounds like rutting hogs emanated from some of the jocks. Jerrod's face registered horror. He grabbed my hand and dragged me toward the entrance. We didn't get far. The jocks stood as a solid muscle wall against our escape.

"Going somewhere Jerrod?" Kyle called.

"I don't think this is really Colin's scene."

"Shouldn't your *boyfriend…*" said with such a sneer it threatened to permanently curl his lip, "know every aspect of your life? Or are you keeping secrets from him?"

Jerrod stood his ground. "I suppose then that Bethany's staying."

She suddenly made an appearance with two of her cheerleaders succinctly putting paid to that question. Quite a number had obviously left. As had some of the jocks. This was ominous.

Jerrod shrugged. "Why the hell not stay. The night is young." He pulled me close enough to whisper, "Just follow my lead and do everything I say and everything will be all right."

I nodded. What else could I do?

The lights dimmed. Kyle paired off with Bethany, the other guys surrounded the two unattached cheer leaders. Jerrod pulled me closer. "Sorry about this. I'll top up the bank after it's all over."

I was nervous. "What do we have to do?"

"Make out. You cool with that?"

Make out with the jock of my dreams? The guy I'd had the hots over for longer than I could remember? Was I cool with that?

"I think I can fake it," I said although the sarcasm seemed to escape Jerrod.

"That's what I pay you for."

I mumbled. "I'd gladly do it for free and I wouldn't have to fake it."

Jerrod wasn't listening because he was watching Kyle and Bethany getting up close and personal across the room.

I pulled Jerrod's focus back to me and decided to go for it. Tilting his head down so our lips met, he obviously wasn't expecting my tongue to breach his defenses. He pushed me away, holding me at arm's length, staring into my eyes. I don't know what he saw, although his face creased in confusion. Then he shrugged almost imperceptibly and dragged me in for the kill. I gave as good as I got. In fact, I gave more, tugging Jerrod's longish hair to keep his face in mine, his mouth glued to my own so I could taste a bit of heaven and hope it wasn't too much like hell for him. Seems it can't have been because he clasped me tighter.

We staggered across to a vacant lounge and fell into it, me on top of Jerrod grinding my hard cock against his…his what? I reached down between our two tangled bodies and…holy shit, Jerrod was as hard as I was. I couldn't help smiling. At least until Jerrod moved my hand off his cock. Disappointment.

"Tug my hair harder while you kiss me," he whispered. "I love that."

If there is one thing I know how to do, it's take instruction. And who was I to ignore demands from the hottest jock this side of the sun? I yanked his hair until I saw tears in the corners of his eyes. Then I nipped his glorious neck as I made my way up to his hard pink lips. Jerrod was panting as if he couldn't draw breath. I pounced and sank my tongue inside him. When we came up for air – and that was only because if I didn't stop I was going to blow my load just from kissing him – he sighed. "Wow. Where'd you learn to kiss like that? You kiss like a demon."

I never thought I was anything exceptional in that department but if Jerrod thought so, I'd take the compliment and wear it with pride. "Doesn't Kyle kiss like a demon?" I asked.

"Kyle doesn't really like kissing." He glanced over to Bethany and his ex-boyfriend who were snogging like champions. "Not with me anyway."

"Fuck Kyle," I spat.

"Been there, done that," Jerrod laughed.

That set me off and we both dissolved in fits of giggles which had the unfortunate effect of having everyone in the room turn their attention to us.

Kyle's look was murderous. "We're all amongst friends here so I guess we can turn it up a notch. Everyone okay with that?"

I saw some of the jocks stripping off their shirts. Mmm, this could be fun. It was until I saw the look on Jerrod's face. Okay, so this wasn't good. This must have been the ultimate humiliation. "Fuck. Fuck. Fuck."

"What's the score?" I whispered.

"I should have guessed. If Kyle thinks our relationship is fake…"

"Which it is," I added unnecessarily.

"Yeah. But he'll want to show us up. It's okay that we've been making out. That doesn't prove anything." Then he added, "Except you're a helluva kisser."

"So…" I was waiting for the penny.

"We call Kyle's bluff. Or…"

"What's the 'or'?"

"We walk out now with our dignity intact."

"And prove him correct? So the sleazy bastard will come after you with triple the effort while he romances his cheerleader?"

Jerrod sighed. "Yeah, that would be my guess."

"Is that what you want? Kyle Jenner to pursue you as his fuck toy?"

He had to think about it for a few seconds. "No.' His reply sounded weak. "No. Not anymore." With those words he seemed to release something he'd bottled up inside and he relaxed.

"So what do we do now?" I asked. Call me naïve – well, I was.

"It's a lot to ask anyone."

"I'm not anyone," I said. Crap, what sort of a line is that?

He gave a little laugh. "No, you're not. I've started to realize that."

"So ask."

"Ah, we have to do *it*."

"It?"

"Come on, think about it."

I glanced around the room at what the others were up to. Oh. They were all naked. I snuck a look at Kyle. Impressive, although Bethany seemed to be having some difficulty keeping his interest. That so did not auger well for their future.

"Oh," I said in a croaky voice. "You want to fuck me?"

Thank you god! Thank you angels! Thank you…

"No, I want you to fuck me."

"What?"

"Jesus, I'm a bottom."

How did I not know that?

"You're a bottom?"

"Power bottom."

"Sorry, my mistake."

Hallelujah! Hallelujah! Hallelujah!

"Are you up to the job?" he asked.

"Are you kidding me?"

"I know it's a lot to ask. Can you get it up for me?"

The easiest response was to place his hand on my erection which threatened to burst through my jeans. He ran his fingers along the outline. I watched him. His eyes grew wide.

"Fuck! Is that all you?"

"Does it feel like a sock?"

He pushed me off him and onto my back while he slipped to his knees. I was about to remove my jeans when he slapped my hand away. He undid my belt and unzipped me slowly, unveiling the outline of my prick like it was a much sought after prize. He yanked my jeans off before he gripped the waistband of my briefs, lowering them slowly until my long thick cock was revealed in all its sticky glory. He put his hand around it and I had to think gross thoughts to stop myself from coming. Jerrod Spicer was holding my cock. Not only holding, he had his mouth over it.

I couldn't help it. I screamed, "Yeah, babe. Suck it! I love the way you suck my cock." I meant it too. Grabbing the back of his head, I pushed his face down until it reached my pubes. He took it all although there was a string of drool on his lips when he came up for air. I needed to stop or I'd come too soon.

My turn. "Strip for me, babe. Let me see that gorgeous body."

He seemed pleased by the compliment and slowly teased his clothes off while concentrating totally on me. It was as if the others in the room didn't exist anymore. I couldn't take my eyes of this magnificent man as he unveiled each little muscle, nipple, and OMG the six pack. His cute navel – an innie – the glimpse of trimmed pubic hair as his jeans and briefs slid down. His gorgeous cock so hard I had to lean over to kiss it, making him shudder. Then he was totally naked. Sometimes dreams do come true. All I could do was stare.

He straddled my hips, my cock bobbing against his balls. He gently removed my shirt. He seemed acutely aware that my body embarrassed me. When I was totally naked he passed his tongue across my nipples then licked up my throat until he forced his way into my mouth. His arousal was obvious. I guess he liked me a little. Surely it wasn't all for show. "Fuck me. Please."

It seemed so perverse that he was begging me.

"Protection?"

"In the pocket of my jeans."

I tipped him off my lap and on to the lounge before kneeling on the floor. I didn't care that I was a little flabby because Jerrod wanted me inside him. That's all that mattered now. I retrieved the condom and small sachet of lube from his jeans hardly believing my luck. Wriggling down the lounge until his butt was on the edge, he spread his legs apart, holding them wide so I could see his snug hole. I moved in to slick the entrance with my saliva, licking down the crack, concentrating on the snug puckered hole until he was spit lubed enough that I could force my tongue inside a short way.

He squirmed, pulling my face tighter against his ass. I ate his hole like a starving man until he was panting. "Holy fuck. That is so good."

I tore open the lube to slick my fingers, smearing some around the entrance before slowly pushing inside. One finger slid in easily. Followed by a second. The third gave him pause. I stopped pushing, leaning over to kiss him, and while he was preoccupied and relaxed sank the three fingers all the way home. He was ready.

I tore open the foil package and had my cock sheathed in record time. I still had difficulty believing this was all happening. I didn't dare question it in case Kyle intervened to stop us. I slicked the length of the condom with the leftover lube then poked the head of my cock at his entrance. His face was a combination of amusement and lust, as if he couldn't believe we were doing this. Then I pushed in slowly. He adapted quickly to the invasion, relaxing as best he could until I was seated fully inside him. Giving him time to adjust I twerked my hips hitting all the right spots because he was groaning, clenching his sphincter around my cock. So tight. I was totally in love with the feeling.

"Now," he pleaded.

Starting off slow and easy to get him used to me, I was stretching him enough with my thickness to make him grunt. Eventually we settled into a rhythm and I watched to see which thrusts brought the best reaction, varying my technique to give him maximum pleasure because I knew this was my one and only time. It wouldn't happen again. Thank you anyway, Kyle.

I picked up the pace, slamming my cock inside him, making him feel it. I wanted him to know he'd been well fucked tomorrow and the day after. I didn't want him forgetting me too soon. As I thrust inside with all my strength I held his head, gripping his hair just enough to sting, forcing him to look in my eyes. Harder and faster. Panting. Breathless. "Holy shit fuck," he screamed and his cock shot all over his stomach and chest. Without touching himself. Wailing like a banshee, he continued to pound his ass back against my cock as if he couldn't get enough. That and the clench of his ass muscles around my cock were enough to pull me over the edge and I shot my load, grunting my satisfaction until I fell on his sweaty chest totally exhausted. He patted my head.

"I think that's enough of a show for one day," he said.

My ego deflated, I removed the condom and just dropped it on the floor to let one of the bastard jocks pick it up. Jerrod and I dressed in silence leaving the others to their own pleasures although they stared open mouthed.

Once we'd let ourselves out of the jock frat house we walked slowly back to my room, Jerrod doing the honorable thing in escorting me, probably not keen to return to the Frat House of Debauchery where there would be a myriad questions which he'd probably find difficult to answer. Plus Kyle. Did Jerrod really mean what he'd said about his ex in the throes of…I was about to say passion but I'm not convinced now that the whole thing wasn't an act.

Jerrod looked sheepish as he said, "I hope that wasn't too unpleasant for you."

I stopped in my tracks and turned to the clueless love of my life. "Jerrod. That was the hottest sex I've had in my entire, albeit short, life. It was all my pleasure."

His eyes sparkled. "Nah, a lot of the pleasure was mine. You sure got a cock and a half on you. Where'd you get that secret weapon?"

"It just grew on me."

We both snickered like schoolboys.

I was desperate to ask how I rated against Kyle in the bed department but Kyle was a lover, I was merely a paid fuck. No comparison.

As if he read my mind, Jerrod said. "You are way better than Kyle."

I couldn't believe my ears. "Really?" I was fishing for my compliments. So sue me.

"He's very much a wham, bam, thank you ma'am sort of guy. Actually there was very little thanks involved. Or anything even remotely reciprocal."

"Then how…?"

"I usually take myself to the bathroom and jerk off. He doesn't like to watch me do myself."

I couldn't resist. "Anytime you need an audience, call me."

"You'd really want to watch me jerk off?"

"Hell, yeah."

He laughed at my enthusiasm. "I need another favor. But I'm afraid to ask."

"You can ask me anything. The answer will always be 'yes.'"

He looked at me strangely. "You need the cash that badly."

"It's not about the cash. I'd do it free."

"Nah. I don't bludge. I pay my debts."

"What's the favor?"

"Um, can I stay the night with you? I don't really want to go home tonight."

"Sure."

"I'll sleep on the floor."

I shrugged. "If that's what you want but the bed is more comfortable."

In the end he agreed with my assessment of the floor and scooted into bed once I'd told him to quit moaning about his back and just get the fuck under the sheet. We sat and talked while we ate takeaway pizza with an action movie playing unwatched in the background. It was comfortable. Our conversation covered nothing too personal, nothing that couldn't already be gleaned from a Facebook profile.

This is cozy, I thought. *Don't get used to it.*

It was difficult not to be up close and very personal in my three-quarter sized bed, especially as he was naked and I was wearing, for modesty's sake, my boxers.

Jerrod turned his back to me but before I had a chance to turn over he asked quietly. "Mind if I get one of those kisses you're so good at?"

Surprised as I was, that was no reason to turn him down. I took him in my arms and the kiss was sweet and slow. "Mm, so nice," he muttered. I brushed some stray hair off his forehead and was about to wish him good night when I realized he was already asleep. I hugged him closer to my body and he sighed.

The following morning I woke with the taste of hair in my mouth. My first thought was a stray pube but on opening my eyes it was Jerrod's hair. He'd backed up against me during the night and had fallen back asleep with the back of his head pushed against my face. Shit. My cock was hard, pressed up against his butt crack. Humiliation. Wait a second. Jerrod was actually rubbing his ass against my erection.

"Is that just morning wood or are you pleased to feel me?" he asked.

"One per cent morning wood and ninety-nine per cent sexy Jerrod Spicer ass."

"You…ah…wanna do something about it. You know, like…ah…let me take care of it?"

"Sure," I said attempting not to sound too enthusiastic. "What did you have in mind?"

"I can…blow you."

"Yeah. Anything else."

"Maybe, if you feel like it, you could fuck me again and…"

"And?"

"You know, pull out and, maybe, blow your load all over my face."

Be still my pulsing dick. Fantasy time.

"You like that, huh?"

"Yeah, I guess."

Not needing any further encouragement I fumbled through the drawer in my nightstand to retrieve a strip of condoms and a large plastic flip top bottle of lube.

"I'm pretty loose from yesterday when you pounded my ass so I don't think all that lube is really necessary. You're not that big," he joked.

"A guy can dream, can't he?"

My comment was meant to keep the atmosphere light but he suddenly grew more serious until he sighed and said, "Yeah."

I greased his ass lightly because he really didn't need much prep and I was eager just in case he changed his mind. I was sheathed, lubed, and inside him before he could say 'fuck me.'

Oh god, I could get to love this.

I took my time, plunging deep, stretching him wider, watching his languorous movements against the sheets, making him whimper every time I thrust harder than normal. He moved like a leopard enjoying the sun. I stroked his cock to show I took his pleasure as seriously as my own. I had plans for that cock later.

Like all good things, our leisurely lovemaking had to come to an end. I ripped my dick out of his ass leaving it gaping and pulled off the condom, already close to coming because Jerrod had been encouraging me to 'spatter your fuck juice all over my pretty face.' When someone asks so nicely, I find it hard to refuse. Another few strokes and my spunk shot out of me like pellets from a shotgun, leaving snail trails from his chin to his forehead. His tongue snaked out to catch any stray spunk near his lips.

"You look so hot lying there well fucked with my cum dripping off your face."

I quickly dropped down to his still drooling cock and wrapped my tongue around the shaft before engulfing it in my mouth. Jerrod bucked but I held him down. I was determined to milk him dry. It didn't take long before I felt his balls clench. I'd taken his cock down my throat but I wanted to taste him so I eased up to feel his spurts on my tongue.

Once I'd sucked him dry I went in for a kiss. He opened up because I knew by this time Jerrod loved kissing. I hoped I'd guessed something else that Jerrod Spicer loved. He opened his mouth expectantly and was surprised when he tasted his own cum that I'd held in my mouth. I licked the remnants of my own spunk off his face and chest to mingle with his own that we swapped from mouth to mouth until, eventually, we swallowed.

"You like that, huh?"

He looked sheepish. "Oh, yeah."

"Me, too," I admitted.

We fell asleep again only to be woken by pounding on the door. I grabbed my robe and stumbled to answer. It was Mason in full Cicely mode. Pushing past me, he saw I had company. "OMG! He stayed the night. This is precious. Tell me all. No, wait. Shall I tell you the stories I've heard. Wake him up. Go on, I hate to repeat myself."

"You're always repeating yourself." I was grouchy from being woken up.

Mason went to the bed and poked Jerrod with his index finger. Jerrod slapped it away until Mason was so annoying that Jerrod had to sit up.

"Oh, did I wake you?"

"Of course you woke him," I spluttered. "You were poking him."

"Like you were reported to have done last night at a very public party."

Jerrod groaned.

As the coffee pot percolated Mason kept up a running commentary on what he'd heard about our escapades the previous evening. It was surprisingly hyperbole free. We corrected a few glaring inaccuracies, mainly to do with Kyle's prowess with Bethany, before Mason turned to me and demanded, "Why didn't you tell me you're a top?"

"Why didn't you tell me it's none of your goddam business, Mason?"

Jerrod's voice was croaky. Probably from screaming instructions on how I was supposed to pleasure him. "It was a set-up, wasn't it?"

Mason nodded. "Of course, but it backfired."

"Big time." Jerrod looked at me. "Thanks to this stud here."

Mason has never felt an awkward moment in his life that I know of but even he withdrew discreetly. "Thanks for confirming the dirt. I'll be sure to straighten out any misconceptions about last night."

"Please do." I shooed him out the door.

We finished our coffees in silence, me at my desk, Jerrod sitting cross-legged (and naked) on the bed. Our next words would be goodbye because we'd convinced Kyle that Jerrod was no longer interested, that he'd found love elsewhere. I'd been paid in advance up to the end of the following week.

"I guess I better shower and get home. Grandmother will worry."

"Okay."

"Colin?"

Fuck. What was I thinking? There's no future with someone who can't even remember my fucking name.

I didn't bother correcting him. "Mm?"

"Thanks. Just thanks."

He grabbed the towel I'd taken out of the drawer for him before he disappeared down the hall to the bathroom. When he returned he dressed quickly. Goodbyes are not my thing so I fled to the bathroom knowing he'd be gone by the time I got back. He was. All that remained of his presence was two crisp hundred dollar bills on my pillow. Was that the going rate? I felt so cheap.

I felt cheap again two nights later when Jerrod turned up unexpectedly to supposedly 'watch that movie we missed the other night because we were so busy chatting.' We missed it that night and the next three times he visited. Much as I wanted to watch it, I wasn't complaining.

That didn't mean there weren't repercussions, particularly after Cicely Trublood's tell-all column although she refrained from naming names. Jerrod played his next football match like his ass was on fire. Perhaps it was because we'd been together the night before and I'd pounded that sexy butt twice. I didn't know how he could walk let alone run and pass the ball after I'd finished with him. But each time there was the cash pile. It pissed me off.

The day after the match, which I had dutifully attended, I'd pulled a double shift at the Burgertorium. I was irritable from the litany of complaints from assholes who didn't know their burger from their buttholes. About two hours from finishing time the crowds had thinned and we were taking it easy. I was on the drive-through window again, praying that Kyle wouldn't show up. Instead this sleek black car slid to the window. I had no order. I called out to the kitchen. "Hey, Jerry, we got anything to go for the dude in the mafia car?" I'd said it jokingly but when the driver lowered his window he was a rough looking dude with wrap-around shades and a dark suit.

"You Bransfield?" he asked with the sort of accent you immediately associate with sudden death or dismemberment.

There was no use denying it as my badge already gave away my identity. "Yeah. Who's asking?"

He leaned over and opened the back door of the car. "Get in."

What the hell?

"Look, that's really nice you want to drive me home but I'm afraid I'm working."

"I'm sure your buddy can finish the shift for you."

"Who are you?"

"It doesn't matter who I am," he said. "More important is who sent me?"

"And that is?"

"When you get in the car you'll find out."

"Um, I don't think so. Thanks anyway."

"That's not a request, that's an order. You want me to come in there and get you."

No way I wanted to get the other staff involved in my shit. "Jerry can you finish the shift for me? I gotta go. Something urgent just came up." I wrote down the rego on the car and a brief request that if I didn't turn up for work on my next rostered day, to go to the police. I grabbed my coat and exited.

The car was empty apart from the driver who looked less scary up close. "So you're Mr. Bransfield? It's a pleasure to meet you."

This was different. Do hit men soften up their targets by charming them first.

"How have you heard of me?"

"Oh, I've heard a lot about you. So just sit back and relax and I'll have you to your destination in no time."

I guess it was nice to be chauffeur driven to my death. Not something I'd ever imagined.

"I'm Chapple," the driver said. That was the sum total of his conversation until we turned through the iron gates and drove up the gravel driveway to Jerrod's place.

The tension drained from my body and I sighed in relief that I wasn't about to meet my doom. Prematurely as it turned out. Chapple led me to a sitting room where I was obviously expected.

"Mr. Bransfield, ma'am."

So I wasn't here to see Jerrod.

"Please stay, Chapple. Mr. Bransfield won't be here long."

Jerrod's grandmother looked me over as if I was some specimen that had adhered to the sole of her shoe. Of course, it didn't help matters that I was still in my wildly unattractive Burgertorium uniform. Her nose turned up, whether at my appearance of the odor of fried grease that clung to my body – or both – I was never privy to.

"I'd ask you to sit but these chairs are priceless, so you may remain standing."

"Thank you," I said sarcastically, "I wouldn't want to get them dirty with honest worker's sweat." Then I added for good measure, "Your majesty."

She paced the large lavishly furnished sitting room in which I'm sure Marie Antoinette would have felt right at home. I merely felt uncomfortable. "So you're the young man my grandson is paying." To emphasize her disappointment she looked me over again. Her opinion obviously didn't improve on a second viewing. She sniffed. "I was always under the impression that although prostitutes were tawdry creatures they were at least good looking. You seem to contradict that impression."

"Perhaps that's because I'm not a prostitute."

"My grandson pays you does he not?"

"For companionship. In order to make his former boyfriend jealous."

"We won't speak of the unspeakable Kyle Jenner. His mother and I have put an end to all that nonsense." My blood was beginning to boil. Who did she think she was? "Just as I will put an end to all this nonsense with you, young man. I can spot a gold digger a mile away and Jerrod has had more than his fair share of those since his parents died."

I laughed out loud. "Gold digger? I have no designs on Jerrod's money."

"Then what do you have designs on?"

"His body. Jerrod is gorgeous."

"Yet he is paying you for…for…for…"

"Sex."

"As you say. That, in my book, and in law, makes you a common whore."

"Oh, I'm anything but common."

"I can't understand what my grandson sees in you, yet he has spoken about nothing but Colin this and Colin that for the past two weeks. And that mouldy bear he brought home. He never parts with it. Named it after you."

WTF? He named the Panda Colin? Okay, just this once I'd forgive him for getting my name wrong.

"You are such an unprepossessing specimen. I'm baffled."

My lips curved in a malicious grin. "Perhaps it's because I have a huge cock and he loves having it rammed up his tight meaty ass."

I heard Chapple almost choke on his tongue as he attempted not to laugh. Granny did one of those stumble double takes as if she couldn't believe she'd heard what I'd just said.

It was time to drive in the knife. I was sick of being insulted. "It's been a long night so if I'm to be insulted some more, at least I'd like to sit down." So saying I flopped into the nearest antique chair. Grandmother spread out her arms as if to stop me and shrieked so loudly I thought my eardrums would burst. Chapple merely stood his ground but put his hands over his ears.

I heard someone running down the hallway. Jerrod burst through the door.

"What on earth is all the commotion? Has someone been killed?" He hadn't seen me as he was concentrating on his grandmother who held the marble mantle above the fireplace for support. Clutching her throat as if she had lost the power of speech, she pointed her aged arthritic finger in my direction. Jerrod turned, his face lighting up when he saw me. "Hey, what are you doing here?"

"I was summonsed."

Jerrod turned to Chapple who nodded agreement. "Grandmother. What have you done?"

She stood ramrod straight. "I will not have this creature in my house."

"He has a name grandmother."

"I will not have Colin Bransfield in my…"

Jerrod lost it. "For fuck's sake, how many times must I tell you. His name is Colm." He spelled it out for her.

My mouth dropped open. I'm sure my face registered a 7.8 shock. "What did you call me?"

Jerrod appeared confused. "Colm Bransfield. It's your name isn't it?"

I scarcely dared to breathe.

"And what did you call your panda?"

He looked at the floor sheepishly. "Oh, that. I called him after someone that I'm seeing on a sort of regular basis at present"

Shell shocked. "You called the panda Kyle? What sort of name is Kyle for a panda."

"Kyle is the past. My panda is named after the man I hope is my future. If he'll have me. I called him Colm."

I was up and out of the chair flinging myself into Jerrod's arms so fiercely I knocked us both to the floor. He opened his mouth to welcome me and I dove straight in. When he'd finished, and without moving off the floor which I thought was quite an achievement, he said authoritatively. "Just to be clear grandmother, this is my house. Of course you have every right to stay here as long as you wish as specified in my parents' wills, but you will not insult my guests nor will you take it upon yourself to judge who is and who is not welcome."

He struggled to stand and then held out his hand to me.

"But he's a common prostitute," she snarled, not about to give in so easily.

"He's no such thing. He was paid to make Kyle jealous when I foolishly thought Kyle Jenner was worth my time."

"He admitted you pay him for…for…"

This woman was impossible. "Sex," I shouted.

"Why would I pay you for sex when we both enjoy it so much?"

"But the money?"

His face went so purple I thought he'd explode. "That money was never for sex. I thought I was taking you away from your paid employment and it was only fair you were compensated. Oh my god. You must hate me."

My heart burst. Tears filled my eyes. "Jerrod Spicer, you are the nicest person I have ever met. I loved you from the moment I first saw you. It was hero worship. But once I got to know you, the real you, then I really lost my heart. I'm sorry." I raced toward the door.

"Hold him, Chapple."

The chauffeur held me firm. "He's made a good choice in you, lad," he said in my ear. "You're a keeper."

Jerrod turned to the old lady. "Grandmother, I think enough has been said tonight. I suggest you retire and think things over. I intend asking Colm to come and stay here over the college break. He's very special. Not just because he won that ridiculous stuffed panda which I love more than any other toy I received as a child. Not just because he took me to an amusement park on a date. Not just because he actually remembers what I tell him. Not just because he bribed a zookeeper. But when you put them together, they're the actions of a man who cares. You will not interfere this time grandmother. If I fail, so be it. It will be my failure and mine alone."

The old woman kept her head bowed as she left the room.

Jerrod turned to me. "Will you come and stay?"

"I've saved every penny you ever paid me. I did extra shifts at the Burgertorium rather than spend any of your money. I would have gladly been your companion for free. I always intended to give it back. I want to return it all to you so we can start afresh."

I could see he was about to remonstrate with me but Chapple shook his head.

"Okay. If that's your wish."

"Oh, you have no idea what I wish."

He smiled. "Will you stay tonight? Maybe I can help you with one or two of those wishes. We can go and collect your things tomorrow."

I nodded because I was too choked up to reply.

We consummated our relationship in Jerrod's expansive king-size bed fitted with such high thread count sheets even my calculator couldn't do the maths. I wrapped him in my arms.

"I do love you, Jerrod Spicer."

"I know," he said.

I slapped him. "Egotistical bastard."

"And there's a very good chance that I may have the same feelings for you."

"Go on, say it properly," I chided.

"I love you, Colin Bransfield."

I just hoped his grandmother could hear our laughter and know how happy we were.

My insecurity made me ask. "What happens after the holidays?"

"You could extend the lease on my heart and stay here until it runs out."

"If it ever does."

"It won't," he said.

I believed him.

ELEVATOR SHAFT

~

$\mathcal{F}$or a few seconds there I thought I was safe. Then a hand thrust into the narrow space between the closing elevator doors, cutting the beam, and they sprang apart like startled children. I took a deep breath, and tensed my muscles, ready to flee.

I never understood: he both terrified me and turned my cock hard, hard as life on this council housing estate — hard as it was for me to forget the taunts, the hard-assed graffiti scrawled across the brick wall outside my flat, hard as the steel blade that sliced me open when my tormentors got tired of my passive resistance. The passive resistance wasn't a Gandhi-like conscious decision, it's just I'm not very brave, not very strong. Especially when there's a gang of them.

I'd been released from hospital ten days before after two weeks flat on my back while my council flat lay at the mercy of my torturers. I knew I'd be lucky if there was anything left of it. My scrapheap furniture would be stolen or else broken up, there would be disgusting accusations scrawled across the walls, and shit smeared on the curtains and windows. Oh, yeah, they'd done it before. While I was at work as a lowly paid shelf-stacker. It's all I can get. I'm not the brightest spark in the lighter, though I'm trying to do something about it. I'm going to community college at night to try to graduate high school. That's a major scholastic achievement on this estate.

Get me: scholastic. That's what comes of education.

Normally I walk up the nine floors, but that day I had no energy. My side still hurt, the bandages tight, making walking a slow and awkward shuffle, so stairs were totally out of the question. However, I was feeling good. I'd totally nailed the exam which meant I'd caught up with all the work I'd missed while I recovered from the attack. The physical wound had just about healed but I was still a nervous wreck around the estate.

The police and the counselors and the others in authority had clucked their concern like chooks in a wired enclosure, especially to the local press, but they disappeared pretty quickly once the spotlight focused on something more compelling and I slipped into the computer as just another statistic.

If the condition of my flat after I'd been confined to a hospital bed had been an exam question, I would have got a High Distinction. I managed to salvage the mattress, but it stank of piss and contempt. It was all I had to sleep on until I begged, borrowed, and cajoled a few items from charitable organizations. The clean-up I did myself, determined I would never allow the bastards to drive me out of my home. Not that I had a choice in the matter. It was my home come hell or high water because there was simply not enough public housing to go around. The waiting list was years and there were unlikely to be any vacancies in the near future just to move one pathetic faggot because he was constantly harassed. I had to make the most of it – or live on the streets.

Then I made the mistake of getting in the elevator again. I cursed myself for the damn fool I was when Trig broke the beam and the doors opened, the evil grin on his face as he saw me was sufficient for me to take a chance on getting out. I mumbled 'Excuse me' as I attempted to brush past him but he stuck out his arm, successfully corralling me inside as the doors closed.

Trig was one of the swaggering alphas on the housing estate and the leader of the gang that stabbed me although I wasn't sure who exactly had done the deed as it had all happened so fast. They'd surrounded me, each of them egging the others on until someone stuck me with a blade. It was an act of bravado, I'm sure no one had actually meant to kill me so when I went down and the blood flowed, they ran off like frightened teenagers shocked by their own violence. By that stage, I hadn't cared much. I prayed to whatever god looked out for me to just let me die, end my misery now, but he or she was not listening.

Eventually, someone called the paramedics but not before a number of my neighbors had walked past and ignored me sprawled on the pavement. It was that sort of community. Nobody wanted to get involved.

Trig stood facing me, his back to the lift door, as the creaky old metal box began its slow ascent. He examined me like some alien disease under a microscope, his brow furrowing as I stood facing him, not flinching under his threatening gaze.

If he thought he could intimidate me, he was wrong. My time in hospital, close enough to death as the blade had narrowly missed a number of vital organs, had given me a taste of what was to come and I was no longer frightened of the future. I wasn't going to go out of my way to encourage it, but I would face my fears and conquer them. I didn't break eye contact with Trig.

He was the first to speak. "You didn't rat on us?"

It didn't require an answer. Of course, I didn't. I told the police I was jumped and had no idea who my attackers were. Lie. I could name every single one, but I knew if I identified them, I would surely end up dead the moment I set foot back in the area. I'm not stupid. It was the code of the estate.

He nodded his head as if he was impressed, then asked, "You really a fag, mate?" His voice was quizzical rather than belligerent.

Faggot was a generic term he and his ilk used to label anyone on the estate who didn't meet their exacting standards, regardless of the accused's sexual inclinations. There was no point denying it. It had taken me long enough to come to terms with it myself. Working class boys were not expected to have those sorts of feelings, it just wasn't done.

Either way I answered was gonna be bad. At the least he'd harangue me or physically assault me for the remainder of my journey. If I admitted it, he'd have to do something more painful about it.

I didn't look away. "Yeah," I admitted without hesitation.

He reached over and jabbed his finger on the Stop button. The elevator lurched to a halt between floors. I couldn't expect anyone to come to my rescue as the lifts were breaking down all the time and people just shrugged and used one of the other two that were still working, assuming someone had reported the breakdown.

I tensed, but he made no move toward me. He did, however, block my access to the control buttons. We were stuck here for as long as he wished. "Shit, no kidding. You're really a fag? You like, take it up your shitter?"

What the fuck?

"Yeah."

"No way, dude."

I shrugged.

"Ah...you got a boyfriend or something?"

"Nah."

God, I hope he doesn't notice I've got a boner. All this talk has got me hard.

Trig was quite a piece of work. Tall, blond, built from his work as a laborer on the wharves. In his mid-twenties. His biceps bulged under his T-shirt. His pecs were a work of art. His ass was sculpted under his denim jeans, and his package was...He noticed me staring. My mind had stopped because I saw he was sporting wood. He made no attempt to hide it.

The air seemed to have been sucked out of the elevator. His breath was almost as labored as mine.

"What's it...um...what's it..." He had real difficulty getting the question out. He took a deep breath and blurted, "What's it like?"

"What's what like?" I asked.

He'd opened the floodgates, so the rest of it came comparatively easily.

"You know..."

But I didn't.

He sighed at my stupidity.

"What's it like to kiss another guy?"

I'd expected anything but that. There's only one sort of man that asks a question like that – a curious man. So, even if it was the last thing I ever did...I closed the distance between the two of us and pasted my lips to his. He was so startled he opened his mouth in surprise and my tongue rammed its way home. His mouth tasted of cigarettes and beer, but I didn't care. I knew the moment he came out of his shock, I'd be shoved away, pummeled by his fists until I couldn't stand up. Oh, it was so worth it.

Just pressing myself against him, my mouth and his locked together, even for a few seconds, was worth any price I had to pay. But he didn't push me away. The moment he overcame his initial shock, he began to respond. His tongue pushed back and I allowed him into my mouth, sucking him gently, opening my mouth wide as he almost attempted to devour me his hunger was so great.

Grinding his body against mine, I felt his cock pressing into my own hardness. He grabbed the back of my head and ravaged my lips, my mouth, my tongue like a man starving. I put every skerrick of my longing for him into that moment and, in return, I felt his loneliness. I understood. That didn't mean I would escape this episode unscathed. I knew from experience that a closet case could just as easily turn on the violence to prove he wasn't gay. Chances were Trig would be one of those people. He had a reputation to uphold. He could not be gay and retain the respect of his gang members. Or anyone else on the estate.

So when he released me I closed my eyes in anticipation. I'd feel the blow soon enough, I didn't want to see it coming. The sneer of revulsion on his face would wound me more than the physical pain.

But nothing came. I opened my eyes to watch Trig wipe the back of his hand across his lips. There was no sneer, no hate, merely a look of surprise. Once he'd cleaned the communal saliva from his mouth, he put his fingers to his lips as if to make sure they were still there. "Mate, you sure know how to fuckin' kiss. That was shit hot." He shook his head in disbelief. "I never knew."

While he was so focused on this unexpectedly pleasant new experience I managed to press the buttons on the lift and after a few wheezing groans and screeches we continued the interminable ascent toward the ninth floor. I was breathing heavily because I couldn't anticipate what Trig's reaction was going to be when we reached my level.

He didn't attempt to stop me as I raced past him hoping to reach the comparative safety of my spartan flat and its door with three deadbolts and a safety chain that a big enough fart from one of the neighbors would probably shatter. He must have realized I was making my escape because he called after me, "Uh, thanks." I was so surprised I stopped in my tracks, turning as the doors on the elevator closed on a man who looked totally bewildered.

While I'm a romantic at heart, I knew better than to read any sort of happy ending to his furtive lip lock. This was definitely not the early stages of our happy ever after. There could be no such thing on this estate for the likes of me. Sure, he could pass and would do so if his brief flirtation with the 'other side' was anything more than mere curiosity. Most of the people who were born here, lived here, died here, usually in not-so-genteel poverty and quiet despair. Sometimes not so quiet. Like Mrs. Marker who tossed herself from her small shabby balcony on the thirteenth floor barely missing the postman who had been at that moment delivering a letter from the hospital informing her they had no beds for someone with her terminal condition.

Mine was the sort of housing estate that if the cops or the fire brigade didn't turn up at least once a day then it was little short of a miracle and old Ma Rossetti would be off to Our Lady of Sorrows to light a candle or two in thanks. Just as she did for poor Mrs. Marker although that wasn't so much in thanks as a bribe to let her neighbor's tired old soul enter the gates of heaven. I was glad Mrs. Rossetti had the comfort of her beliefs, but her god was simply not mine. I had no faith, just a stubborn instinct to survive. And I was as far from Darwin's fittest as it's possible to be.

I saw Trig around the estate over the next few weeks without him spying me. An ultra-invisible profile suited me so that I blended in with the background, refusing to draw attention to myself. I dressed as shabbily as the rusting swings and slippery dip in the forlorn children's playground in the main square. I hunched my body to be as inconspicuous as the stunted drab olive-colored bushes that passed as the estate gardens.

His gang left me alone. If they saw me coming, they scattered in case social workers were still on my case but, as time passed, they became more openly belligerent again, my camouflage no longer keeping me invisible. Apart from a few juicy epithets to do with my fagdom and the occasional spit of contempt I was generally left physically unmolested. It did not escape my notice that the bullying always occurred when Trig was not around.

Each evening I would head off to my job at the Shop'n'Go convenience store on the edge of the estate. It sold all the essential requirements of the denizens of the housing estate: alcohol, cigarettes, microwave pizzas, crisps, and sugary soft drinks. Okay, I'm generalizing here but give me some slack – I pack the shelves so I know what people are buying. I also knew there were people in the surrounding high-rise flats dreaming of getting out. I was one of them.

I had another semester to go, one final exam to nail and I would have my high school diploma. Maybe that doesn't seem much to you but it was a major achievement to me, a means to a better life. I'm not talking a quick trip up the ladder to the millionaire's club. Hell, I'd be happy with something just a bit better than a zero hours contract. As Bernie, the night manager at the Shop'n'Go, said to me one night when I told him my dreams. "Good for you, mate. Take it one rung at a time." The second bottom rung on the ladder to a better life would be a big step up for me. It would mean getting my own flat. It wouldn't matter how dingey, how delapidated, it would be mine.

So after I finished my shift at the store, I'd head home, keeping to the shadows in the early morning so I wouldn't draw attention to myself. With luck I could slip upstairs to my apartment, throw the three deadbolts, slip the safety chain on, and collapse into bed. If I'd been less determined I could have spent my life in bed all day and at the store at night. It was a life that had seduced too many of those in the public housing complex, people who dreamed small or simply had given up dreaming at all.

When my alarm woke me after exactly seven hours of sleep, I would bounce out of bed and make myself a healthy breakfast, reading one of my textbooks as I ate the scrambled eggs and baked beans on toast, making notes as I discovered points salient to my exams. After washing the mismatched plates and cutlery, leaving them to dry in the sink, I'd scurry downstairs as inconspicuously as possible and catch the bus to the big library in the center of town.

The seventh-hand laptop that I'd owned had been destroyed when my flat was trashed – no great loss as it barely worked anyway. By that stage I'd learned to save all my work to a stick. That had escaped the attention of the vandals. The whole world was available to me at the library and I'd spend my time there researching and writing my essays. If there was enough time, I'd allow myself to dream, not of Trig (I classed that as fantasy) but of a new life far away from the grind and bullying of the community housing. To feed my dream, I'd pore over real estate rentals disappointed to discover that even as my modest nest egg was increasing the rents were outpacing it. Then I'd turn my attention to Positions Vacant. There were a number of factory positions available for the unskilled which is exactly what I was. My talent was my proficiency with numbers although I was far short of being a maths wizard but if the way I handled my savings was any indication, maybe my future lay with a course in accountancy. Plus, I was good at organizing. I had to be, what with my rather full schedule of eating/sleeping/classes/study/ shelf-stacking. Not much of a life if I thought about it but it was all I had. For the present.

There's nothing so private as your own dreams.

I packed up and headed to class followed by the mind-numbing replenishing the cans of dog and cat food purchased mainly by dispossessed people who had no pets that I knew of, directing clueless customers to the correct aisles for cheap luncheon meat, and explaining how to cook certain vegetables to heavily pregnant newly-married teenagers. It wasn't part of my job description but I like helping people even if some of them thought I had to be mentally deficient to work at shelf-stacking.

I was bushed as I made my way home. One of the stackers was off sick and management expected the rest of us to make up the slack. No extra pay, not even a thanks for helping us out of a mess, merely the smug superiority that we could be ordered about like sheep because this was a job of last resort. Bastards. Bernie at least attempted to make it up to us by letting us loose on the expired drinks and biscuits that didn't sell even in the Dollar Bins.

The last thing I needed was to run into Trig smoking on the steps of the apartment block. If I didn't know better I would have thought he was waiting for me. As I approached he stood on shaky feet, almost toppling over sideways. Drunk as a skunk.

"Where have you been?" he snarled indignantly.

Too tired to play his games, I went to push past him but he grabbed me by the arm. My body went into high alert, adrenalin pumping through me, flight was my only option, fight totally beyond me. "You're hurting me," I said calmly trying my best to defuse the situation.

He let go of my arm as if it had burnt him. "Oh, shit, sorry, mate."

Sorry?

If he wasn't here to hurt me what did he want? I walked into the building to the elevator, pressing the button as he followed. I felt his breath on my neck as he sidled up behind me. I knew what he wanted. Curious had led to curiouser. There was no need for words.

The doors seemed to take an eternity to close. Trig swayed as if the building was rocking, his eyes closed as if he were asleep. This time it was me that reached for the stop button between floors. The elevator creaked to a halt.

"What do you want, Trig?" I wasn't going to give him the satisfaction of assuming.

I wouldn't describe his actions as lunging at me, it was more of a stumble, but the intention was plain. He missed my lips so I got a tongueful of slobber down my cheek. Once he'd perfected his aim, his kiss was dynamite – so full of need it broke my heart for him. Then he gripped my hand and placed it over his crotch so I could feel the heat and steel hardness of his erection. I wanted him – badly – but not when he was drunk so that he could justify it in the morning as an alcoholic aberration or even pretend that he had no memory of it at all.

Almost shyly he ran his hand down over my chest and belly toward my cock which was equally as hard as his, hesitating only slightly before he wrapped his hand around as much of it as he could through my chinos. He must have been satisfied that I was liking this as much as he obviously was.

His kiss was languid but just as sexy as when he was gasping for it and I could have stayed glued to him all night if that's what he wanted. No, it wasn't. He disengaged his tongue, staring into my eyes as if trying to fathom the attraction. Then he made his intentions perfectly clear. He put his hands on my shoulders and tried to push me to my knees. For an instant I began to buckle but then my common sense kicked in. I fought to stay on my feet.

I was brusque. "No."

Anger flashed across his face. He probably wasn't used to people turning him down. Then he looked confused. "I thought...don't you want to?"

His pleading almost made me laugh but it didn't seem appropriate in a situation that was still fraught with the possibility of violence. "Trig, you're pissed."

"So? Some of me best blow jobs were when I was fuckin' off me face."

This time I did smile. "If you were as pissed as you are now, I'm surprised you remember."

He looked sheepish. "I don't."

Just as I thought. "Yeah." I nodded sadly. "And that's why you're going to bed to sleep it off. If you ever want a blow job that will rock your world and one that you'll remember the rest of your life, then ask me when you're sober." Okay, I was a bit cocky – a lot cocky – and a lot disappointed. He wanted the experience but needed the cover of alcohol to get up the courage. Clearly I was besotted with the guy but not enough to grasp at any opportunity. Trig wasn't marriage material; he was a quick fumble on the back seat of his car kind of guy. I wasn't gonna turn that down but it would be on my terms and it would have to be without the fortification of beer.

Bringing the lift back to life, I pressed his floor. Trig had sort of collapsed against me and was snuffling against my neck. I helped him along the passageway to his flat number, knocked loudly and scampered away. It would not do to have anyone catch me helping the top cock of the housing estate. I was around the corner and climbing the stairs when I heard cursing from his front door. Sounded like his stepdad.

Around lunch the next day, after a night of very pleasant dreams that included Trig and lashings of sex, I was heading off to the library when I ran into the man himself looking much the worse for wear, pacing and smoking outside the front entrance. He looked about furtively as I came out the door to the building. Normally he was at work this time of the day. He must have read my look of surprise because he muttered just loudly enough for me to hear although without looking in my direction, "Too plastered for the morning shift so I swapped with a mate."

Obviously he had more on his mind but couldn't afford to be seen chatting with me. I fumbled at my mail box, set along with countless others in a brick wall just outside the main entrance.

"Where are you going?" he asked quietly.

Not that it was any of his business but if he had gone to the trouble of intercepting me at least I could be civil. "The library then to work." I wanted to add "What's it to you?" but refrained.

"We need to talk," he stage whispered as he moved off, flicking his cigarette butt onto the ground.

"They're bad for your health," I whispered after him.

"Living is bad for your health," he replied.

I didn't give his comments much thought as I was snowed under with school assignments. At least at work I had the luxury of switching off my brain so my body got a chance at exercise. The stacking was mindless and I could almost do it on automatic as long as I shelved items in the right spot and moved the nearest expiry dates to the front. The store gets quiet in the early hours of the morning so I wasn't paying much attention to my surroundings, examining a load of expired instant veggies and quinoa salad – not a lot of demand for quinoa in the area – perched high on a ladder when my daydream was interrupted with, "What time's your break?"

I was so startled I almost fell but strong hands gripped my waist, lifting me to the floor. It would have been so easy to relax into his arms but I was at work and, more importantly, anyone from the estate might see us. It's no exaggeration to say our lives would have been forfeit had that happened.

"Well?" he said. "Are you deaf as well as cute?"

WTF. Did Trig just call me cute?

He must have uttered his smart-ass response without going through a filter because he turned bright red when he realized what he'd said. I couldn't resist. "Nah, just cute, not deaf. I have a break in twenty."

"Meet me outside. I'm in the car park."

"Okay." I clambered back up the ladder because Mal, who worked the register, could watch everything in the store on his security monitor. I didn't want to give him cause to wonder what was going on in aisle F: health foods and vegan cosmetics. It was a very small aisle, squeezed between the freezer for frozen chips and the shelves of Coke and Pepsi. Bernie had believed that sales might increase if the section had a higher profile which is why it was wedged where it was. Made no difference and as the healthy items expired, they weren't replaced. Soon Aisle F would be subsumed by sugary drinks and frozen spicy potato wedges.

While I worked I heard mumbled conversation from the check-out, Trig had obviously made a purchase so his visit looked legit. After Trig left, Mal called, "Isn't that one of the guys who sliced you open a few weeks back?"

"Yeah," I yelled back. "Leader of the gang."

"He gives you any trouble, let me know. I'll ban the cunt." Mal would, too. He was a big bastard. Ex-marine with enough weaponry under the counter to ward off an army – or a gang of estate punks.

"Nah, he's cool." I didn't want him barred.

Mal laughed. "Just as well cause he'd find it hard to get his supplies this time of the night anywhere else around here."

"Why? What'd he buy?" I hoped I didn't sound too inquisitive.

"Mainly booze. He'll go the way of his oldies if he's not careful."

"They drink?"

"They siphon up liquor like mother's milk. Killed his dad. Mum is a wreck. His stepdad's no better. Mean drunk."

I felt a twinge of sympathy for Trig, but only a twinge, his story much too common in the area. Unemployment was way above the national average. Boredom, depression, despair and alcohol are a lethal mix.

"Strange," he went on. "He usually buys smokes, not tonight but."

I detested people who smoke. I gave Trig a Get-Out-of- Jail-Free card because I fancied him. I'd fancy him even more if he gave them up.

"Someone's in for a wild night though," Mal continued as he tore open a packet of Use-by-date expired vinegar crisps, stuffing his mouth, spitting remnants all over the front counter as he spoke.

"Why's that?" I wondered if Mal was getting suspicious of my interest in Trig's shopping habits as I normally put in my ear buds and listen to music because Mal likes to talk boring shit. Early in the week it's just the two of us, maybe a third. Come Wednesday the other stackers come in, frantic to get Thursday's specials on the shelves.

"He bought two packets of rubbers and some lube. That girlfriend is gonna get a right fucking. Silly bitch."

"Why?"

He made that 'duh' sound used to indicate supreme stupidity on the part of the questioner. "Because he bought packets of condoms."

"I meant why is she a silly bitch?"

He snorted. "She thinks she's gonna marry him. And that he'll join her family's business. Not gonna happen."

"Why not?"

"You are an inquisitive little monkey tonight. Wanna marry him yerself?" His belly wobbled with laughter at his joke.

I was indignant although Mal didn't seem to have a homophobic bone in his body. His motto was 'Leave me alone and you can do what you want.'

"It is legal now you know," I said.

"Never said it weren't."

"Why then?" I really wanted to know.

"It's simple. He's an escaper."

"What? From prison, you mean?"

He laughed again. "Nah. You can tell the ones around here who are gonna get out. Most of us are reconciled to our fate. We don't care enough. Life kicks you in the balls often enough you stay down. Get yourself a pair of concrete undies and settle for what you got. Trig's not like that. He was born into a shitheap but he's one of those that will get out. Not saying he's gonna be president or prime minister. Not saying he'll be richer than that Bill Gates bloke. But no matter how hard life kicks him in the scrotum, he'll pick himself and keep going. You can see it in him. Same as I can see it in you. Youse'd make a great pair."

My preening at Mal's words was interrupted by someone after cigarettes. When he left I needed one more answer. "What's his girlfriend's family's business?"

"Her dad's a drug runner. Nasty piece of work. Will break your legs for an ounce of cannabis. You can say a lot of things about Trig but he don't do drugs. Got to have a clear mind to clear out of here. Isn't it your break? Clear out, sick of the sound of me own voice."

I grabbed two Pepsis (sugar free) from the large fridge, smacked the money on the front counter and strode out the door.

"Thirsty bugger, ain't you?" Mal shouted.

It wasn't hard to find Trig's car parked in shadow on the edge of the parking lot as far away from the well-lit highway as he could get. It was impossible to see the color of his vehicle let alone the number. I sauntered over, Trig opened the door for me and I clambered in, handing him his soda. He took it with thanks, popped the ring pull and guzzled it down, letting out a godawful burp at the end. I suppose some people would find that vulgar, I just thought it was cute that he felt he could be himself in front of me. So I followed suit and belched louder. That developed into a competition until we drained our drinks.

He crumpled the can and was about to chuck it out the window until I put out the palm of my hand. Sheepishly, he handed it to me without a word. I stored them to recycle later back at the store. Turning sideways in my seat, I looked at him. He was nervous. When I didn't say anything to start the conversation he cleared his throat loudly. "Look, Michael–"

"Micky."

"What?"

"Micky. My friends call me Micky."

He seemed pretty impressed that I might number him among my friends.

He cleared his throat again. "Look, this is hard for me." I wasn't about to make it easier. "What we did to you was wrong."

"No shit."

"But I took care of it. He won't do anything like that again."

I was horrified. "You didn't...?"

He saw the look on my face. "No, nothing like that. But he won't be using his fingers or his hands for a while."

"Okay."

"You're an okay guy, Micky. And...and..."

"I kiss like fuck, eh?"

That was all the encouragement he needed. Grabbing the front of my shirt he pulled me across the seat to him and buried his face in my neck, nipping and sucking before searching out my lips and plunging his tongue in. I reciprocated. It wasn't any more comfortable than the elevator as a space to make out but I wasn't complaining.

We had to pull away from each other to breathe, our panting fogging up the windows.

"I gotta get back to work, Trig." I attempted to straighten up my hair and tuck my hard-on down so it wouldn't be obvious when I walked back into the store past Mal.

"We gotta talk, Micky."

"It's okay. I won't tell anyone about what we did. You can trust me."

"Yeah, I know that. This is something else."

"Oh."

"Shit, it's so hard. Everyone knows everybody's business around here. There's no privacy."

"Come to the library tomorrow, we can talk. There's a coffee shop."

"Okay. I finish work at three. Probably take around thirty minutes to get there."

"See you between three-thirty and four tomorrow then." I was smiling as I got out of the car to walk across the deserted parking lot. I heard his car start up and pull away toward the main road. He gave me a coy beep as he drove out.

My grin was a mile wide as I went back to my job. I had a date tomorrow. With Trig. Yeah, right. I don't think Mr. Closet Gang Leader wanted to date the likes of me. He might want a blow job but that would be as far as it went. I'm not fussy, as long as he's sober.

But he didn't turn up. I waited as long as I could which meant I was almost late for class. My expectations were low but, yeah, I was disappointed. Especially when he didn't call into the Shop'n'Go later or wait for me at the front of the building when I got home. I'm such a sap.

I didn't see him for weeks afterwards, almost like he was avoiding me. Don't know why he'd bother as he never spoke to me on the estate where he could easily be seen and his motives questioned, especially if he didn't beat me up after or at least spit at me. I worried someone had seen us in the convenience store car park although I realized I would have heard about it before now. Just in case, it was head down, blend in with the concrete and rust of the estate in clothing the colour of lost hope.

It worked. I was pretty much left alone apart from the occasional spat jibe of 'faggot' or string of expletives that seemed more a mechanical reaction to me than a heartfelt putdown. It felt eerily like the calm before a storm, a marking time before something cataclysmic would occur. There was nothing for me to do but get on with my life, pathetic as it was, and look to the future when I could leave my dull grey existence.

Head down, concentrating on my monetary situation, calculating what I would need to get out, I sped through the estate on my way home, looking neither left nor right, my head resolutely focused on survival. Relieved I made it without a can or bottle thrown in my direction, I barged into the lift as the doors opened, and banged straight into...

"Sorry," I mumbled, waiting for the inevitable curse or stinging slap.

Nothing.

The doors closed but the elevator didn't move. The passenger I'd bumped into made no effort to push me aside and get out. Maybe...

Looking up, I made eye contact. Yep. It was him.

His kisses had made me foolish. "You didn't turn up," I blurted, revealing more hurt than I'd intended.

"Yeah," he replied. It was more honest than making excuses. "Sorry."

An apology?

This was awkward. I turned to press the button for my floor knowing full well Trig would stop me if he'd wanted to get out.

"Hold on a minute," he said retrieving a folded piece of paper from the pocket of his frayed black leather jacket. The paper had some of that blue rubber cement stuff people use to stick posters to walls. Pressing the button for Doors Open, Trig quickly got out of the lift, stuck the paper, on which he'd hastily scrawled 'Out of Order', on the silver metal floor panel and jumped back in before the doors closed.

"What's that for?" I asked, keeping my eyes on the floor. I'd learned young it was best to show humility in the face of superior strength.

"Protection," he said.

But self-preservation will get you only so far, sarcasm when you're hurting can't be bottled up. "Ah, you mean like that box of condoms you bought from the Shop'n'Go for your girlfriend who has no idea you're kissing me on the sly?"

He laughed. "You're feisty when you're angry. I like it."

The lift began its ascent but he stalled it pretty quickly between floors. I was grateful I didn't suffer from claustrophobia. If I'd had any pride at all, I would have told him to fuck off as he reached over and pulled me against his body. What can I say, I'm a sucker for strong men, especially strong men who are as handsome as Trig. I stretched up to meet his mouth and melted into him as he put his arms around me to hold me steady.

There was something different about the kiss that night. Sure, it was still desperate, it was still furtive, it was still mind-explosively brilliant, but it was seasoned with tenderness and a pinch of confusion. I really needed to stop overthinking whatever this was. I knew for certain it wasn't love. It was a straight boy, a well closeted straight boy, experimenting. I didn't mind playing guinea pig just to get my wet dream man for a moment but I knew there was no future. I'm not up there with Einstein and Stephen Hawking but I'm not stupid either.

I could feel Trig's hard-on pressing against me, rubbing to get relief, the kiss reinforcing his desire. Oh, fuck it. It was worth taking a chance.

His kiss made me light-headed, or stupid – take your pick – as my hand found the top of his jeans and undid the top button, then slid the zip down until I could get my hand inside his briefs. He gasped as my hand found its target. He was not the biggest I'd ever felt, though he was well-endowed. He moaned as I took more of his tongue and saliva, fingering his balls and rubbing his shaft as he clasped his hands on my ass.

I couldn't have stopped even if my life had depended on it. I'd dreamed about Trig, jerked off to fantasies of Trig for so long there was no way I would give it up now that it was within my grasp. They say reality is never as good as the fantasy. Bullshit. Trig was better than I could ever have imagined.

I slid his jeans down over his ass, and then pushed his briefs down under his balls so his cock sprang free. Much as I hated to leave his kisses, I slipped to my knees, engulfing his cock in my eager wet mouth. There was no time for foreplay here, this was a spur-of-the-moment passion, and I was determined to taste him before he changed his mind and reverted to the housing estate thug he was.

His crotch smelled of sweat and salt and masculine funk. I breathed deeply as I took his thick oozing cock in my mouth. I wanted him to want me. I wanted him to scream his orgasm so loudly the entire building heard him. I wanted to give him the best blow job he would ever receive. I wanted him never to forget me.

He writhed in exquisite agony as I took him into my throat, praying my gag reflex would take a holiday just this once. He leaned back against the wall of the lift, moaning his appreciation of my technique. I thought I could take a little time to appreciate his balls so I released his cock to concentrate on lathering his nut sac with my tongue. He held my head, attempting to insert his cock back in my mouth while I sucked each of his balls in turn. Only then did I satisfy his urgent demand for satisfaction. I took his prick so far into my gullet that his pubes tickled my nose.

Flexing my throat muscles made him cry out until I released his cock in order to gasp for breath. I returned to my task determined to milk him dry. "I'm close," he whispered.

Whether he informed me as a courtesy, which I doubt, or because he expected me to spit him out and jerk him to final orgasm, I wasn't sure. But I wanted to taste him and I sucked like a Dyson while he held the back of my head and spewed his cum into my gob. I swallowed those spasms that didn't shoot straight down my throat, relishing every drop. I kept sucking until his cock was so sensitive he jerked in an effort to extract his prick from my mouth. Reluctantly, I let him go.

Now would come the onslaught, the guilt, the name calling, the violence. It would have anyway. At least now I'd got something out of it.

His body skidded down the wall until his ass hit the floor. I was still on my knees so he looked me in the eye. "Is it always like that?" he asked.

I decided to be cheeky. "If I like somebody."

He was impressed. I could see it in the way his body had turned to jelly. I sat back on my heels, praying the moment would last a little longer.

"Mate, you got a magic tongue."

I had to be careful what I said. Any misjudged joke, such as 'Spread the word,' was likely to be met with violence. He wouldn't want his gang members to know he'd just let a fag blow him, no matter how good it was. The only way to have sex with a fag was to force him with the utmost violence. At least I'd been spared that.

Trig shook his dick before tucking it away. It was the signal our relationship was at an end. I stood, dusting down the knees of my jeans, offering him my hand to help him stand. To my surprise, he took it and, for a moment, our eyes locked. Then, abruptly, he turned away from me, jabbing the lift buttons with a force that belied his recent calm. The elevator shuddered back to life and we continued on our upward journey.

When we stopped at my floor, he neither looked at me nor issued a warning. I knew better than to go blabbing. Not that anyone would believe me anyway. Trig's reputation was rock solid. I must admit there was a spring to my step as I walked along the corridor to my flat. I think I may even have hummed.

If I expected my tormentors to leave me alone, I was sadly mistaken. If anything, their verbal abuse seemed to increase, spurred on undoubtedly by my sly smiles when I saw Trig lurking among them. To give him a little credit, he didn't join in the name calling and he did prevent any physical violence. Still, the last thing I wanted to encourage was the attention of a closet case who liked man sex but then set about bashing his partner in public for his fagdom. My self-esteem had never been that low. Besides, I knew from experience that once tasted, forbidden fruit was addictive. Especially if that taste was part of your nature.

I couldn't expect that Trig would automatically come back to me. In fact, it was more likely he would seek to slake his sexual thirst off the estate – it was safer. Or else, he was in a state of denial, damming his feelings until they threatened to overflow or burst through. I didn't think for a moment Trig's experimentation with me was based on a genuine emotional attachment, but I also knew it was more than mere curiosity. The way he kissed, the way he clamored for that male-to-male connection.

He surprised me when he turned up at the library a few days later while I was searching for jobs on the computer.

"Hey."

"Hey yourself," I replied.

"Mind if I sit down?"

There were so many ways I could answer that from sarcasm to over-eager. Instead, I just pulled out the chair beside me. He hesitated momentarily, glanced around the library to see if anyone was watching – it was unlikely any of his gang would be here – and then sat backwards on the chair facing the computer.

"What cha doing?"

"Looking for jobs."

"You don't like working at the Shop'n'Go?"

I snorted. "It's not exactly a career is it?"

"It is for Bernie." Trig shrugged as if that was all there was to it.

"Bernie's a stayer. I'm not. There's got to be more to life than living in this shitheap, working long hours for fuck-all wages."

"Yeah, I get ya." Trig sighed. "What sort of work you looking for?" he asked.

"It's more a matter of what's available to someone with no skills."

"Yeah, but what would you like if you had any choice in the world?"

I didn't like being set up to be laughed at and Trig must have realized how sensitive the subject was to me, so he added, "Me. I'd like to have me own car repair shop. A garage, a couple of blokes working for me. Maybe a flat over the garage long as it didn't stink of petrol. Maybe a dog. You like dogs?" Before I could answer he added, "Or maybe a cat. You like cats?"

"I like both."

"One of each then."

"Perfect."

We both sat silently for a few minutes, obviously with our dreams of a better life unspooling in our minds. He snapped out of it first. "Only one thing would make it even better.

"What's that?"

"Sharing it with someone." For a moment he stared straight at me. My face must have been a mass of confusion – was he suggesting something? – so he quickly looked away.

Not wanting to embarrass him, I said, "That would make it better than perfect."

He relaxed. "Yeah." As if to shake the dream off, he went back to his original question. "I told you mine, what about yours?"

"Mine would be much the same but instead of a flat above a garage, I wouldn't mind a small house somewhere, with a garden so I could grow some vegetables, somewhere for the dog and the cat to play instead of being cooped up in a flat all day. Some chickens."

He looked disappointed when I failed to share his dream apartment over the garage. I made amends as best I could. "Of course, the house could be next to a garage."

"Yeah. That would be good, too."

"My own special bloke to come home to."

He seemed intrigued. "Like, you'd live with another bloke openly? You know, as…um…"

I completed the question for him. "Partners? Lovers?" He nodded. "Fuck, yeah. It's my dream."

"Can…you know…two blokes sort of be in love with each other. Together. Exclusive like?"

"Of course. Two men can get married now."

"Yeah, my stepdad thinks that's sick. Never stops going on about it and the fags on the estate."

So that's where the self-loathing came from. It explained a lot. "I expect he wouldn't like you mixing with me then."

"Hates your guts. Prayed you'd cark it in hospital." My horror must have registered on my face. "Sorry, mate, that was uncalled for."

"Is that what you hoped for as well?"

He stared at me as if I'd struck him. "Fuck, no. What do you take me for? I don't pray, but if I did, I would have asked god to get you through it as quick as fuck and back on the estate."

I was entitled to feel a little bitter. "Oh, so the cops wouldn't get too involved and you and your gang could threaten me to keep my mouth shut."

"No, you got it wrong. Real wrong. If you'da died, I would have killed the bastard that cut you." He was so worked up people in the library were watching us. I put my hand on his arm to calm him down. He looked at my hand as if it burned him. I removed it quickly.

"Sorry," I mumbled. I thought I'd better explain myself. "It's just that people were looking."

His mouth was open in surprise. I hoped he wasn't going to explode in violence because I'd touched him. Best to get away as quickly as I could. "I guess I better go."

He made no effort to stop me. He just looked at me. "No one's ever touched me like that before."

Did he think there was something sexual in the gesture? He was confusing me. What was he after?

I grabbed my gear and walked from the library before there were any repercussions. Trig didn't run after me and as I rounded the corner of the building, I glanced through the glass frontage and saw he was still seated, stunned, peering at his arm where my hand had rested on it.

Fearful I'd done something to piss him off I made myself even more invisible than usual. I dressed in dark clothes and the night enfolded me in its embrace so that I could stick to the darkest edges of the streets and alleys of the estate where the few street lights that hadn't been smashed failed to make any difference. I avoided the lift; I changed my usual habits where I could although my job as a shelf-stacker didn't allow much flexibility.

So it was inevitable that's where Trig would run into me again.

I was perched on a ladder trying to dislodge a carton of baby wipes from above the shelves. "You avoiding me?" a voice asked. It didn't sound aggressive or angry, just a little miffed. "What did I do to, you know, piss you off?"

The carton dislodged, I lost my grip, and it slammed onto the shop floor with a resounding thud, missing Trig by a matter of inches.

He didn't budge. "I'll take that as a 'yes' then."

I clambered down the ladder and although he hadn't been hurt, I started brushing his coat as if to wipe away any pain or humiliation he might have suffered.

He grabbed my hand. "Take it easy, you'll wear it out." It was his favorite leather coat.

"I'm so sorry. I didn't mean it. It was an accident."

"Everything okay there?" Mal called from the check-out.

"Yeah," I shouted back. "Just a box of baby wipes fell from on top of the shelves."

"Anyone gives you any trouble, just let me know." Mal made it sound as threatening as he could.

"Thanks. I will."

"He looks out for you?" Trig nodded in Mal's direction.

"Yeah, he's good like that." I tore the carton open and began stocking the shelves. There were a lot of births on the estate.

"You need someone to look after you full-time, not just when you're at work," he said.

"You volunteering?" I said it flippantly so he could laugh it off.

"Maybe."

That got my full attention. I was squatting to fill the lower shelves and had to look up so he wouldn't misinterpret what I was about to say. "I don't need a bodyguard, I need a boyfriend." I went back to the shelves. He had no response to what I'd just said. I heard him pad away down the aisle after a few minutes. It was going to be a long night.

He must have been mulling it over for a few days because when he turned up at the library, me preoccupied with my lack of skills as I searched the job market – I was good for factory work, zero-hour contracts, and a lavatory cleaner – the first thing he said was, "Okay, I get it now. But boyfriends sounds so frilly knickers teenage shit. There's gotta be a better word."

It was pointless trying to follow where his thought patterns were headed. Best to just give in and go with the intellectual overflow. "Well, there's husband, if you're married, partner, spouse, lover, couple, other half," I listed them off on my fingers, "Oh, husbear, if you're into bears."

"What the fuck?"

I couldn't conceive where his mind went with that one so I quickly added, "A bear is a hairy gay guy, usually a bit overweight."

"You mean some blokes go for that sort of thing?"

He sure had a lot to learn. "Plus there's all those other terms of endearment like honey, babe, snookums." I stopped when I thought he looked as if he was gonna puke. "Okay, not them."

"Partner. Yeah, partner. It makes it sound like we're equals. I like that."

I knew he was talking generically and not about him and me, but… "I hate to sound thick, but are you hinting that you might just be the tiniest bit gay inquisitive?"

"I dunno," he sighed. "It's all so fuckin' new. Well, maybe not that new but now I sorta put a toe in the water it's doin' my mind in."

Much the same effect he was having on mine.

Trig calling into the library for a chat was like a class in Homo Elementary. Everything about gay life was alien to him except what he'd learned from his stepdad and the gang members on the estate. He'd unquestioningly swallowed the negatives and was finding it difficult to equate them with the pleasure he got with kissing me, without going into the tsunami of pleasure he'd got from a simple gay blow job. But he'd never taken it any further.

I enjoyed his company and I could see him struggling with his same-sex desire, so I persevered answering his questions which any modern ten-year-old could have answered. "Thanks for not treating me like an idiot," he said one evening as he got up to leave. The big breakthrough that session – they really did feel like a psychological session or a catholic confessional – he'd admitted that, perhaps, he was bisexual although I could read the lie on his face. It frightened him to admit even that much out loud.

Inevitably, that old perennial came up one afternoon when I'd abandoned my job search to give my full attention to Trig's dilemma. The question? "Don't it hurt?"

I didn't have to ask what 'it' was as he'd admitted he'd been watching gay porn on the net to get a few pointers. I'd already told him there was no mystery to gay sex, "It's just like doing it with your girlfriend except there's no vagina and there's an extra dick."

"I ain't never done anal with Ange. She don't like the idea. You do that?"

That was his opportunity to learn a bit more terminology: top and bottom. Or versatile.

"Which one are you?" he asked eagerly. "Don't answer that if it's too personal."

There was no point not admitting the truth. "I'm a versatile bottom."

"Meaning?"

"I mainly like to take it but I will give it if the occasion arises and the partner wants it."

And that led into the Six Million Dollar question. "Don't it hurt?"

"Not if you're doing it right. If the partner's rough or his dick is too big, then yes, it can sting for a while, but it usually goes away quickly, especially if your prostate is stimulated."

Anatomy lesson anyone?

"Some straight guys get their girlfriend to shove a finger up their ass while they come. Or, they even go so far as to buy a vibrator to try it out."

That snippet of information was about all he could absorb on that occasion. His education was advancing at a rapid rate and he'd soon pass his Homo entrance exam with honors. I wasn't so sure about the practical application, however.

It came sooner than I expected.

Trig had disappeared for about two weeks. I didn't see him anywhere on the estate, not even with Ange who was usually possessively draped over him, and he didn't visit me in the library or at the Shop'n'Go. In fact, our meeting again was by sheer accident.

I was coming home late from my shelf-stacking job, keeping to the shadows in case some testosteroned kid was lurking, bored or drugged off his tree, just itching for a bit of ultra-violence so his life didn't seem a total shitheap.

I heard the voices before I got near enough to confirm it was Trig and his girlfriend, Ange, who had every intention of leading him down the aisle by his balls. She was as bad as the more violent members of Trig's own gang as she headed a posse of local vixens who intimidated both sexes, particularly the elderly, offering protection from harassment and physical harm for a large slice of their pension cheques each fortnight. The Queen of Extortion. With threats.

She and Trig were arguing. They were notorious for their bitter feuds which normally lasted for days and dragged in all other gang members who had to swear allegiance to one side or the other.

Trig sounded exasperated. "I am not gonna marry you."

I did so not want to be involved in this discussion. I'd heard enough already of Ange's pleading and whining to set my bowels on edge. It was the usual cause of friction between them. As I edged my way toward the door to my block, I must have dislodged loose stones because the sound of crunching gravel drew their attention to me. All I could do was look straight ahead and keep going as if I hadn't heard a thing. It's not like the entire estate wasn't privy to what was going on, Ange had a voice like a fog horn. It carried for miles.

Her voice dripped venom. "Well, if it isn't the faggot," she sneered. "Gettin' your rocks off in the dark, eh?"

"Leave it, Ange," Trig snapped. "This is about us."

Ange changed tack. "What is it with you an' the faggot lately? You're always defendin' him. You in love with him or somefink?"

Something in Trig's face must have given him away. Ange shrieked in triumph. "Oh. My. God. You fancy the little fag, don't cha? Is that why you wanted me to shove my finger up your date while we were fucking the other night?"

I didn't want to hear this. I used the distraction as an opportunity to escape, to try to get into my flat and bolt the door as quickly and quietly as I could, Ange's parting shot to Trig, "Well if you like him that much why don't you marry the fuckin' poof then? It's legal now. Are you waiting for him to propose?"

I thought I was safe. The elevator door was closing, my breath was steadying, my heart was thumping less urgently. Then, fuck me dead, the fist burst through the small opening and again the doors leapt apart. His face was deformed into a snarl that threatened anyone in its path. That would be me. He turned his back, jabbing savagely at the floor buttons until the lift jerked upwards. I would have to struggle past him to get out. I doubted I'd get that far.

He turned suddenly, smashing his fists into the walls of the elevator either side of my head, his face so close to mine I swear I could smell his hunger. I dared not breathe as he simply stared into my eyes as if searching for something that he thought was hidden there. I kept mum.

"Well, would ya?"

My throat was so constricted in terror I couldn't answer. Would I what?

He must have read the question in my eyes.

"Like she said, would ya marry me?"

WTF?

I didn't need to think about it. "Yes," I croaked.

This wasn't the time to go into the fact that my lust had slowly turned to love during those afternoons we shared furtively even though the most we ever did publicly physical was a clap on the shoulder or a quick hand on an arm. But it was enough. Of course, there were obstacles: The fact he smoked and that I swore I would never go into a relationship that included an ashtray, or that the likelihood of me and him marrying was on a par with the chances of Jupiter colliding with Mars. "If you give up the cigarettes," I added. No use making it easy for him.

His whole body relaxed when I gave him my reply.

"Why?" he asked.

I hit the button to stop the elevator this time. If he wanted to talk, this was about as private as it got. I'm sure Ange would be gathering her gang of harridans to make an assault on my flat at this very moment. I didn't want to be there, especially not with her boyfriend, when she arrived.

If I was going to get personal, I was going to be comfortable. I sat on the floor. He paced a while longer then sat opposite me. He asked again.

I shrugged. "Lots of obvious reasons. You're hot. Great looking, sculpted body, dick of death—"

"How's me dick compare to other guys?"

"Bigger than average." It was only a small lie.

"Go on."

"But besides that, I think you've got potential. You're intelligent."

He made a dismissive sound at that.

"Yes, you are. You got dreams, you got the chance to escape from here. You gonna take Ange with you?"

"She don't wanna move. Her family's here."

"She been here so long, she don't smell the shit no more," I said.

He looked at me like I said something deep.

"Yeah," he said. "But you smell it, don't ya? It clogs your nostrils. The stinkin' smell of desperation and small dreams gets in your clothes, in your hair, and in your mind."

For Trig, this was waxing lyrical.

His foot touched mine. It wasn't an accident.

"Would ya come with me?"

"Yeah."

I would, too. My exams were over, I was free.

"I got a new job lined up. In the north. Away from here. Pay's good. I could look after ya till ya got set up like."

"Sure, I want to get away but I don't want a sugar daddy. Besides, you couldn't afford me."

He took it as a joke and cuffed the side of my head lightly.

"You could get a job. They got courses in book-keeping at the local community college."

How the fuck did he know I was trying to get that sort of job? I'd always been good with numbers, much less so with words.

"I saw what you was lookin' at in the library a couple of times I was there. Is that what you want?"

"Yeah."

"I can pay for your course and you could get a part-time job. Maybe help out round the garage where I got a job. It's me uncle's place. Me mum's brother. He got out of this shithole when he finished school and ain't never been back. No contact with anyone from around here. Me mum won't have nothing to do with him. I had to track him down. He said he's glad I take after him. He's, um, like you."

I bunched an eyebrow. Trig looked shamefaced. "Like us."

I had a simple question. "Why?"

He slithered over to where I was and put his arm around me. "I can't get ya outa my mind. What is that, eh?"

I thought it was a bit early to mention the L word.

"I give great head," I joked. "But wait till you try my ass."

"How about right now?"

"An elevator doesn't exactly scream romance but, what the fuck, it's probably the most romantic spot I'll ever get around here. Or we'll make it that way."

He bear hugged me into a kiss, his desire obvious. As I began to undo his jeans, a couple of sachets of lube and a strip of condoms fell out of the pocket.

"Oh, shit." He looked at me as if expecting the worst.

I laughed. "You came prepared."

"Is that okay?"

I replied by way of standing to shuck my jeans, kneeling on all fours and wiggling my ass at him. "I dreamed of this so many times," I admitted. "Of you ploughing my ass."

He undressed even faster than I had. First he tore one of the rubbers from the strip using his teeth, sliding it smoothly on his gorgeous hard cock before slathering my hole liberally with the gel, then greased his sheathed pole. He pushed the head of his prick into me, penetrating the sphincter.

I saw stars for a moment but I knew the pain would subside once he got into his rhythm.

He slid his cock all the way in.

"Oh, fuckin' Je-zus."

I could tell from the timidity of his technique he was trying not to hurt me but he was taking so long my knees were feeling the strain.

"How about I lie on my back, so I can watch your face as you fuck me," I suggested.

He was a gentlemen. He removed his favorite jacket, spreading it on the floor for my comfort, before I lay down so he could push my legs onto his shoulders and sink inside my guts again. I watched him as he tried out various different angles and strokes, then found one to his liking, concentrating on that.

"Mate, your ass is so fuckin' hot."

I drew his face down to mine and kissed him deeply as he pounded my butt. When we broke the clinch in order to breathe, I panted, "I'm not made of glass. You can fuck me as hard as you want."

Now that he had the go-ahead, he ploughed me like he did in my dreams. This was better than any fantasy. But that's really all it was. A fantasy. Sure, I was getting what I craved, a right royal buggering for a man I had feelings for, but if I thought anything else would come of this, I was even more naïve than Trig's girlfriend, Ange.

It didn't bear thinking about so I shut down my mind's skepticism and relaxed into the best sex I'd had in forever although it was hard to ignore the whimpers and groans and the murmurs of appreciation that Trig whispered in my ear. It made being used a little less hard to take.

As we were hitting our stride, someone on the upper level began kicking the elevator doors in frustration. I wondered if they'd heard the sounds we were making. But Trig ignored the interruption, holding my waist tighter as he increased his pace, eventually moving his hand down to touch my prick. I'd been working it so that I'd come about the same time as Trig. I wasn't about to miss out on my own orgasm just to please him.

To my surprise, Trig slapped my hand away and grabbed hold of me. It was so unexpected I gasped loudly which led to more cursing and fists banging against the lift doors a few floors above. It didn't matter because I could tell from Trig's breathing he was close and just the feel of his hand around my cock made it impossible to hold back. If there's such a thing as a quiet roar then that was the sound Trig made as he blew his load just a fraction after I did, my ass clamping down around his cock to milk every drop.

He held me tightly as he came down from his sexual high, nibbling at my neck and whispering, "Fuck, if everyone knew that was what gay sex was like, they'd be instant converts." I could have argued but the fact he hadn't freaked out was a positive. I knew he'd forget all his shit about marriage and liking me and going with him to his uncle's by the time he left the building, but I'd treasure the moment and the compliment.

"I guess we better clean up and get out of here," he said with a note of disappointment in his voice. Holding the base of the condom, he pulled out, tied a knot in the rubber and rather than dropping it on the floor like most of the animals in the building did, pushed it into his pocket.

I wiped myself down with a hankie I always carried with me — it was to staunch blood mainly – while Trig shoved his sticky cock into his jeans. He watched as I finished up and pulled on my clothes before he put his arms around me, kissed me much more tenderly than I expected, and said, "Thanks." Looking into his eyes I was hoping to see something, anything, of what he was thinking, but he revealed nothing. I guess I didn't know him well enough.

"You ready?" he asked, now assuming his hoodlum persona once again.

I nodded and he deactivated the Stop button and pressed my floor. We both feared anyone would be waiting to get in. Luck was not with us. As I stepped out of the lift I almost knocked over poor Mrs. Hubble who seethed irritation. She never liked me. I was about to apologize when Trig explained. "Lift's fucked. We got stuck between floors. Thought we'd need the mechanics to haul us out."

Mrs. Hubble humphed and pushed me aside to get in, sniffed and said "I can smell what you boys got up to while you were caught between floors. It's a disgrace."

I stepped out and as the doors closed on the two of them I saw Trig put his arm around Mrs. Hubble and drag her close with just enough menace as he said, "I don't think you really want to go around spreading rumors now, do you?"

That brought home to me how close we were to being discovered. And discovery would be fatal, at least to me. Trig was a survivor, he'd fight his way out of the predicament, besides he had an out now, what with his uncle's job, and the idea that people might discover our little trysts would probably spur him to leave sooner. And then where would I be? Fucked, that's where. And not in a pleasurable way.

I took extra precautions locking and bolting my door that night but still found sleep elusive.

To my surprise, Trig proved to be more attentive, taking to calling in to see me at the library where I sought peace and shelter away from my small flat and harassment, or else at the Shop'n'Go where Bernie and Mal began to get suspicious of our friendship even though we played it cool. "I think that boy likes you," Mal called one night after Trig left.

"What makes you say that?" I asked as innocently as I could manage.

"Well, for starters, he's always in here now. Never useda be. Never buys anything so I'm guessing he has things to discuss with you. Not a friendship that springs readily to mind. Unless…"

"Unless what?" I was snappier than I intended.

"Unless you have a lot more in common than it seems on the surface," he said.

I could scarcely keep the fear and anger out of my tone. "Just what are you implying?"

"Whoa, boy. Not implying nothing, but I ain't as stupid as the other bastards around here. I can see it in his eyes the way he looks at you."

He does? I couldn't help my smile.

"And the way you look at him."

"You're imagining things, old man."

"I don't care what you get up to in private, son. I've seen things in my life that would make your hair curl. Probably why I'm bald as a billiard ball. But if you want my advice, and I know you don't, get out now. Go as far away as you can. Take him with you. Before it's too late."

I had to rub my sleeve across my eyes they were watering so much. "I wish," I said quietly.

Mal didn't say anything else and after I told Trig about the conversation the next day he never came back to the Shop'n'Go. But his excitement never abated. He was all plans and finances. His uncle this, his uncle that, what he would do once he got his apprenticeship. The fact his uncle offered to make him a partner if it all worked out. And always there was room in his new life for me. I always thought it was a sop to my ego so I'd listen to his dreams because he couldn't share secrets with anyone else. He hadn't told his parents or even Ange about his job offer or contacting his uncle. He wanted a clean break. He told me because I couldn't betray him without betraying myself.

That's what I believed until the afternoon he turned up with a booklet and slapped it down on the table.

"What's this?" I asked.

"I thought you said you passed your exams," he chuckled. "And I know English was one of the subjects so you should be able to read the cover as well as anyone."

"No need to get snarky. I can see it's the community college brochure. So?"

"Open it. Page 16," he said proudly.

I flipped through the brochure until I found the page. "Book-keeping?"

"I know that's what you want to do. I saw you looking on the computer. You're good with numbers, yeah?"

"Better with numbers than with words," I admitted.

"So? What ya think?"

"About what?"

"About the book-keeping course, ya dummy." He said it with a smile in his voice.

"I'd have to look at it more carefully," I said.

"Take it home, let me know what you think of it," he said, his eyes sparkling with mischief. He couldn't sit still for a minute. "I've got news."

I was about to ask what it was when a voice cut through our conversation like the knife that cut through my flesh.

"There you are," Ange squealed from the end of the aisle of books that separated the computers from the general reading area. "When Charmaine said I'd find you here, I didn't believe her for a minute. But here you are, and here's the fag. I should have known."

One of the women seated at a computer nearby hissed her disapproval, whether at the slur or Ange's piercing voice I wasn't sure.

"Blow it out your minge, you slapper," Ange screamed at her.

All eyes were on us.

"Hope you're not asking your fag mate to be Best Man," she went off into peals of laughter that threatened the ear drums of anyone within a five-mile radius. "Best *man*, get it. Though he might make a passable flower girl." She laughed again but when no one joined in she sort of choked it off, sounding like a throttled chicken.

"Could you give us a moment, doll. I have something important to discuss."

"Okay, but don't take all day about it. I gotta lot to prepare for the wedding."

"Wedding?" I couldn't believe my ears.

"Yeah. Wedding." Ange draped herself over Trig, obviously claiming property rights. "And yeah, him and me."

I was so shocked it must have shown on my face. "O. M. G. The ugly fag didn't know. You didn't tell him."

I stood up, grabbing my pen and notebook, and shoved them in my backpack before heading for the front door of the library, muttering, "Gotta go."

I heard Trig turn on Ange, "Look what you've done, Ange."

"Not my fault if the little queer is in love with you."

"What?" Trig exploded.

"You blind. It's written all over his face. Plain as day. God, you men are so clueless."

The door closed behind me and I raced away hoping, but not expecting, Trig might follow. Nope.

I didn't want to go back to my depressing flat, and the library was out even after Trig and Ange left, because I couldn't stand the pitying looks of those who'd witnessed my humiliation. I needed to keep busy. I needed not to think. I headed to the Shop'n'Go. Bernie was on duty, all sympathy when I said I'd start work early as I had nothing better to do. "Don't think you're getting paid overtime," he said before heading back to his cubbyhole that he called an office.

After I dropped off my backpack in one of the staff lockers and put on my Shop'n'Go dust coat, I brought in a pallet of goods from the loading bay.

"So you heard the news then, huh?" Mal was at the check-out.

"I must have been the last to hear it," I sniffed.

"If it's any consolation, it's none of Trig's doing." Mal patted me on the shoulder in sympathy.

"Can't be much of a wedding if Trig's not involved." I was barely keeping my feelings in check.

"Listen here, son." Mal had on his serious voice. "It's a marriage of convenience. Ange has got her way and that boy has been forced into a situation that's none of his doing."

"How so?" I asked, ready to grasp at any straws.

"His stepdad, the silly fucker, owes Ange's dad enough dosh that they'll be around with baseball bats soon if he doesn't pay up."

"What's that got to do with Trig?"

"His dad doesn't have the sort of money that's owed what with interest rates that'd tear you heart out if you cared, and his mum is beside herself with stress and worry. No, listen." I was about to interrupt again.

"Ange's dad would do just about anything for his little girl. He dotes on her. She can twist him around her little scrubber finger. So little Ange has been whining about how she wants to marry Trig but Trig isn't willing to commit, isn't there something daddy can do to change his mind. Solution? Trig marries Ange, Ange's dad wipes the debt Trig's dad owes. Everyone's happy. Except Trig."

"And me," I said.

"You love him?" Mal asked, not unkindly.

"Yeah. Fuck it. I thought I had a chance. Slight, but still a chance."

"Then fight for him, mate. Fight like you've never fought before."

I went back to the stock, my head teeming with confusion. It hurt that Trig would sacrifice himself for the stepdad he despised, yet he didn't think enough of me… What about all those fancy plans he had to work for his uncle, get an apprenticeship, get out, take me with him? Nah, it didn't make sense.

I spent the next two hours morosely stacking shelves but my mind wasn't on it and I had to undo a lot of the angry mistakes I'd made to the extent Bernie called me aside. "Get your head out of your ass. I could stack those shelves faster than you and everyone knows I'm a useless bastard."

"Hear, hear," Mal called from the check-out.

"No one asked you," Bernie shouted. "Now get yourself a coffee – it's on the house – and take yourself outside or to the loading dock and have a fifteen-minute break. I want to see an improvement in attitude when you get back. Or else."

I felt like demanding "Or else what?" but I couldn't afford to lose this job. I had savings but I didn't want to eat into them now that it was imperative I leave council housing. My life here would be rubbish if I had to watch Trig and Ange married, or even worse, pushing their sprogs around in a pram. No. I'd buck up, tuck my heart back where it couldn't hurt anymore, or at least not much, and get on with my plans that had been so rudely interrupted by the tsunami that was Trig.

I grabbed my backpack and went to sit with my coffee on one of the pallets in the comparative calm out back of the store. I kept a few energy bars on hand in case of emergencies like this one when I hadn't gone home first to make up a sandwich – the Shop'n'Go version were rubbish and the staff discount was not nearly enough to make edible cardboard bread with Best-By-Last-Week luncheon meat filling palatable.

I told myself I wouldn't cry. Really, I wouldn't. I reached into the backpack dislodging the college booklet Trig had given me. A sheet fell out from between the pages. I picked it up merely glancing at it in case it was something I needed to return to Trig or something I could dump in the bin along with the brochure and my shattered dreams. Shit. I really needed to stop being so dramatic.

I saw my name on the page. It wasn't my address though. It was an address to the north, the city where Trig's uncle had his garage. Why was my name on it? On closer inspection it proved to be an application form for a course in basic book-keeping. WTF? My name. An address in the north. But I couldn't afford the fees. I would have told Triq that if we hadn't been… Holy shit. Trig had filled in the credit card details and signed it himself. All I had to do was sign on the dotted line. I'd like to say my fate hung in the balance or that my future flashed before my eyes or there was some great epiphany but all I felt was numb. I got up, stuffed the application back in my bag, slung it over my shoulder and walked robotically back into the store, speeding up until I reached the check out.

"Tell Bernie I had to go," I said to Mal as I pushed through.

"I'll tell him you've got a stomach bug. He hates that. You coming back?"

"I dunno," I said truthfully.

"Go get him, son."

I was all fired up, a feeling completely alien to me. I felt brave. I felt elated. Trig was gonna pay for my course. He really did want me there. And I ran out on him. Okay, he wasn't totally blameless in this marriage fuck-up but I could forgive him anything. Well, anything but tying himself to Ange. Fuck what his parents want.

Didn't know how he intended to sugar coat his forthcoming nuptials but I pushed him away without giving him a chance to explain. I raced back toward my flat without a clue where to find Trig. Ange probably had him holed up somewhere to keep him to herself. I didn't dare go to the flat he shared with his parents. And, of course, the one day I really wanted to meet him in the elevator, he wasn't there. I'd go home, change out of my work gear and go looking. Hopefully it would come to me where to start.

When I reached my floor and went to unlock the door I noticed it had been tampered with. I pushed; it opened much too easily. Sighing in expectation of the place being trashed and graffiti covering the walls, I entered carefully, but not carefully enough. I was grabbed in the semi-darkness and pushed against the wall. It wasn't until I felt his mouth on mine that I realized it was Trig.

"What kept you?" he panted when we broke for air.

"Doesn't matter, I'm here now."

"You didn't let me explain and I couldn't while Ange was around." He sat down on my bed. I sat beside him and held his hand.

"You're doing it to cancel out your stepdad's debts."

"You heard?"

"Yeah." I tried to keep it light. "So it's not a love match then?"

He laughed. "Hell, no. It's not a match of any sort."

"What do you mean?" He seemed remarkably happy for someone being forced by circumstances into a relationship he didn't want.

"I have no intention of getting saddled with Ange and her family of pimps and drug pushers."

"But your stepdad." I was still having problems getting my head around what was going on.

"The bastard hates me. So what makes you think I should sacrifice my life to pay off his debts? Fuck him."

"I hope I'm around when you tell him that. And Ange. So I can pick up the pieces. If there's anything left of you."

He looked at me strangely. "You won't be here."

"Where will I be?"

"With me. Up north. Working for my uncle. You'll be in classes."

"You really want me to go with you?"

"What have I been telling you for weeks?"

I launched myself at him knocking him to the floor, smothering him with kisses.

"I haven't saved up much money but I'll pay my way as soon as I get a job stacking shelves. They must have convenience stores where we're going."

"You won't be stackin' any fuckin' shelves."

I was about to ask him what I would be doing when someone started hammering on my front door. "Trig, I know you're in there. What the fuck are you doing with that fag?" There was a murmur of voices so she wasn't alone.

"Shit. Shit. Shit." Trig cursed but his mind seemed elsewhere. "We only have seconds before they bust in. You trust me?"

"With my life." I knew it had come to that.

He said nothing but produced a knife and slashed at me. I felt hot blood on my face as Ange and members of his gang burst through the door. He slashed again. More blood.

"You filthy fuckin' faggot," he screamed in my face.

WTF?

"What's going on?" Ange demanded as the gang members crowded in.

"The little poofta made a pass at me. Said he wanted to suck my dick. Made me want to puke my guts out. Poxy pervert." He spat in my face. His gang advanced ready to do me injury.

I was totally defeated by the change in Trig when he was caught out. I expected better than being tossed to his mates. Kill me now.

I got my wish. He drove the knife into my stomach and pulled it out bloodied. It hurt less than I expected. Then he delivered the final touch, knocking me to the floor. The last thing I heard was Angie screaming, "You killed him."

***

My head hurt, my shirt was covered in blood, and… I was alive. And I wasn't in hospital. "Where am I?" I groaned.

"You're in the car." He turned to look at me as if to ensure I was all right.

"We on the way to the hospital?"

"Nope. We're headed north. As far away from that shitty housing estate as we can possibly go."

"But you fucking stabbed me. Are you just gonna dump my body on the side of the road and drive off?"

"You only think I stabbed you," he said in the most patronizing voice I'd ever heard.

"I saw the knife go in. And what about all this blood?"

"I had to make it look real otherwise they would have killed both of us."

"Okay, I'm confused."

He passed over a bottle of water and a pill. "Take that. It'll help your head."

"If I do, will you please explain what's going on?"

"If you'd stop interrupting me. Are you gonna be like this when we're married?"

My mouth dropped open. "Are you asking me to marry you?"

"See, there you go interrupting again."

"Okay, but I'll be going back to that question as soon as you've finished. Just so you know." I pretended to lock my lips and put the key in my pocket.

He took a deep breath. "Okay. I had to think on my feet. Real fast. I knew what would happen to both of us even though they hadn't caught us doing anything. It was still too suspicious, me being in your flat. Best I could do was turn the tables on you and call you every filthy name I could think of. That threw them. Especially when they saw all the blood on your face. I nicked your ear. Ears bleed a lot and in the confusion I cut my arm and managed to get some on you so it looked worse than it really was."

"But you fuckin' stabbed me." To emphasize the point I lifted my bloody shirt to show him the wound. "What the... Do you have miracle healing powers?"

"I didn't stab you. Sure, I cut you with a knife I carry for protection, but this one," he produced a nasty looking weapon from between the seats, "is the one I used on you." He stabbed his stomach. I gasped and went to grab it until I noticed there was no blood and no cut in his shirt. "It's a fake. No way did I want to end up in jail so I carry that for show. Sure, if my life depended on it, I'd use the real thing but otherwise you'd be amazed how many people back off when I produce that monster. I've never had to use it, bar once on a guy who led a gang of nutters. I stabbed him and the look of shock on his face, the gang ran away. I couldn't use it too often cause word would get around. Even my gang didn't know about it. Lucky for us."

He leaned over and kissed my cheek.

"In the blood and confusion, they all thought I'd really stabbed you. If they'd looked close enough they would have seen how fake it was. But you were out cold after I socked you so I bent down and felt for a pulse. 'He's still alive. Just,' I told them. I tried to look as panicked as they were but I was totally calm. I had to be to get us through this shit.

"Ange asked the perfect question. 'What do we do now?' They all looked to me. 'Don't touch him. You don't want your DNA on his body.' There was lots of moaning about what would happen with the cops. Everyone just wanted to get out. It was easy to take control. 'Look,' I said. 'We can't take him to the hospital. The cops would be on to us big time. You guys, pack up all his gear. Everything you can find.' 'Why can't we just trash his place?' one of the guys asked. I shook my head. 'If we make it look like he just moved out, then no one will care. If we trash the place with his clothes and his shit still here, they'll come looking. So pack it all up and take it down to my car.' I tossed the keys to one of the guys and they got to work carefully avoiding you on the floor.

"I picked you up and lay you out on your bed cover. It's probably ruined by the way. Sure enough, someone said, 'Cover him up. I don't want to see his bloody dead face.' See, people will believe what you want them to if you just suggest shit. So I wrapped you in that tacky chenille bedspread thing and told them I'd take you down to my car. 'What are you gonna do with him?' Ange asked. 'I know someone down on the docks who'll take the body out to sea and dump him far enough out he'll never be found. And I'll get rid of his stuff so it looks like he moved on to somewhere else. They may wonder for a week or two but they'll be busy with other shit soon enough to forget the fag.' 'What'll you do then?' Ange asked, 'Cause there'll be rumors.' 'I'll just disappear for a few weeks until it all blows over.' 'Where will you go?' 'I got some mates over Bristol way,' I lied. 'They'll help me out. Best if you don't know all the details, that way the cops can't catch you out. I'll be in touch in a coupla weeks to see if things have cooled down. Maybe I can use the excuse I got cold feet about the wedding. Okay?' 'You haven't, have you?' she asked. I just grabbed her and put everything into that kiss. I could only do it because I imagined I was kissing you. Ange bought it. 'Ange, can you get your girls to wash down the blood. Doesn't have to be forensic clean cause they won't think he's dead or missing, just moved out.' I had to wind it up quick in case you came round and blew the cover.

"I hoisted you over my shoulder in that bedspread and carried you downstairs to my car and dumped you in the back seat. The guys had already put all your gear in the boot. They scattered. I took off."

"Won't people be looking for me?"

"Nah, while you were playing Sleeping Beauty in the back seat I went to Shop'n'Go. I persuaded Bernie to give me the pay he owed you, oh, and told him you wouldn't be back. He gave me the cash but that wasn't important. I wanted someone to know you were going and you didn't just disappear. That bloke, Mal, at the checkout asked about you, wished us both luck. Said we deserve it. Slipped me a couple hundred for the trip. That's when I moved you to the front seat."

"I'll miss him," I said, getting choked up. "It was because of him I came looking for you."

"I owe him then."

I yawned. It had been one of the most stressful days of my life. My old life. I had a new one stretching out ahead of me like the motorway we were speeding along.

"You got any plans for when we get to your uncle's?" I asked.

"Hell, yeah. You're really bad at this teaching me about gay life shit."

"What?"

"Yeah, you haven't made me suck your dick or shoved it up my ass."

I was amazed. "You want that?"

"I want everything with you, babe."

I smiled. "Then you better give up the cigarettes."

NICE WORK IF YOU CAN GET IT

~

"*I* DON'T NEED your fuckin' sympathy, I need your help." Vinnie suddenly heard himself, loud, shrill, shouting like a banshee. Horrified, he lowered his head in embarrassment as his friends stared wide-eyed at his outburst. Vinnie was the last person to ever lose his temper. He knew he had to make amends. "Look, I'm sorry, but I just lost another job." There were groans from around the table. This was the group's weekly ritual: Friday night drinks at the Hammered & Tickle Bar to catch up on the week's gossip. It was almost inevitable that, added to the salacious rumormongering that usually prevailed, Vinnie's latest disaster would be a prime topic of conversation.

"I just couldn't seem to get the bloody orders right. Caused a near riot at the café." He smiled at the memory of the shemozzle he caused but then frowned at its aftermath. He got a right pasting from his boss and an immediate severance pay that would scarcely buy him a six-pack of baked beans to tide him over until he moved on to his next humiliation.

With luck it would be a matter of days before he found himself another position that was totally unsuited to his skills. The simple fact was – he had no skills. Zilch. Nada. Zero. Diddly squat. He was confident, but at the same time depressed, that his ability for rapid re-employment was based on his looks and his physique. He was blessed. Everyone kept telling him so. Unfortunately, with every new economic position, he was most likely to find himself in a new position sexually. Like, bent over a table in a restaurant, a dumper bin in a back alley, behind a bar, the boss's office in a manual labor factory —you get the picture. So did the predators, but once Vinnie wriggled from their grasp it also meant the loss of another job as well as his self-respect. Not that he had that in great abundance. He wasn't a prude – he loved sex – he just wasn't very good at it. He was as inept in bed as he was in positions vacant. He wished he was better at both.

His mates sighed.

Vinnie was annoyed. "I don't do it deliberately."

"Of course you don't, sweetie," Maurie said, patting his arm. "You can't help it if guys come on to you just because you're gorgeous." Vinnie bristled at being patronized. He detested sarcasm even more. Lenny, who had never been one of Vinnie's biggest fans, snickered across the table. Their animosity grew in proportion to the number of times Lenny had unsuccessfully propositioned him, usually when he was pissed as a newt and all handsy so that Vinnie felt like he was being attacked by a tentacled creature from the Black Lagoon. Lenny was never going to take 'no' for an answer. The others at the table were a lot more subtle but he noticed how his drinks always tasted stronger in the alcohol department as the night wore on, how they all argued over who was going to drive him home (and not to Vinnie's apartment if he knew anything about their devious plans for his body). Even the devoted couple, Glenn and Adrian, had suggested quite openly that he join them for a threesome.

It's not that Vinnie was averse to most of the propositions – apart from the sleazy Lenny – it's just, ewww, they were his friends. He just didn't know how to be rude, how to turn down men who kept pestering him long after he'd told them to stop. In his innocence he thought telling them once was enough. But they took his quiet rejection as a "don't stop", as a signal he was flirting and wanted them to persist. He just wished he could let himself go. Get lost in the moment. Surrender to the warm exhilaration of sex. The only member of the group who seemed totally immune to what little charm he seemed to possess was the self-proclaimed kinky manslut, Zeb. They loathed each other. It had been mutual on their first meeting. They bickered and snarled and…

"If you're so bloody useless why don't you just stop faffing about and get down to that corner where all the twinks hang out. You can make good money on a busy night." Zeb was totally not the caring type. He abhorred self-indulgence as much as he disliked Vinnie. It may have had something to do with the fact they were the two most attractive men in the circle of friends although Zeb was everything Vinnie wanted to be: confident, charismatic, sexually alluring, unafraid to grab life by the ass and fuck it into submission. He shuddered just thinking about being submissive to Zeb. Then he remembered the slur his nemesis had just muttered.

Vinnie raised his voice again. "Fuck you!" It felt good to use an obscenity every now and then although his face flushed at the naughtiness. He was such a loser.

"In your dreams, honey. You couldn't cope. Besides, you'd keel over once you learned how kinky I am."

The imputation of kink was a mystery that surrounded Zeb and he wore it like a cloak. It made him dangerous. Not one of his friends knew what his kink was although he alluded to it frequently, almost as if it were a badge of honor.

Vinnie was tired of the secrecy. He was tired of all the shit in his life and his temper got the better of him. Normally he was the mildest of people, this time he uncharacteristically struck out. "So what exactly is this kink of yours? Macramé? Golf? You kiss with your eyes closed?"

Zeb was the opposite – quick to anger – but this time he managed to control himself quickly even though the sarcasm hit home. He laughed a little too loudly, dialing it back as he said much more calmly than he felt, "Mate, if you knew my secret you'd turn a nice shade of puce and empty your breakfast, lunch and even the supper you're yet to eat all over this table."

"Funny that no one seems to know what it is. I can only suppose that not many people share your predilection or, possibly, you don't get to indulge it all that often." Vinnie was poking a stick at the tiger. Losing yet another job made him reckless. That and the alcohol he was throwing down his throat in order to forget his predicament.

Zeb sighed. "You're not wrong. I have such a refined taste in kink it's not shared by the masses. What can I say, I'm a connoisseur."

Vinnie couldn't help himself. "Nah, you got the pronunciation wrong, you really are just a sewer."

Zeb stood up angrily.

Maurice noticed his glass was empty. "Whose round is it?" Perfect save.

"That's my cue to leave," Vinnie said. "Can't afford to shout you guys now that I'm down to my last coupla hundred bucks."

"I hope you're not thinking of going back to your place and drowning your sorrows, mate?" Adrian, at least, was concerned.

The guilty flush on Vinnie's cheeks gave testimony to the fact they knew him too well.

Glenn had a better idea. "Why don't we all head over to Vinnie's, order some take-away, watch a movie, commiserate?"

The others shrugged looking to Vinnie to gauge his reaction.

What the hell? He could be miserable on his own or he could be miserable in company. "Sure. Why not? Beats drinking on my own."

"And we may come up with a few good ideas for your future. Right, guys?" Lenny wiggled his brows suggestively to plant the seeds in the guys' minds. If Vinnie noticed he didn't let on.

In the end it was a dispiriting group who congregated at Vinnie's place for beer and pizza, the atmosphere rife with sexual tension and despair. The more he drank, the more Vinnie's spirit sank, until they were lower than a winter sunset, and so he little realized his mates were doing their hardest to get him pissed and more suggestible in the self-serving belief that their concept of group therapy would cheer him up. That was their handy solution to just about any of life's problems. That, and pizza, or finding out Zeb's secret kink. How bad could it be?

Some of the social gang's peripheral hangers-on had not bothered joining what was bound to be a gloomfest – Vinnie lost his employment on a regular basis – so that just five of them sat around the coffee table littered with the greasy cardboard remains of their pizza banquet, and crushed beer cans littering the floor. Vinnie was once again wailing about his lack of skills to the consternation of those who merely wanted to test his skills *a la bed chambre.*

Vinnie, even in his inebriated state, noticed Zeb remained aloof from the sexual tension in the room. Odd that Zeb seemed to watch the behavior of his friends with growing alarm and not a little petulance, whilst striving to run interference on every attempt at the utterly predatory idea of sex as therapy.

No one was in the mood for a movie unless it was porn but Vinnie vetoed that, so the compromise was an easy-listening radio station playing softly in the background. So mellow was the music, Lenny was almost asleep. It was his cock's anticipation of action that kept what little interest he had in the unfolding evening.

Lenny stirred, finally ready to get his hands, and his cock, in that fantastic butt. He nodded to Glenn who, like the others, had been waiting for a signal that it was on. Although they'd need the rubbish out of the way if they were going to lay Vinnie over the coffee table and fuck the gloom out of him.

Maurie, got the hint. "I'll just clear this mess up, mate. Can't have your flat looking like a pigsty." He grabbed the boxes, piled the cans on top and headed to the kitchen. He'd only been gone a moment when he called. "Oh my god, guys. Come and take a look at this."

The urgency in Maurie's tone got their attention and they sprang up to head toward the kitchen. They'd never been to Vinnie's small apartment before so it was all new to them. Not a one of them had expressed any more interest in his habitat than the living room and the shortest possible distance to his bathroom to piss away the excess beer.

"Shit, look at that," Adrian enthused. "Does he even cook?"

"The place is immaculate," Glenn agreed. "I wish we could keep our place this tidy."

"Fuck me dead, he even recycles." Lenny pointed to the bins sitting neatly beside the fridge which Maurie opened to peek inside.

"I guess that answers the question about whether he lives on takeaway. The fridge is full of food. And the freezer has leftovers all neatly labeled in plastic containers."

"You a fuckin' neat freak, mate?" Lenny called through to Vinnie who was slumped on the lounge.

"Nope, just tidy." Vinnie was getting to the stage where he wished they'd just go away and leave him to wallow in peace but was too polite to say so. Especially to that asshole Zeb who hadn't gone to the kitchen with the others but remained in the living room, hovering much too closely like a concerned mother hen. He knew what they were expecting. He may be clumsy but he wasn't stupid. Hell, maybe a good gangbang would make him feel better. Sad that his self-esteem had sunk so low. Not that he had issues with gangbangs, just when they were used to positively reinforce self-worth. Like if he did it now. Knowing that his friends were in it to get their rocks off and add another notch to their bedposts rather than for any actual concern about him pushed his libido down to practically nil. He really needed to find better friends. But he was as inept with friendship as he was with everything else.

So preoccupied was he with his misery he didn't notice the gang of four doing a top to tail inventory of his apartment. It was a modest one-bedder but it had a number of personal flourishes that made it feel cozy and comfortable. And it was neat. He guessed it was close to obsessively neat. So kill him, he liked to clean.

Adrian was effusive in his enthusiasm. "Holy shit, Vinnie, your place is so tidy and so clean you could eat out of the toilet bowl." They all trooped back into the living room with a fresh brew for Vinnie, forgetting totally to bring another for Zeb. Didn't matter, he was an asshole.

"Look guys," Vinnie began, "I guess I'm not up to having mates over tonight. What's say—"

Lenny saw the evening getting away from them. "Hey, you got the latest issue of *Gay Blade* here?" He had an idea to get the party mood lifted to ramp up the evening. He'd spent too much time getting Vinnie into this situation to give up so easily.

"Sure, it's with the other mags in the rack," Vinnie slurred. He was exhausted and perhaps a little under the weather from the drinks he'd hoped would assuage his despondency.

"Drink up, Vinnie. Nobody likes warm beer." Lenny called as he rummaged through the newspapers and journals leaving a mess in his wake.

Vinnie looked about for his drink. He remembered he had one a few minutes ago. Or had he? He scratched his head. He was sure…ah, that was it. Zeb had pried it from his fingers and put it down…there it is.

Vinnie leaned forward to grab his unfinished beer but, as he did so, Zeb swept it up and kept it out of reach.

"What the fuck is wrong with you, Zeb?" Vinnie asked. It was a rhetorical question because he knew *everything* was wrong with Zeb. He stumbled to get up and retrieve his drink but Zeb moved it farther from reach. WTF? It made no difference, Vinnie would just go into the kitchen and get another one. Or he would have if Zeb hadn't grabbed the back pocket of his jeans and pulled him back down onto the lounge.

Vinnie wondered why none of the others were commenting on Zeb's odd behavior but they were concentrating on Lenny pawing the magazines. "You're the only person I know who has a magazine rack let alone one where everything is stacked in alphabetical order." He found what he was looking for. "Ah, here we go."

"You so bored you're going to read while we try to cheer him up?" Maurie asked.

"No, dickwad. I know you only ever read this bar freebie to look at the pictures of hot guys at clubs and dance parties—"

"And to see if his photo is featured," Glenn laughed.

They were regularly featured in the photo pages because even though they were all individually photogenic, as a group – especially shirtless – they were off the chart. In fact, they got frequently propositioned by men who'd ogled their hot sweaty torsos in *Gay Blade*.

"But," Lenny said to still the interruption. "if you actually learned to read, you would know the back pages are full of classifieds. There may be a job that Vinnie can do. You never know."

Vinnie choked. "You want me to set up shop as a hooker? Is that why the concern about how neat my place is?"

Zeb snorted. "Hookers are female. You'd be a hustler."

His erstwhile friends glared at him.

"Vinnie's right," Glenn said seeing the look of horror on Vinnie's face. "Those classifieds are mainly for paid sex or massage with a happy ending."

"I had one the happiest nights ever with this muscle massage giant." Lenny was off in his own little fantasy. "Okay, not so little. He was enormous. Buns like steel. A dick that wouldn't say 'no'. I'm getting hard just thinking about him." He massaged his crotch to show his obvious excitement. "Anyone here want to take care of my problem?" He looked straight at Vinnie.

"Hold that thought," Maurie suggested taking the rag from Lenny and turning to the back pages of the *Blade.* Before he could look for Positions Vacant Lenny retrieved the paper from his hands. "I wonder if he's still around?"

"Asshole," Maurie snapped as he snatched the paper back. "This is all about Vinnie tonight not your fantasy masseur. This is about Vinnie's happy ending."

And if Vinnie's happy ending involved them all getting one as well, there was no arguing with that.

"I'm not selling myself as a fuck toy. And I'm not doing massage. With my luck I'd probably get some terrible sexual disease or take the skin off someone's back." Vinnie slumped in the corner of the lounge, dejection getting the better of him.

"Here we are, Positions Vacant." They crowded around Maurie hoping there'd be something that would lift Vinnie's spirits so that he'd be amenable to a bit of group passion later. They didn't want him so pissed he wouldn't remember. Unless that's what it took.

Maurie ran his finger down the page. "Handyman, plumber, pool cleaner. That's not a bad idea. Pool cleaner."

"Nah, he'd probably drown," Glenn suggested.

The others nodded. It was all too true.

"Tennis coach, waiter, waiter, waiter, barman, barman, barman, security." He paused, glancing at Vinnie. "Nah, don't think so. Shelf stackers, parking attendant." Lenny sighed. Vinnie had already tried most of the advertised positions – and failed miserably.

"Keep looking, there's has to be something." Adrian sounded desperate.

"What about…?" Glenn said.

"Cleaner." Zeb had raised his voice to be heard over the hubbub.

Vinnie looked up. He liked cleaning. He was good at it.

They began flipping the pages back and forth frantically searching until Adrian stabbed the newspaper with his finger so hard it almost tore the page. "Shit, look here. How ideal is that?"

The guys all looked at one another, smug satisfaction that with that solution their night of friendly fucking was back on course. At least until they turned around and saw Vinnie sprawled across the couch, his head lolling back, his mouth drooling, snores wracking his body.

"Shit!"

They all thought it. Did it really matter he was unconscious. A hole was a hole even if it didn't grip back. They were in. Until they saw the set of Zeb's jaw and the steel of determination in his eyes.

"Since when did you become Mary Poppins?" Adrian asked sarcastically.

"Oh, I get it," Maurie sneered. "Your little kink is you like to fuck 'em while they're unconscious and you don't like to share."

Glenn patted Zeb's cheek. "You're secret's safe with us, honey."

Then, disappointed that they hadn't got to fuck Vinnie, they headed back to the bar to try their luck elsewhere. All except Zeb. He heard Lenny mutter as they walked down the hall toward the elevator, "Maybe Zeb's kink is he likes dead bodies." The others guffawed. At heart, they liked Zeb about as much as Vinnie did.

Zeb stayed to place Vinnie in a less painful position on the lounge, covering him with a rug he found neatly stored in the hall closet, leaving a bottle of water and clearly labeled headache medication on the coffee table for the morning. He moved a small rubbish bin within reach just in case, then highlighted the classified advert calling for cleaners and left it where Vinnie would see it when he woke up.

THE NEXT MORNING, Vinnie stumbled from the couch remembering little of the previous evening. He careened into the wall as he half blindly felt his way to the bathroom to search, unsuccessfully, the shelves behind the mirror for his pills – his head felt like he just wanted to scrub it clean with bleach until the pain went away – was then sidetracked by his need to piss, which he did loudly and unceremoniously into the bowl, before stumbling back into the living room.

"Ah, there you are," he muttered when he saw the pills and the bottle of water. He had a flashback of his mates coming over to cheer him up. They'd been disastrously unsuccessful and he'd had too much to drink. Ergo, he was now suffering. The memory of their disinclination to take 'no' for an answer to their suggested group session sobered him quickly. He stripped off his trousers now so crumpled they'd have to go to the dry cleaners, sheepishly feeling between his ass cheeks almost afraid to touch the hole. He felt no pain. No wetness. Pushing in he felt little more than the muscles clamp down. He relaxed. He wondered whether his suspicions said more about him or about his friends. Maybe he needed to get new mates.

He took two caplets, guzzling the entire contents of the bottle to rehydrate. It was warm and wet but helped clear his head. He hadn't been so pissed that he'd need a day to recover. A bite to eat and an energy drink and he'd be back to normal. Okay, not so normal. He was out of work. Again.

Not feeling up to cooking he poured himself a bowl of muesli topping it with milk and a dollop of Greek yoghurt then sat on the couch, curling his feet underneath him before he noticed the newspaper with something circled and a small business card nearby.

He seemed to recall his mates pushing him to get a job but he wasn't going to sell his ass for all the rice in China. He didn't have any great moral objections, he just didn't believe anyone would be willing to part with hard cash for what he'd be offering. And the idea of converting his refuge, his apartment, into the Happy End Massage Parlor turned his stomach. He barely glanced at the ringed advert, preferring to examine the card. It was Zeb's – just what had been up with him the previous night hovering like a great harbinger of doom? – and under his address and social media there was the handwritten message 'Call me as soon as you wake up.' Well, that would have to wait. He was having his breakfast and a shower before he did anything that stupid.

Funny that not two hours later, Vinnie was standing at the front door of a rather grand apartment block in a part of town that was so expensive he couldn't even afford to breathe the air. When he buzzed, Zeb's cheery voice greeted him, "Floor twelve," and he was buzzed in.

Zeb had never had a kind word to say, but now that Vinnie came to think about it – he'd only ever had negative thoughts about Zeb – the guy didn't indulge him like the others did. Zeb was straight to the point, an enemy to self-indulgence, called bullshit when he saw it. Vinnie had to admit he was so inculcated with dislike for the guy he'd failed to notice Zeb's few – oh so very few – admirable qualities. That's if you classed making Vinnie feel small and inadequate an admirable quality.

The building's foyer was all marble and mirrors. It was far grander than anything he'd ever set foot in before. If Zeb hadn't told him when he called in response to the business card message that this was his residential address, Vinnie would have thought it was where Zeb worked. He knew his friends weren't what anyone would call poor, but this? Zeb obviously had a great job to afford to live here. But what was it? He realized he had no idea what Zeb did for a living. He knew Maurie was in finance, Lenny in pharmaceuticals (mainly testing them out on himself it seemed), Glenn was a stockbroker and Adrian was an NLP therapist. Zeb never talked about his work but he obviously had money. Then the conversation of the previous evening came back in crystal clarity: "Hookers are female. You'd be a hustler." Zeb was a hustler. Zeb had a Sugar Daddy. That's the reason he could afford to live in such luxury.

He almost turned around and walked away. This had to be some awful joke at his expense. Vinnie was quick to jump to conclusions but just as quick to jump out of them. So what if Zeb was a kept boy? That was his business and nobody else's. Vinnie had no great moral qualms about well-regulated non-exploitative prostitution. In fact, when he looked around this apartment building he was more inclined to consider it as a choice of profession.

He shook his head to dislodge the idea. Let's see what Zeb had to say. He may merely have rich parents who indulged him. So what if his Daddy was of the Diabetic variety? Maybe that was his secret kink. Well, one way to find out. Vinnie was lots of things but coward wasn't one of them.

There was no concierge so he made his way to the bank of elevators. They, too, were mirrored and immaculately presented. In fact, everything in the common areas of the property screamed quality. Pressing the button, the elevator rose swiftly and silently announcing the level in hushed tones as it reached the correct floor and then settled. The doors opened onto long hallway carpeted in rich burgundy pile that looked as if it were mowed regularly rather than merely vacuumed.

Treading warily lest the carpet cops suddenly appeared to fine him for sullying their pristine hallway he found the apartment and knocked. Vinnie almost expected a liveried butler to respond but it was a matter of seconds before Zeb himself opened the door.

"Come in, come in. How are you feeling?"

Vinnie couldn't help but notice that Zeb appeared nervous. Then he realized it was the first time they'd been alone together without the safety net of their mutual friends. "Not too bad. Considering."

"Good. You recover quickly it seems."

"Why are you being so ostentatiously polite?" Vinnie asked. "It's doing my head in. And I don't need that today. I think I prefer you snarky."

Zeb was unable to contain a burst of infectious laughter. It did something to his face and for the first time Vinnie wondered if his opinion of his nemesis was too harsh.

Finally back in control, Zeb said seriously, "Snarky is so much hard work. It's exhausting. Don't you find it that way?"

Vinnie was shocked. "What? You mean it's all an act?"

Zeb sighed. "Look, I know you don't like me and so sarcasm and ridicule are my default positions. It's the way I protect myself." Vinnie went to reply but Zeb held up a hand to signal he hadn't finished. "So let's, just for once, act civilly and pretend we actually like each other."

I'm not that good at pretending. The thought made Vinnie nervous.

He couldn't be more gobsmacked. Zeb expected a reply and Vinnie took a breath to explain that he didn't like Zeb because Zeb didn't like him but that seemed so petty. He let his breath out and relaxed as best he could in an otherwise tense situation. Zeb was right. Just for once they could let it go. No use poking a stick at the wild animal. Besides, he was intrigued as to the purpose of the meeting. He shrugged.

They'd been standing in the vestibule to the apartment while they negotiated a temporary peace pact. Zeb ushered Vinnie inside.

"Wow." Vinnie's gob was smacked all over again. The apartment was gorgeous. Pity that Zeb appeared to be a bit of a slob with food containers, magazines, and beer cans scattered about with scant regard for the impeccable furnishings, the subtle recessed lighting, the artwork – original, not prints – and that view from a cozy private terrace overlooking the city. Vinnie was envious and not a little put out that Zeb lived in such a beautiful space but regarded it with scant appreciation. "Come on, I'll give you the official tour," Zeb said.

A glance into the modern stainless steel kitchen revealed grease-smeared dishes and wine-stained glasses stacked on the benches and in the sink. Zeb seemed unconcerned about the mess. "I had guests over for a dinner party. It got late and I didn't even have enough energy to load the dishwasher. That was three days ago. I guess I just never have the energy for anything to do with cleaning up after myself." The bathroom was a cyclone of dirty clothes dropped anywhere, wet towels bunched up in a corner, and that toilet bowl. Ewww! Vinnie felt it best to avoid the bedroom, not that he thought Zeb would try anything – after all he was the only member in the group that hadn't hit on him. No, his reluctance was that he didn't want to be knee deep in used condoms and crusty tissues left over from Zeb's prolific sexual escapades.

The apartment was simple, dignified, not ostentatious. Zeb, however, lived like a pig. It was not Vinnie's place to say so. He struggled to form words when Zeb looked at him expectantly after the brief tour of his abode of which he seemed inordinately proud.

"Um…it's a beautiful apartment."

Zeb was obviously looking for a little more enthusiasm because his brow bunched up. He sounded disappointed. No, he sounded hurt. "But?"

Don't say it. Don't say it. Don't say it.

Vinnie bit the inside of his cheek but the effort was futile in view of Zeb's apparent disregard for cleanliness. He said it. "You live like a slob."

Zeb's reaction was totally unexpected. He looked pleased. "Exactly. That's why I told you to contact me. Here, sit down, I'll make us a coffee and some snacks and we can talk it over."

"It?" What the hell was going on, Vinnie wondered.

While Zeb busied himself in the kitchen, the clatter of plates giving away the fact Zeb really needed to clean up after himself so he could find bench space for coffee mugs, Vinnie looked at the collection of CDs scattered around the upmarket player. He gritted his teeth to stop himself from screaming at Zeb about putting discs away in their plastic cases after use and not leave them lying about. They'd get scratched or at the very least get dust all over them. Zeb's taste in music partly assuaged the promised outburst. Here were all the classics Vinnie loved. Ella, Sarah, Nina, Della, Etta, and even Elisabeth Welch. He could love a man who had these singers in his collection. That's not to say he didn't enjoy Kylie, Beyoncé, Lady GaGa, Madonna, Cher. Yep, Vinnie was a cliché gay man with a cliché gay man's taste. But he was also much more than that. Just like Zeb appeared to be.

He wondered about Zeb's reading material but there were no books visible. Either Zeb eschewed reading or the books were in his bedroom and Vinnie wasn't about to sneak in there.

"Here we go." Zeb placed a tray with coffee plunger and some finger food that must have been already prepared then took one of the luxurious lounge chairs opposite Vinnie who was perched on the settee. Vinnie found it difficult to reconcile domesticated Zeb with the version he constantly knocked heads with at the bars.

When Vinnie's stomach grumbled he realized all he'd had to eat that day was the bowl of cereal. His belly was demanding more. Zeb must have heard the commotion because he handed Vinnie a plate. "Help yourself. Sorry, it's not lunch but…" he shrugged as if he couldn't think of a reason it wasn't.

Vinnie grinned at Zeb's obvious discomfort. "If I'd known I was invited to dine, I would have dressed up for the occasion," he said placing a few sandwiches on his plate and grabbing a paper napkin so he wouldn't get crumbs everywhere even though he thought it was unlikely anyone would notice what with all the rubbish lying around. Zeb mirrored his actions and piled his plate high. When Vinnie couldn't help but raise an eyebrow, Zeb replied, "What? I'm an active growing boy. Besides, I keep in shape." So saying, he lifted his T-shirt and smacked his abs with his fist. "See, solid muscle."

Vinnie eyes widened as his throat constricted at Zeb's sudden reveal of his favorite part of the male anatomy – he would kill for abs like those. He choked on his cheese and chutney sandwich – Manchego cheese if his taste buds weren't deceiving him – and reached for his coffee. Zeb sped across the room, patting him heavily on the back until Vinnie's coughing subsided and he held up his hand for Zeb to stop. Vinnie reached again for his coffee and swilled down a mouthful.

"Can I get you some water?"

Vinnie cleared his throat loudly. "Something went down the wrong way."

"It's a bastard when that happens, but some guys just won't take 'No' for an answer." Zeb smirked at his own filthy joke.

Vinnie blushed and looked away. Getting a chance to ogle Zeb's luscious abs had been enough to bring on the choking fit, god knows what would happen if Zeb opened up about his sex life. Vinnie could already feel his cock getting chubby. He gave it a good talking to – silently, of course. *Down boy! This is Zeb, slut supremo, and we don't do casual sex. Especially not with smug bastards. Not that Zeb would be interested in me.*

He probably could have kept the inner monologue going for days in an attempt to keep his libido in check. What was wrong with him? He hated Zeb – abs or no abs.

Zeb's smooth brow furrowed. It was almost as if he'd waxed any imperfections or stress lines away. "Is something wrong?"

"I was…uh…wondering why you called me to come over. It's not like we have a lot in common." Vinnie wanted to get to the point and get out of there. Such close proximity to a friendlier than usual Zeb – let alone the casual clothes that showed off his lean muscular body and his…um…package. His mouth-watering, rather large crotch that appeared ready to burst from his jeans. Just like Vinnie's less impressive but still perfectly adequate…he was staring. Shit! He raised his eyes. Caught. Zeb had that superior look that said he knew that Vinnie was salivating over his tackle. Bugger. It was also obvious that Vinnie was erect now. He tried to adjust his cock as casually as possible but he wasn't fooling anyone.

Zeb put on his serious face. "Look, there's no hidden agenda here. I just think I might be able to help you. Okay?"

Vinnie was not convinced. "O-kay."

Encouraged to go on, Zeb leaned forward to get his point across. "I think you and I have a lot in common."

"Fuck me! Really?" Vinnie exploded with indignation. "You think I'm a slut?"

Zeb was taken aback by the outburst.

Vinnie turned purple in the face. "You think I share this kink of yours, is that it? Well, let me tell you," Vinnie raised his voice to get his point across, "I've had so little experience I barely know if I'm a top or a bottom. Let alone have some perverted kink that's beyond my wildest imagination."

"Hey, Vinnie, tell me what you really think of me." Zeb didn't appear to be offended by Vinnie's outburst. Quite the contrary, he seemed to relish it.

Vinnie had felt good getting the spleen out of his system but now he was embarrassed, especially as Zeb seemed inured to the insults. Zeb said quietly, "Why do you have to define yourself by such limited criteria? Can't you be both?"

Vinnie was confused. "What?"

"It doesn't have to be an either/or situation."

Vinnie thought he must be in a parallel universe. Nothing was making sense. "What doesn't?"

"Top or bottom. You can be both. You can adapt to any given situation. It's not like you're gonna have it tattooed permanently on your ass."

"I guess not." Vinnie didn't want to discuss his sex life with Zeb.

"Hell, you don't even have to do it at all. If you don't want to."

Did Zeb think he was a prick tease? That he was a virgin? "I want to, I really want to. It's just..." *It's just what?* He really didn't know.

Zeb finished the sentence for him. "You're waiting for the right man. For that connection that will make it feel worth the wait."

Vinnie nodded his head. When did Zeb get to be so smart? Or become a mind reader?

"I think I can help you out with a paying position."

And there it was. Finally. Zeb was going to pitch the idea of a sugar daddy to pay Vinnie's bills. It wasn't going to happen. Not now. Not ever. He'd starve first.

"I'd rather not be paid to discover my favorite sexual position. I think I made you well aware of that last night."

Zeb chuckled. "You're a good looking guy, Vinnie. I wish you could see yourself as others do."

Really? Zeb thought he was good looking? No, no, no. He wasn't gonna let himself be seduced into a life of debauchery. Paid sexual companion was not on the list of career choices he'd been given in high school. He had to shut this down. "Look, it's okay for a hot guy like you but—"

Zeb interrupted. "You think I'm hot?"

"Oh, come on, you know you're hot as fuck." Vinnie wondered if Zeb had feelings of insecurity deep down.

"*You* think I'm hot?" Zeb repeated with emphasis, appearing surprised by the revelation. "I thought you hated me."

"Just because we have this…um…social difficulty going on between us doesn't mean I can't appreciate what a good-looking guy you are."

Now he'd done it. Zeb's ego would be mammoth-sized next time they all met at the pub. He'd be crowing that Vinnie thought he was hot as the sun. "Anyway, you know you can have any man you want. And you do."

"Who said I want them?" Zeb said it so quietly that Vinnie wondered whether he'd heard it correctly.

Vinnie was confused. He wanted to get this uncomfortable meeting over and get the fuck out. "I think we got off the point of why I'm here."

"I guess we did." Zeb seemed to be no more eager to bring the meeting to a climax than he did before. Vinnie wondered what was going on.

"Look, Vinnie. I know how difficult things are for you. I know you don't have a lot of cash stashed aside. I think I've got a solution to your problem." Zeb leaned forward to touch Vinnie on the thigh. That was just too intimate.

"Okay, I'm out of here." Vinnie swigged the last of his coffee, stood and headed for the door.

Zeb raced ahead of him and blocked his exit. "What's the matter with you? You're more jittery than the battery bunny."

Vinnie lost his cool. "What don't you understand, Zeb? I thought I made it clear that I don't want to be a slut like you selling my ass to the highest bidder."

Zeb deflated. "What the fuck, Vinnie?"

Vinnie was on his high horse now. "I'm not making moral judgments about your life, Zeb. But it's not for me. I won't give away your secret to the other guys."

"What secret? What are you talking about?"

"Zeb, I know your intentions were probably honorable but I'm not in the market for a sugar daddy."

"A sugar daddy? Where did that come from? "

"Oh, come on. Look around. Like someone your age can afford all this." Vinnie swept his arm around to encompass the apartment. "I may be naïve but I'm not stupid. It's okay. I get it. You're trying to be helpful in your own funny way. I appreciate that side of it. But, no, sorry."

Vinnie was startled when Zeb bent double unable to contain his laughter. He had tears running from his eyes and even snorted his amusement. Vinnie stood, mouth agape, wondering what was so funny.

"You think…" Zeb could scarcely get the words out between gulping breaths, "You think I have a sugar daddy?"

"Don't you?"

Zeb wiped his eyes. "That's the most bizarre thing anyone has ever said to me. Look, come and sit down." Zeb grabbed him by the shoulders, turned him around and steered him back toward the lounge. "Vinnie, I promise you that what I'm about to suggest has absolutely nothing whatsoever to do with sex or prostitution. And just FYI, I don't have a sugar daddy."

"How…" Vinnie finished the question by waving his hand around to signify the living arrangements.

"I have a mortgage so big and far enough up my ass it's threatening to come out my mouth."

"How can you afford a mortgage?"

"I'm careful with my money, Vinnie. That was drummed into me by my dad. I may seem a little loose with my dick and my ass to you – although you're mistaken there as well but we'll let that pass – but I'm sure as fuck not loose with my money. I own an advertising agency, Vinnie. It's small but it's getting there. I pitch to the LGBTQI community. A lot of it currently is gratis, mainly for charity events, but the agency is getting a reputation. It's not easy but I make my monthly repayments and have enough left over for a bit of fun now and then."

Instead of being sheepish, Vinnie got snide to cover his embarrassment. "I've noticed."

Zeb ignored the insult. "So, sit. Let me tell you what I had in mind."

Somewhat chastened, Vinnie sat back on the lounge while Zeb went to brew more coffee. "I'm sorry I jumped to conclusions, Zeb," Vinnie called. "I feel so stupid."

Zeb came to the kitchen door while the coffee brewed. "You really thought I had a sugar daddy, eh?"

"Don't. I feel pretty small right now." Vinnie felt utterly humiliated.

Zeb walked over and ruffled his hair. "Hey, don't fret. In a funny sort of way it's the nicest compliment anyone's ever paid me. So, you think I'm a prime candidate for a sugar daddy. Hm, might get the mortgage paid off years early yet."

Vinnie looked up. "You're not seriously considering… Oh, you're making fun of me."

"No, doofus. I'm making fun of me." Zeb went back to the kitchen to get the coffee. When he sat back down in the armchair and had filled both their mugs, he launched into his plan. Vinnie remained silent – he thought he'd done enough damage for one day although Zeb seemed to be taking it all in good fun.

"I've given your situation a bit of thought and--"

"Why?"

"Why what?"

"Why have you devoted even a single second to my fucked-up life?"

"For starters, your life is not fucked up, Vinnie. It might be a little messy but I think I've come up with a solution."

"I'm useless at everything. I'll just get fired again."

"Not if you do something you like. Something you do well."

"What part of loser don't you understand?"

"You're not a loser, Vinnie. Stop saying that. Just stay still until I tell you my plan. Can you do that?"

Vinnie nodded.

"Look around, what's the difference between your apartment and mine?"

"Money."

"Yeah, yeah. I expected that one. Now look. Apart from the monetary angle, what's the difference?"

Vinnie took his time and really looked. Sure the apartment was bigger – big enough for a family – whereas Vinnie couldn't even find enough room in his to share with a cat. No, that wasn't it. It was obviously something so simple that even a loser like Vinnie could see it. Time stretched until Vinnie thought it would snap. Or Zeb would. Everything was too obvious. This had something to do with himself. But what? Wait a minute…

"My place is clean and organized, yours is…" he hesitated, unsure if this is what Zeb wanted to hear, "a bit…untidy?"

"Ding, ding, ding! We have a winner."

"Okay." Vinnie wasn't sure where this was going.

"So, what is it I need, taking into consideration I'm a very busy businessperson, I have commitments and, let's face it, I'm a bit of a slob?"

"Duh, you need to up your game and clean up after yourself." Vinnie totally missed the point.

"Failing that ever happening?" Zeb encouraged.

"Obviously you need to hire yourself a cleaner."

"And who's the best cleaner I know? And just so we're on the same wavelength, who is the best cleaner I know and who is currently unemployed?"

Vinnie couldn't believe the nerve of Zeb suggesting such a thing. "You want me to clean your apartment? Get a life. I'm not your slave. You think giving me a peek at your abs will have me down on my hands and knees?"

What had he just intimated? "I meant scrubbing your floors not anything else."

"Nice picture you conjured up there, dude. But why not? Be my cleaner, I mean? I'll pay you."

"Really?"

"Of course really. You said you enjoy it."

"I do. I really do."

"Then how about it? Say, once a week. How about it?"

Vinnie had difficulty sitting still. Getting paid to do something he enjoyed. It wouldn't pay his bills but it was a start.

"Oh my god, that's so generous of you. Of course, I'll work cheap and I won't let you down, Zeb. I'll do a good job. If…when I find a new position I'll keep doing your apartment if you can work around my hours."

"Vinnie, I was thinking maybe you could turn this into a full-time career."

"Cleaning?"

"Why not?"

"Baby steps." It was all Vinnie could manage at present. "Let's see if you're happy with my performance."

Zeb wasn't going to push. He'd let Vinnie ease into the task and hope things blossomed from there.

"When would you like me to start?"

"What about right now? Are you doing anything this afternoon?"

"No, I was gonna go home and look at Positions Vacant."

"You can't get much more positions vacant than right here. What do you say?"

"No offense but I don't like people looking over my shoulder while I work."

"That's okay, I have some things to catch up with at the office. I'll leave you alone."

"I'm not dressed for cleaning. By the time I get home to change the day will be gone. And I have no cleaning cloths or liquid or mops or…"

"Stop!" Zeb didn't want to hear any more excuses. "Come with me." He led the way down the hall to a small room. When he opened the door, Vinnie discovered paradise. "Wow." It was a laundry with washing machine and dryer. And enough cleaning product to stock a supermarket.

"I think you'll find all you need," Zeb said.

"It all looks brand new," Vinnie said examining all the mops and brooms and liquid detergents. He turned to Zeb and gave him a quizzical look.

Zeb shrugged. "What can I say? I had the best of intentions but not the will."

"Still, I can't afford to ruin my good…goodish clothes." Vinnie looked crestfallen that he couldn't get his hands on all the new cleaning apparatus at his disposal. He was so into instant gratification when it came to washing and polishing.

Zeb smirked. "You can always do it in your undies. Naked even. There'll be nobody here to see you." Vinnie was about to object so Zeb backed down. "Okay, I'll lend you an old T-shirt and a pair of old shorts, how's that?"

"Yeah, right, like they'll fit."

"I think I have just the thing. Hold on."

Zeb disappeared toward the bedroom and Vinnie heard the sounds of doors opening, drawers slamming, cursing, until finally, "Here they are." He came back and handed the 'old' clothes to Vinnie. They weren't his idea of old or worn. "You sure?" he asked.

"I have a closet full of shit I don't wear so I won't miss these."

"Okay. I'll do it."

It was the first time Zeb had seen Vinnie genuinely happy in, well, forever.

"Good. I'm off to the office for a couple of hours. I should be back by the time you finish so make yourself at home and I'll drive you back to your place. Okay?"

"You don't have to do that."

"Shut up, Vinnie. I'd like to."

Zeb grabbed his keys but before he could get to the door, Vinnie asked sheepishly. "Um…do you mind if I put some music on. I work better when I listen to music."

"Of course, Vinnie. Treat this place as if it was your own. See you this evening."

Once Vinnie was alone he turned to survey the apartment, a broad grin on his face. He couldn't believe his luck. He couldn't believe Zeb had thought of him. But here he was and there was work to be done. First, though, he rifled through Zeb's collection of CDs, chose some Kylie – he needed something up-tempo to start, mellow could come later – and changed into his cleaning clothes.

He could smell Zeb on the T-shirt. It didn't exactly hug Vinnie's body but he didn't care. When he slid Zeb's sweats on he found his cock was hard. What was that all about? He hitched them up and tied the cord so they wouldn't fall down, ignoring the excitement he felt tugging at his balls. Where to start? He decided on the kitchen.

Singing and dancing along to Kylie, he wiggled his butt provocatively just like he did in the privacy of his small flat. He loved moving like that, he was just glad no one could see him jut his ass out – they'd get the wrong idea.

He gathered everything he'd need for the kitchen and began to work. When that room was finished, he went to the living room and worked his magic there. He felt sorry for Samantha from *Bewitched,* all she had to do was wrinkle her nose and the job was done. Same with Mary Poppins although she used magic not her nose. They would never know the sheer pleasure, the relaxation that came from cleaning. To Vinnie it was the closest he came to orgasm without sex.

ZEB KNEW enough to disappear and give Vinnie time to relax and adapt to his surroundings. He wondered if Vinnie would be curious enough to snoop through drawers and closets to discover more about his 'employer.' Didn't matter, there were no secrets regardless of what everyone believed. Zeb was an open book, wore his heart on his sleeve, it's just that people were so busy looking at his ass or his crotch they failed to see what was on open display if they really wanted to know him. That's what he wanted, someone to really look not just at the packaging but what was inside.

He'd never hated, or even disliked, Vinnie. He saw the guy as a bit of a loser, an opinion reinforced by his sleazy friends who saw an advantage that they were forever attempting to take advantage of. It amused Zeb that Vinnie was smart enough to see through their ruse although the constant subtle belittling had ingrained itself in Vinnie's soul. What Vinnie wasn't smart enough to see was that to succeed he had to find what he was good at and work on that. It wasn't genius and Zeb felt smug that he'd figured it out for him, giving him a warm buzz to think he may have propped the ladder of success against the right wall for Vinnie to climb out of his depressing rut and clamber into the light.

That was all the justification Zeb needed to focus his do-gooding on Vinnie. It had nothing at all to do with his recognition of Vinnie as a fellow soul even as the idea twanged at his subconscious. Or that Vinnie had a certain naïve charm. Zeb smiled. Vinnie was hot, damn it! He'd thought so from the first moment they'd met but, in a tragic attempt to impress, Zeb had made an ill-advised snarky comment about losers. Pity then that their initial meeting, in the pub amongst their mutual friends, was on yet another occasion on which Vinnie had lost his job.

The freeze from Vinnie could have been used to house an entire village of Inuits. Zeb had apologized as best he could and genuinely admitted that he wasn't name calling Vinnie in particular, but that was just digging himself an even deeper grave. It wasn't like him to back down and in exasperation at his own faux pas, he snapped. "Fine, if you feel more comfortable playing the poor-me-I'm-so-badly-done-by card then please feel free to wallow in your self-congratulatory misery all you want. Just don't expect me to commiserate."

Okay, harsh, but he'd meant well. He couldn't abide those people who used setbacks and bad luck as an excuse for self-pity. In his mind every negative attracted even more negativity. You could either use disappointment to learn from or you could take it onboard and drown in your own despair. Zeb had believed Vinnie was one of the latter on first meeting. As the weeks passed he was genuinely pleased to learn there was a lot more to Vinnie than incompetence and sheer bad luck. He suspected he was the only one who noticed as Vinnie proved his resilience time and time again. He didn't indulge

Vinnie, nor did he groan and bitch about how inept Vinnie was that he couldn't keep a job.

No, Zeb marveled that Vinnie just kept on going back for more no matter how badly his ego was bruised. That's why he'd help him overcome the latest brush with unemployment.

He hurried upstairs after securing his Volvo in the secure underground parking bay that came with his apartment. He'd been absent for over three hours and hoped Vinnie had waited. He'd made a detour on the way home to withdraw cash from the ATM realizing he and Vinnie had never discussed hourly rates. He considered himself a generous employer but he didn't want to offer too much. He'd learned to his dismay that many people on low incomes were embarrassed or insulted as much by over-payment as they were by under.

Vinnie was standing, now back in his own clothes, their threadbare nature which no amount of cleaning and pressing could disguise, on the terrace watching the lights of the city below and the tall office and apartment buildings nearby whose windows were lit up like squares on The Wheel of Fortune board. Maybe this time the wheel would spin for Vinnie and he'd emerge a winner.

He must have heard Zeb come in because he turned, his face anxious as if he'd been caught doing something he shouldn't. "I…um…I didn't know whether you wanted me to wait. It's okay to come out on the terrace, isn't it?"

It pained Zeb to see Vinnie's insecurities writ so large in his behavior. "Of course. Make yourself at home."

Vinnie came inside sliding the glass door closed behind him. "You should check I did everything you wanted."

"I trust you, Vinnie," Zeb said and meant every word of it but he sensed that Vinnie didn't want his trust, he wanted confirmation of a job well done.

Zeb was mildly irritated as Vinnie took him on the tour. He trusted Vinnie to have done a good job considering the pristine state of his own apartment. Vinnie's pride in the job he'd done was obvious and Zeb wondered if he should add a couple more dollars to the payment he had in his pocket. Vinnie avoided the bedroom. "I didn't…um…go into your bedroom so if you want that done I can do it now."

"Why, Vinnie?"

"Bedrooms are personal space. I don't like people going into mine unless I invite them."

Zeb couldn't stop himself. He smirked.

Vinnie hurried to add, "Not that I've got anything to hide but, you know…" He shrugged as if what he was saying was a given.

"It's okay, Vinnie. There's nothing in my bedroom that I'd hide from my mother or my friends." So saying, he strode to the door, opening it to reveal it was the tidiest room in the apartment.

Despite himself and his headlong dive into assumptions, now proven wrong, Zeb's bedroom was an oasis of calm and Vinnie chastised himself, albeit briefly, for jumping to conclusions. His new belief was that Zeb had tidied everything away in his bedroom in expectation of his visit. Vinnie was not one to let go of prejudices easily. It was very Elizabeth Bennett of him. Only after he examined the en suite bathroom and swung open the small mirrored cabinet set in the wall which revealed…well, nothing out of the ordinary… his faith in assumptions was rattled.

Zeb noticed the look of consternation and said, "You look disappointed. What were you expecting, a cache of hard drugs?"

Vinnie blushed. Zeb was a mind reader.

Zeb's gasp of incredulity made Vinnie's cheeks redden even more. "You did. You did think you'd find drugs in my bathroom, didn't you?" Vinnie took the Fifth. "Go on, admit it. And that's why you didn't clean my bedroom. What? You expected to see some poor twink bound and gagged in a sling, his ass hanging down to his knees because I fucked the shit out of him." Zeb needed to stop. He was sounding increasingly bitter as he spewed out the accusations so that he could almost taste Vinnie's humiliation.

"I think I'd better go," Vinnie mumbled heading for the front door.

This couldn't be happening. Shouldn't be happening. Everything had been going so well. For a few short hours Vinnie had been happy, truly happy in his work. He was proud of what he'd accomplished, something to be so rare he couldn't remember the last time. Maybe in high school…

"Wait," Zeb called. "Don't go." He removed Vinnie's hand from the front door and led him back to the living room. "I'm sorry, Vinnie. You just took my breath away. I didn't think you were the type to make those sorts of judgments. You really must think very little of me. But that's no excuse to say those things to you. So, I'm sorry."

Vinnie was in agony. He'd screwed up again and just wanted to get out of there as soon as possible. He'd have to avoid his group of friends for a few weeks until they forgot what a fool he'd made of himself and the fact he'd been fired after only three hours on a job he was supposed to be good at. That was a record, even for him. His lips quivered but he kept his head lowered so Zeb wouldn't see how moist his eyes were. That would merely compound his distress. "Okay, I'll be off now." He headed back to the door.

Zeb had to stop him. Okay, there was fault on both sides but it was up to him to salvage the situation. Adopting a tone that bore no tone of sarcasm – not so easy when it was his default position – or in any way patronizing, Zeb tried for light and humorous, as if the last ten minutes had never occurred. "Well, I have to say, I'm amazed."

Vinnie stopped at the door. "It's a bloody miracle," Zeb added glancing about the spick and span apartment. Vinnie had really surpassed himself. The only evidence of the slovenly disaster when Vinnie had arrived was three large black garbage bags, neatly tied, in the kitchen waiting to be taken to the dumper bins downstairs.

"I sorted the recycling into glass, plastic, aluminum, and paper. I would have taken it downstairs to the bins but I didn't have a key," Vinnie said.

"My fault," Zeb admitted. "I don't usually recycle."

Vinnie's head bobbed up and his eyes widened in shock. Damn. He knew he was just being rude.

"Okay, don't call Serial Mum," Zeb said, his conscience stricken. "I promise I'll do better." He handed Vinnie an envelope. "We didn't negotiate a rate so I just estimated what I thought your time and the quality of your skills was worth. I hope it's okay. If you think it's not enough, then let me know."

Vinnie was sure it was enough but he couldn't accept it. "I can't take this. Not after…" He couldn't bring himself to say it so he just pointed toward the bedroom.

"You did the work, you take the pay." Zeb pushed the envelope of cash into Vinnie's pocket. While Vinnie was struggling to extricate himself from the awkward situation, Zeb added, "Oh, I almost forgot, same time next week suit you?"

"You want me to come back?" Vinnie's insides did a little happy dance. He quickly pulled the rug from under those feelings. "I don't think I should after, you know."

"Look Vinnie, you did an amazing job. This place has never been so clean. You're doing me a favor. I'm a busy man and I need help, the sort you're really good at. So, I thought once a week. If you find a new job and you can't fit me in I'll be disappointed but I thought the same time every week until you don't want to do it anymore."

Vinnie really liked the apartment. Spending just a few hours a week there would be a balm for his battered soul but he couldn't bring himself to accept the offer.

Zeb shrugged. He didn't want to push back against Vinnie's obvious reluctance. At least not yet. "Let me know. Okay?"

AS VINNIE waited for the elevator he heard a shout. Turning he watched as Zeb jogged down the hallway. He was breathless by the time he caught up with Vinnie. "Glad you're still here. Can you forgive me for being so unthinking?"

"What?" Vinnie didn't understand. Did Zeb want his payment back?

The lift pinged and Zeb shuffled Vinnie inside. He pressed basement. "The least I can do is drive you home."

Breathing easier, Vinnie tried to deflect Zeb's concern. "That's not necessary. I can catch the bus."

"Hell, what sort of a Scrooge do you think I am making you slave away all day and then not offer you a lift. I don't like the idea of you traveling alone this hour of the night."

"You don't have to do that." Belatedly, Vinnie realized it was much later than he'd expected and the public transport was less frequent. He wasn't about to labor his half-hearted response.

"Yes, I do. So just shut it and accept a bribe."

"Bribe?"

"I want to make doubly sure you come back next week."

Before Vinnie could respond they were in the basement car park, Zeb striding purposefully toward the sort of vehicle Vinnie had only ever seen in the movies. He couldn't name the make but he knew it was the sort of thing James Bond might drive. Zeb pressed the key fob in his hand and the tail lights lit up and there was the tell-tale shriek that the vehicle was ready and waiting. Much to Vinnie's surprise, Zeb went to the passenger door and opened it for him.

The drive started in silence. Vinnie searching his brain for things to say, watching Zeb out of the corner of his eye. He caught Zeb studying him on one or two occasions.

Finally, Zeb took a deep breath, and said, "Okay, what's up?"

"Nothing's up," Vinnie lied.

"You're never this quiet at the pub," Zeb countered.

"You're never friendly to me at the pub."

"That goes both ways." Zeb blasted his car horn at a driver who cut in front of him. "Asshole."

Vinnie giggled. "That's more like it."

"What? You think I'm some sort of major aggressive shithole?" Zeb feigned shock.

"Duh," Vinnie snorted.

Zeb got serious for a moment. "I've never once put you down for who you are, Vinnie. Only when you go all negative on yourself."

Vinnie knew the truth when he heard it. "Thanks."

"I hope you'll come back next week. As you can see, I need your help." Zeb changed the subject.

"You're not wrong," Vinnie agreed.

"So, it's a date?" Zeb turned a nice beetroot color. Vinnie thought it suited him, smoothed his edges out a bit. He was quick to add, "Of course, I don't mean that sort of a date." Zeb sounded flustered. "That came out wrong as well."

"It's okay," Vinnie said but there was grit to the tone of his reply. "I know it's not a date date. No need to talk it into the ground. No need to underline how bad my track record is at dating."

"Oh, my god, Vinnie. I didn't mean it that way. I'm sorry."

Vinnie looked. He was no real judge of character but Zeb really did appear contrite. It was his choice now how the conversation played out by either taking offence or shrugging it off. He tried for light-hearted.

"Who are you and what have you done to the real Zeb?"

It had the desired result and Zeb smiled. "This is the real me. Take it or leave it."

Vinnie liked it and his brain point blank refused to censor his mouth. "I'll take it."

"Be careful what you wish for," Zeb said mysteriously.

The remainder of the journey was lightened by meaningless banter and the revelation of minor personal information. From such small acorns, friendships grow. Or so Vinnie believed. He wasn't sure of Zeb's position on the cliché.

Once Zeb delivered him home safely and he was inside, Vinnie was finally able to get some equilibrium back in his life.

"What the fuck happened today?" he asked out loud.

His mind was a whirl of conflicting emotions. Yes, he disliked Zeb like a lobster dislikes a hot pot, at least the Zeb he knew so well for his snarky comments at the pub. But he liked the quieter Zeb away from the toxic atmosphere of a bar. Above all else, though, he loved cleaning Zeb's apartment. He hadn't made any blunders – a miracle in itself – Zeb seemed to be happy with the result…

Exhausted, emotionally and physically, he flopped down on the bed still fully clothed. It was only when he felt the bulge in his pocket as he turned over that he remembered the payment.

He really should return it. He didn't deserve it. But he was curious. Was it a pity job or did Zeb think he'd work for peanuts and so save himself cash on a cleaner? Mate's rates were shit. Vinnie knew from experience. It took no time at all for his mind to cheapen his labor.

Better to get it over with now than stew over it until the morning. Vinnie took the envelope out of his pocket and tore open the top. Now he would see what value Zeb had placed on his hard work. And let no one say otherwise, cleaning is bloody hard work, especially when you have to pick up after a slob like Zeb. Such a contrast to Zeb himself who was always immaculate in grooming and fashion. Oh, well, nobody's perfect.

He pulled out the wad of notes stuffed in the packet. What the hell? Was this some sort of a joke? Was Zeb having a lend? Who paid a cleaner that much? Not even scrubbing the Taj Mahal from top to bottom until it gleamed was worth this much. Vinnie was suspicious. Zeb had never liked him so why did he give him a handful of cash for a lowly paid apartment clean, unless… Was Zeb going to accuse him of theft? Was it a set-up? Money laundering? Vinnie's mind did somersaults in an attempt to come to terms with enough cash to pay his rent for the next month without having to stress over looking for work.

No, Zeb was direct and to the point, a no-bullshit man to Vinnie's exasperation, but he wasn't mean or nasty. There had to be a simple explanation for the payment. Zeb mentioned a bribe. Was that it?

After wrestling with his paranoia for ten minutes he came to the only solution that fitted the circumstances. He would ring Zeb and ask what the fuck? Too simple as Zeb didn't answer his mobile – Vinnie left a message on voicemail but it was so garbled even he didn't understand what he was saying – and his landline didn't answer. He probably wasn't home yet or, more likely, had gone out prowling at one of the kink bars that catered to Zeb's…preference. He briefly called it 'perversion' in his mind but then scolded himself for being so moralistic. He had no idea what Zeb liked in a partner, and it was none of his business anyway.

He'd sleep on it and contact Zeb in the morning for an explanation.

But he was no closer to an explanation the following day because he couldn't raise Zeb on either phone and had no intention of going to his private residence for an answer. He didn't want to run into the man (men?) Zeb had picked up at the bars last evening. Of course, there was the possibility that Zeb hadn't got home from his exploits yet. Or maybe he was lying in a gutter somewhere. Vinnie's mind went off in so many different tangents he felt ready to explode.

Taking deep breaths to calm down, he decided he'd phone cleaning agencies on Monday to ascertain the going rate for domestic cleaners. It was bound to be much less than what he'd received. Then he would calmly and quietly confront Zeb about what the fuck was going on. As a result, his Sunday was a write-off. He briefly toyed with the idea of ringing one of his friends to ask advice but as Zeb was part of their group, the call would get back to him and Vinnie realized he wouldn't like it if they discussed him behind his back either.

It just brought home the awful crushing truth of his situation. Vinnie was lonely, he had no lover much as he desperately wanted one, his desperation leeched from his pores like a bad smell which turned off prospective suitors, and more importantly, he had no close friend in whom he could confide. He was no fool, he knew the guys at the bar were as superficial as their professed friendship. Scratch the surface and they saw Vinnie as just another bedpost notch. They hung around only so long as he rejected their all-too-obvious advances hoping to change his mind.

Cleaning his own apartment usually took his mind off his problems; but not today. That was his go-to solution and it rarely let him down. It was a measure of the stress he felt that it didn't work this time. His life was a mess. He couldn't keep a lover. He couldn't keep a job. And he needed both for his own peace of mind. What he didn't need on top of everything else was Zeb insinuating himself into the cracks in his existence. He'd enjoyed cleaning Zeb's apartment: a little too much. More surprising, he found himself warming to Zeb although that would almost certainly evaporate once they got back to their sarcasm brawl at the pub on Friday.

As a very last resort, a last-ditch plan to get his life in order, Vinnie knew exactly where to go. He'd seen it in the past but had been too embarrassed to do more than browse. It was now or never. Strangely, his job at Zeb's had not only confused him but it had given him a boost to his self-esteem although he realized it was an unfinished work and that he couldn't do it on his own; he needed professional help.

After putting away his mops and brooms and squeegee, he showered and dressed in fresh casual clothes that always made him feel good, he knew they showed him off to best effect, and took himself off to the large multi-level bookshop in the city. He was resolute in what needed to be done. He walked to the elevator ignoring the detour his body normally made to the graphic novel section before he looked at anything else. No, today he would be strong and wouldn't be deflected from his chore.

He waited patiently for the elevator without glancing at the New Releases nearby which he had been known to pore over for a good hour or more in an effort to find reading material, allowed other browsers out of the lift before he entered and pressed the floor that he knew by heart. It was only when he was deposited on the appropriate level and the elevator doors closed behind him that he doubted his mission. Deep breaths, then he strode to the shelves, knowing exactly the position of what he sought. He'd done this so many times but had never followed through. It was now, or forever be a loser.

He could see the item from a distance. He knew it by heart. There were others browsing nearby and Vinnie felt such a conspicuous fool as he pulled the book from the shelf without a second's pause, strode to the sales counter, paid for it with his almost maxed credit card, thanked the salesperson for the paper bag (he was much too embarrassed to be seen with the book in public), and almost ran from the store, only able to breathe easily once outside. He'd done it.

Mark up a win for Vinnie.

Once back in the security of his apartment, he tore off the bag and held the book in his trembling hands. He opened at the back page and extracted the CD from the plastic pouch adhered to the back cover. Calmly he retrieved his old Walkman (he liked to call it his walk-person as it sounded less sexist to his ears), changed the batteries which had long since expired through lack of use, took out an old Madonna CD which he thought he'd lost, inserted the new disc, and went to the bedroom.

He stripped down to his briefs and a favorite T-shirt before slipping under the covers. Once the head-set was in place, he pressed Play, adjusted the sound level, and lay back to listen to the first track of *Positively Change Your Life and Make Your Dreams Come True*. He hoped he wasn't a fool to think it might help. He wasn't expecting miracles, but…

He slept through both tracks even though the self-hypnosis was supposed to wake you up on the count of ten. Sometime during the night he must have had enough waking moments to remove the headset from his ears and he'd slept right through to the following morning.

Hunger drove him out of bed and he prepared himself a hearty breakfast considering he'd eaten so little the previous day. Amazingly, he found himself humming one of his favorite songs as he concocted the hot meal. His good mood continued through the cleaning up and on into the bathroom for his shower. A quick glance in the mirror revealed no outward change to his appearance although something had clicked inside him. Or was it just wishful thinking. Didn't matter really, all that he cared about was that he felt…good.

One play of the CD was not a game changer, he knew that much, he would have to continue using it until the exercises were ingrained. He had plenty of time to do that. After he showered and shaved he went to his dining table with a lined pad and a ballpoint pen to draw up a list. He entered only three items for that day: Ring cleaning companies for a list of going rates. Ring Zeb to find out why he paid so much. Find a new job.

The first was easy and he took great satisfaction in crossing it off. He'd rung three different agencies, all of whom had offered him a job but the application process was so convoluted it made him wheezy with stress, but he got the hourly rate of each, the variation only slight. His first surprise was that Zeb hadn't been quite as generous as he'd first imagined. Okay, it was at least half as much again as the most expensive hourly rate he'd been quoted over the phone, but it wasn't profligate.

He had to take a break and down a very strong cup of black coffee to get up the nerve to ring Zeb on the private number on his business card. Vinnie hoped he wasn't calling at an inopportune time given Zeb's busy schedule, but Zeb answered right away, "Hey, Vinnie, I was just thinking about you and how great my apartment looks. I hope this call is to tell me you'll be there next Saturday. I got your message but it was a really busy weekend…"

Zeb hadn't paused for breath and Vinnie was stunned at how friendly the whole conversation seemed. It was a little too familiar to be comfortable. "You don't have to explain to me –" Vinnie interrupted.

"But I want to. I don't want you thinking I'm a rude asshole," Zeb said.

Vinnie's mouth ran away with him. "Too late, I already think that."

OMG! Did I just say that out loud. Vinnie was mortified until he heard Zeb. "I suppose I deserve that," he said but Vinnie could hear the chuckle in his voice. "So, what's the call about, Vinnie?"

Vinnie hated talking money. "It's about the, um, payment –"

Zeb couldn't get the words out fast enough. "Oh my god, Vinnie. I'm so sorry. Is it not enough? I didn't know what the going rate was so I just put what I thought was fair in the envelope. I hope you don't feel insulted. I'll make up the difference this week. Please say you'll still clean my apartment. Please." He was begging.

"No. It was too much," Vinnie said. Why did he have to be such a moral bastard? "The going rate is much less."

Zeb spoke quietly. "You know, most people would have just pocketed the money and kept mum."

"But I'm not most people," Vinnie said.

"I'm beginning to see that side of you, Vinnie. And I like it."

He'd had people like him before but that usually led to a swollen sphincter and a broken heart. He shook his head to get the image out of his brain. Zeb did not like him like that.

"What's say you keep it for this time as a show of good faith and we'll adjust the next job according to what you and I agree is fair. How's that sound?" Zeb suggested.

"I appreciate it, Zeb. You know my situation and you could have taken advantage of it. So I'm grateful for the extra just at the moment until I get back on my feet. I'll make it up to you somehow."

"You don't have to do anything to make up for it. I paid you what I thought the job was worth. Okay?"

Vinnie mumbled acknowledgment. "But I don't want a pity job, understand?"

"Vinnie, I'm not into pity, giving or taking, so set your mind at ease. This is all above board. I have a need and you fulfill it."

"Thanks. Regardless of what you say, I owe you and I pay my debts."

"If it makes you feel better, Vinnie."

"Um, we didn't discuss it before, but what do we tell the guys at the pub?" Vinnie would need a thick skin to withstand the withering comments when they discovered he was working for Zeb.

"It's none of their business. We tell them nothing. That okay with you?"

Vinnie gave a sigh of relief. That was more than okay. "Thanks."

"I'll see you at the pub on Friday?"

"Yeah."

"Oh, and Vinnie, I'll be the same asshole you know and detest like always."

Vinnie laughed.

But not for long. Searching for a new job was a daunting task, especially when his reputation preceded him. Or else he lacked the necessary training or qualifications for others. Frequently he was asked if he'd work for free during the training period and when he refused (how was he supposed to live?) people hung up on him. His heart wasn't in it. He'd enjoyed cleaning Zeb's apartment and was looking forward to the weekend. It couldn't come fast enough. Sure, cleaning was an option but the large agencies required competency with industrial floor polishers, long night hours, or else paid poverty wages. They made Zeb's payment look like Steve Jobs. By Friday, he'd all but given up.

Come Saturday, he'd thought of a way to compensate Zeb for his generosity. But first he had to get through the Friday night ritual of a boys night out. Vinnie didn't have the ready cash to splash out on drinks but he knew his friends would want an update on his job search and how he survived his alcoholic haze from the previous week. He had no intention of telling them about the truce with Zeb. He'd have to remember to toss back snarky comments as usual. It would be more difficult now that he'd got to know Zeb a little better. He wanted to know him a whole lot better and it was best done in private, not with an audience.

He needn't have worried because Zeb didn't turn up. Vinnie couldn't help but wonder if he was avoiding him until Maurie arrived with the news that Zeb had been called to an important meeting and wouldn't be able to make it. That meant they turned their focus on Vinnie and the snide remarks and putdowns kept right on coming. He realized that Zeb did often act as a buffer against the nastiness, something he'd never really acknowledged to himself. He was tired of his friends belittling him, especially as it was part of their chipping away at his reluctance to fuck them. He begged off staying long with the excuse of lack of funds and as none of the others offered to shout his drinks he gladly left them behind.

ZEB CURSED. He was running late. He'd got caught up with a GLBTQI+ collective who wanted some posters and artwork done for a forthcoming retreat. They'd spent the afternoon arguing back and forth – that was the problem when no one person was in charge. After a completely exhausting few hours Zeb had been forced to throw his weight around, informing them they were paying him by the hour and if they didn't make a decision shortly they'd have blown their entire budget and be no closer to a decision. Ten minutes later, the meeting wrapped up.

Now he was on his way home. He'd picked up takeaway hoping Vinnie would still be there and would join him for a scrappy meal. Mainly he hoped he'd be there so he could pay him for the work. He'd tried ringing but Vinnie had not picked up, not that Zeb had expected him to while he was working. He smiled at the fact Vinnie had become his regular cleaner.

Zeb bounded up the stairs rather than wait for the elevator, hurrying into his apartment puffing for breath. His relief was instant when he heard music and Vinnie half-singing/half whistling along. He couldn't help smiling. But what the hell was that smell? His nose could distinguish vanilla and...was Vinnie baking?

Not wishing to startle him, Zeb crept into the apartment scarcely able to control his good humor when he saw Vinnie pottering about in the kitchen grinding his butt off to the music. Somewhere along the line while on the job, Vinnie had divested himself of his sweats, his cute butt now covered only by his tighty whities. It was innocent but also, to Zeb's consternation, rudely arousing. He couldn't help himself – he applauded the performance. Vinnie turned to catch Zeb's eyes on his ass. Embarrassment all round. Vinnie stopped his seductive ass pumping while Zeb pawed his semi-erection into submission.

"Oh my god! You saw me?" Vinnie screeched. He ran for the bathroom, his screaming reaching almost pain level before the slammed door cut it off. Zeb's mouth was agape at Vinnie's preposterous behavior before his good humor got the better of him and he chuckled. Striding to the bathroom door, he found it bolted from the inside. He knocked lightly.

"Vinnie. Vinnie?"

"Go away."

"I can't, I live here."

"Then go away for half an hour and let me escape with what little dignity I still have."

"Uh huh. Can't do that either. Our dinner will go cold." To emphasize the point he went back to retrieve the takeaway he'd collected on the way home. Opening one of the containers of food, he fanned the aroma under the door. He swore he could hear Vinnie's stomach rumble.

Vinnie snapped. "You bastard, I love satay chicken stir fry."

"I know," Zeb chuckled.

The door opened a sliver and Vinnie peeked out, his face still crimson from being caught in his underwear. "You do?"

Zeb screwed up his face as if to suggest it was a stupid question. "Of course. All your friends know that. You order it every time we go for a meal at Thai Tanic."

Vinnie's face lit up. "You noticed?"

"Come on out. You want to sit in the kitchen or the living room?" Zeb asked.

Vinnie opened the door wider, he now had a bath towel wrapped around his waist to cover his modesty.

"The kitchen is cozier, we'll eat there," Zeb decided.

Vinnie trailed along a little like a lost puppy. "Oh, shit." He raced ahead of Zeb to the kitchen, flung open the oven, grabbed the mitts and pulled out a baking pan. "I forgot it. Almost burnt but it should be okay."

Zeb took a deep breath, there was nothing that felt more like home than the aroma of pies baking in the oven. "It looks perfect. What sort is it?"

"Well, you don't exactly have a lot of ingredients so I went out for a few minutes – I hope that was okay – I found a set of spare keys on your bureau." Zeb nodded. "I went down to that convenience store on the corner. That nice Mrs. Mosto…"

"I hope you were wearing more than, you know." Zeb pointed to Vinnie's state of undress.

"Of course, I was. You think I'm an idiot." Vinnie was getting riled.

"No. No, I don't think you're an idiot. Sorry. It was my attempt at a joke." Zeb looked suitably chastened.

"Oh? My fault. I didn't think you knew how to joke."

Zeb sputtered indignantly. "There's lots you don't know about me."

"Ditto," Vinnie said, leaving the pie to cool on a metal rack.

Vinnie decided to leave it there and change the subject.

"Plate or bowl?" Zeb asked.

"Bowl, please."

Zeb was opening and closing cupboards getting more and more frustrated. "Fuck, where the hell do I keep the dishes?"

"Oh, my fault." Vinnie went to help, finding the bowls in the first cupboard he opened. "Um, I rearranged things a little." Zeb just stared at him. "Well, you have no system. Everything's just thrown in where you think it fits. I just made it more methodical. That's all. I can change it back if you don't like it."

"Nah, it's fine."

"I guess I was enjoying myself so much, I didn't know when to stop. I arranged it all as I would if this was my place," Vinnie added wistfully. "I guess that was a bit presumptuous."

"No, you're right. I just shove things where there's a space. No system at all which means I spend more time looking for something than I do actually eating. I've even bought the same kitchen utensils twice because I couldn't find the first set."

Vinnie placed the bowls on the counter before opening the plastic container of rice, scooping equal shares into each. He snapped the lid off the stir fry and the succulent smell of sweet chili sauce, basil and satay had him groaning with expectation. "Smells divine."

He shared it out, spooning more into Zeb's bowl than his own. If Zeb noticed he didn't let on.

"Spoon or chopsticks?" Vinnie asked, breaking the takeaway wooden utensils apart.

"Spoon for me," Zeb muttered. It sounded as if he was almost ashamed. "I've never mastered the skill of eating with knitting needles."

Vinnie laughed. "Here, shove over. I'll teach you."

Zeb moved aside and Vinnie moved in closer bringing his food with him. "The first thing is to position the chopsticks in your fingers the right way." He demonstrated and even though Zeb tried, he kept dropping them or they splayed awkwardly like a long-legged skater fallen over on the ice. They both laughed.

"Here, it's easy." Vinnie grabbed Zeb's hand to position the implements correctly. Then he controlled the hand as Zeb reached into the bowl to pick up one of the larger pieces of chicken. Between the two of them they managed to wrangle it into Zeb's mouth. "See."

Concern suddenly scarred Vinnie's brow. Had he been too familiar? He'd lost all sense that he was merely an employee of Zeb's – at least for this one-off occasion. "Oh my god, I'm so sorry."

"What are you sorry about?" Zeb was attempting valiantly to salvage a snow pea and raise it to within striking distance of his mouth.

"For assuming too much," Vinnie replied meekly.

"For fuck's sake, Vinnie. We're just two friends having a meal together." Zeb seemed annoyed. "You're teaching me an important skill which I'm obviously far from mastering." The snow pea dropped back into the bowl.

Friends? Vinnie thought not. Maybe they could come out of this situation as frenemies. Vinnie was actually enjoying himself more than he'd anticipated. He was chuffed to discover he was good at something that Zeb wasn't. He was less than thrilled that Zeb had caught him, in his undies, wiggling his ass while cleaning. He'd never live that down once Zeb revealed all at their next group get-together.

"Show me again?" Zeb asked.

It took a few more practices before Zeb started to get the hang of it and managed to get more food into his mouth than dropped back into his bowl. Vinnie moved aside, he'd been cramping Zeb. It was only once he was back in his own seat he realized how comfortable he'd felt against his arch-frenemy. They ate in silence – Zeb was concentrating too much on simply getting the food into his mouth to chat, although he watched Vinnie closely to pick up the finer points of chopstick dining. Zeb was nothing if not competitive.

Vinnie slowed down so he didn't finish his meal so quickly it would make Zeb look inept, although he still finished first. He watched patiently as Zeb emptied his bowl. By meal's end Zeb was managing just shy of expertly. Vinnie felt a stab of satisfaction that he'd been the one to teach him a new skill.

Vinnie carried the plates to the sink for a rinse before stacking them in the dishwasher. "Where do you keep the rinse aid?" he asked. "I notice it hasn't been topped up in ages."

"You're not my slave, Vinnie. Sit down. Give your meal time to digest." He smiled. "Now there's a fantasy – having you as my slave." Zeb realized too late he'd said it out loud. He was almost afraid to look at Vinnie's reaction.

But Vinnie just laughed. "Oh, so that's your kink. You want a slave to do your washing up."

Zeb breathed easier. "If it ever does become my kink, you'll be the first person I call."

Vinnie covered his embarrassment by repeating his earlier question. "Rinse aid?"

Zeb shrugged. "I don't even know what that is." He got up to help Vinnie search through the kitchen cabinets. While Vinnie scrambled about on his knees examining every drawer and shelf under and around the sink, Zeb stretched over him in an attempt to get at those at head height. There was a muffled "Ah, gotcha!" from somewhere inside a cupboard before Vinnie's head popped up, his hair laced with a few grey cobwebs. While still kneeling, holding the plastic bottle of dishwasher rinse aid victoriously in one hand, Vinnie's face was just a little too close to Zeb's crotch for comfort. He swallowed loudly, the situation rife with sexual tension. Vinnie stared at the bulge scarcely able to swallow. He thought he saw a slight twitch from the material covering Zeb's crotch.

"While you're down there," Zeb said.

Vinnie had heard that joke too many times before to see it as anything other than predatory. He attempted to stand up, his dignity bruised by Zeb's crude assumption. But a hand on his shoulder held him down. He was about to shrug it off in disgust when Zeb ran his hand through Vinnie's hair. "Hold still, you've got cobwebs all over your head." He held up a strand as exhibit A.

Vinnie bounced to his feet frantically rubbing his hands through his hair in an obvious effort to dislodge the strands of web. He was freaking out. "Ewww, I hate spiders. Quick get them off me." He was jumping up and down on the spot in fear.

Zeb held him still. "Calm down, Vinnie. There are no spiders just webs. Here, let me get them."

Vinnie calmed although his phobia meter was still on apocalyptic. "You know what they say: Where there's a web there's a giant arachnid just waiting to dig its venomous pincers into your flesh."

Zeb laughed loudly. "I think you watch way too much 1950s science fiction. There, that's got it." He flicked the last ball of web onto the floor.

Vinnie shrieked. "What are you doing" I just cleaned that floor." He bent down to retrieve the wads of web which were small enough they were hardly visible. When he stood back up again, satisfied he got them all, he said in a voice that threatened dire retribution if he were not obeyed. "Hand out." Zeb was amused but did as requested. Vinnie dropped the evidence into his palm. "Now, go put that in the trash where it should be."

Snapping to attention, clicking his heels together and saluting, Zeb barked, "Yes, sir," before marching to the bin and, with military precision, disposing of the dreaded threads. He turned and snapped back to attention. "All disposed of, sir!"

Vinnie looked sufficiently embarrassed. "Um, I suppose that was a bit of an over-reaction, huh?" He hated he'd made himself a figure of fun in a way that would ensure ridicule at the next gathering of his friends. Zeb read the meaning in his face.

"Look, Vinnie. I have no intention of telling any of the guys what goes on here so just relax. And, before you ask, Lenny is the absolute last person on earth to whom I would reveal anything at all, or certainly anything that he could use as ammunition to humiliate you more than he does now."

Vinnie was surprised that Zeb had even noticed let alone would not take this perfect opportunity to add to his misery.

"What's say we have some of that fantastic smelling pie of yours?"

That was enough to galvanize Vinnie into action. Baking, as well as cleaning, was safer turf. He gave quick silent thanks to whatever god was looking after him that day hoping they might stick around long enough to shower him with a little more good luck. Zeb had already found dessert bowls and had them lined up on the bench top as Vinnie retrieved the pie from the cooling rack. "If I'd had more time and a few more ingredients…" He almost said 'better' ingredients but that was an implied criticism and he wasn't going to go there after Zeb had been so…nice. "Maybe next time." He had no idea if there would be a next time – he was on a week-to-week basis – or why he wanted so badly another opportunity to impress Zeb. He just knew that he did.

THERE WAS definitely going to be a next time. Especially after Zeb had gorged on the most delicious pie he'd ever tasted this side of his mother's own baking – and he had to admit Vinnie's pie had a slight edge – there was no way he would let Vinnie go.

He drove Vinnie home again but this time the conversation flowed as if the words had been oiled for smoothness, Zeb finding Vinnie to be delightful company when he wasn't uptight about his job or his love life (or lack thereof).

They both tended to avoid the personal, concentrating on the general: favorite movies, TV shows, food, color, the sort of inane chatter that marks the beginning of a friendship. Vinnie was best when Zeb had him in a one-on-one situation because the following Friday bar night was fraught with tension.

"We missed you last week," Lenny sneered. "You find someone into the same perversions you are?"

Zeb didn't bite. "Bad day at work this week, Leonard." He always used Lenny's full name as a warning not to pursue that line of questioning.

Lenny backed off but turned his attention to Vinnie who was not participating in the usual snarky banter with Zeb. The guys all thought he was depressed over the lack of job opportunities and left him alone. But Lenny was not in any mood for conciliation. "You still an unemployed loser, Vinnie? Or have you got some poor mug to employ your hot ass for a week or so before they discover how inept you are at work and at fucking?"

Zeb got in first. "Lay off, Lenny. Go and jerk off in the men's and leave your foul mood in the bowl."

That attracted everyone's attention. "My, my, what's got into you, Zeb, defending the little loser? Since when have you and the king of losers become buddy buddy? Something you'd like to share?" Lenny was persistent.

There was nothing either of them cared to share with Lenny. Vinnie made it an early night, partly in expectation of a much friendlier Saturday at Zeb's, partly the cost of drinks, a further expense he didn't need.

"WHAT'S that lovely smell?" Brigid asked sniffing the air like an addict in a parfumerie as she and Zeb entered his apartment.

"Vinnie's doing a bit of baking. It relaxes him after he's done the cleaning," Zeb replied without thinking.

"Vinnie? Cleaning?" Brigid's eyebrows shot up. "Is there something I should know?"

"Nothing like that, Brigid. Get your mind out of the gutter. Vinnie is one of the guys I meet at the pub on Fridays. He was looking for work, I needed a cleaner, voila, Vinnie comes in on Saturdays to do the shit I'm much too lazy to lift a finger to do."

"Smells divine."

"I know that look, Brigid. You want a taste. And you want to meet the cook."

She nodded enthusiastically.

"Vinnie. Vinnie, where are you?" Zeb called.

"Hey, Zeb. I'm in the bedroom."

Brigid's eyebrows shot up even higher, especially as Vinnie wandered out in his T-shirt and skimpy shorts.

"Oh my god," Brigid said breathlessly. "He's gorgeous. Where have you been hiding him?"

"Please don't frighten the staff, Brigid," Zeb pleaded, hoping Vinnie wouldn't revert to default position and lock himself in the bathroom until Brigid was gone.

Fortunately, Vinnie just smiled. That did it. Brigid began fanning herself with her hand to alleviate the effects of Vinnie's hotness. Instead of looking startled or embarrassed, Vinnie appeared to be pleased by the brazen appraisal. "I like her," he said. "She's good for the ego. I'm Vinnie." He held out his hand and when Brigid went to shake it, he pulled her into a hug.

Zeb made a mental note that the self-improvement CD Vinnie was using was actually working. Who'd have thought?

Vinnie snapped away from Brigid. "Oh, I'm so sorry. I must stink."

Brigid ran her finger along Vinnie's muscular arm. "All I smell is testosterone. It's an aphrodisiac, you know."

"He's gay, Brigid," Zeb warned.

It didn't faze her. "Pie. I smell pie."

Vinnie was pleased at her reaction to his baking. "Would you like some?"

"As long as I don't leave you short."

"Nah, I made two this time. Experimented with a new flavor. Rhubarb and pomegranate. You'll be a guinea pig."

Brigid screwed up her face. "Not a big fan of rhubarb. Just a small taste."

"The other one will be to your liking," Zeb cut in. "Traditional apple and cinnamon."

Zeb led Brigid to the living area, knowing Vinnie didn't like to be crowded while he worked and Brigid was an expert crowder and interferer. Vinnie took the pies out of the oven and left them on the rack to cool while he whipped up a brandied cream to complement his baking, then he divided up the pies because Brigid was getting impatient and kept asking when they'd be ready and put a generous portion of each in bowls before scooping the cream over the luscious desserts. Vinnie hoped Brigid wasn't lactose intolerant. Or a recovering alcoholic. The coffee was ready and Vinnie took it out, placing it on the small table for them to help themselves before heading back to the kitchen to fetch the pie. With great ceremony he handed a plate to Brigid and another to Zeb.

"Aren't you having any?" she asked.

"Later," Vinnie said, eager to get her impression of his ability. It was all very well Zeb praising him but he was a friend, well a sort-of friend, while she was a total stranger. She would be more truthful. Apart from cleaning, baking was the only thing Vinnie did well.

Brigid forked a piece into her mouth, closed her eyes, and … wham, he eyes flew open in surprise. "Oh. My. God."

Vinnie tapped his feet impatiently.

Brigid finished swallowing the mouthful before shoveling the other piece of pie into her mouth. She hummed in bliss. When she could speak again, she asked, "You made these?"

"Uh huh," Vinnie replied. "Are they okay?"

"No, these are not okay," Brigid exclaimed. "As far away from okay as it's possible to get. These are magnificent. They belong in the Smithsonian as an example of what a pie can be."

Vinnie knew she was exaggerating but her enthusiasm was infectious. He blushed as he thanked her. "And the rhubarb?"

"I've done a total backflip over rhubarb as a pie filling. It's divine."

Vinnie smiled shyly and sneaked a look at Zeb who was looking on in admiration, as if he was proud of Vinnie. But that couldn't be, could it?

Brigid gave them both the strangest look and, after demolishing the luscious pie samples, disappeared to the bathroom leaving the two men to clean up. When she returned ten minutes later she beamed.

"It's so neat in there. I've never seen it like that before. You even have his bathroom cabinets so precise that everything, including toothpaste, is in Use By date order." She looked about. "In fact, the whole place is spotless. And everything in its place. Everything is as it should be. I don't know how you managed it but you're a miracle worker, Zeb doesn't like change and you have surely turned his world upside down."

Vinnie was ODing on compliments.

As Zeb helped her on with her coat, she suddenly slipped out of his grip to turn to Vinnie. "How would you feel about doing a bit of cleaning for me? I'm having a party in a few weeks and I want to impress my husband's boss and, particularly, his wife who's house proud and looks for it in others. You maybe could give me a few pointers."

Vinnie was about to answer that he'd love to when Zeb intervened. "What's in it for him?"

Brigid turned sharply. "What are you, his manager?"

Vinnie was momentarily pissed off at Zeb's interference until he realized he was about to volunteer without asking who would supply the cleaning agents, the mops, the buckets, if payment was involved, how he'd get there. Now, if Zeb was offering to help…

Vinnie looked up at Zeb, his anger gone, and hoped he sent the message through his eyes.

"Yes, as a matter of fact, I am Vinnie's manager."

Vinnie relaxed, Zeb had got the message.

If Brigid was offended she didn't show it. "Okay, manager," her voice oozed skepticism. "I have a party coming up in three weeks at my home. The refreshments are catered but I'm a total failure at housework. It's always the same old same old but the boss's wife, who has far too much sway with her husband's decision making, judges people by their home…well, you get the picture. I'd really like to knock her on her ass with how pristine my home is. What do you say? Help a girl out?"

Zeb winked. "What do you say, Vinnie? Should we chance your reputation with the house-proud hausfrau?"

Vinnie looked heartbroken. "I don't have any of the necessary…"

"Not a problem. You'll use mine." Zeb was taking over and Vinnie liked it. He could just turn up and do the job, someone else could look after the detail.

"Okay. I think I can manage that."

"My partner has given the okay. Send me a list of what you need and I'll get a quote to you. How's that sound?" Zeb obviously knew what he was doing.

"Mate's rates?" Brigid asked hopefully. "I'm not made of money."

"I think I can offer a discount in exchange…but I'll have to discuss it with Vinnie first."

She kissed Zeb on the cheek and then did the same to Vinnie. "It was lovely meeting you," she said. "And your delicious pies."

Zeb saw her out and Vinnie waited in barely contained excitement, bouncing up and down on the spot until Zeb returned.

"She really wants me to clean her house." Vinnie was delighted.

"Of course, she did. Who wouldn't?" Zeb was so matter-of-fact.

"Um…can I…um…can…"

"Spit it out, Vinnie."

"I need a hug."

Zeb pulled Vinnie into his arms and held him tight. They were a comfortable fit. Vinnie liked the way it felt and couldn't prevent a loud sob from escaping.

"What's that for?" Zeb asked patiently, stroking a few stray hairs from Vinnie's face.

"Happiness," Vinnie sobbed.

VINNIE'S confidence grew each time Zeb saw him on the Friday night pub meet where he gave as good as he got in their verbal exchanges. They were having fun throwing barbs at each other although it was more in jest than in anger or genuine dislike. Neither of them realized it was an unusual form of foreplay. Only Lenny was suspicious of how friendly the banter sounded and how much Vinnie seemed to enjoy the exchanges. It was easy, however, to put it down to the self-confidence CD Vinnie was listening to. The self-help CD was a constant source of humor and bollocking of loser Vinnie for the group although Zeb was careful not to use Vinnie's conviction about its efficacy as fodder for his banter.

The Saturdays were a different matter altogether. An understanding, if not a friendship, had developed. Vinnie was still looking for permanent employment but until he found it, Zeb's weekly, generous fee was enough to survive on if he followed a stringent budget. It helped that Zeb had become habitual in returning after Vinnie's work was complete with lavish takeaway meals that they shared while chatting amiably. Vinnie was wary at first of revealing anything too personal in case Zeb used it against him so he dipped his toe in the water as a test and revealed a crumb of childhood embarrassment. When Zeb had the opportunity to use the revelation as a source of ridicule and black humor at the pub, and hadn't, Vinnie opened up more. It was almost like having a friend he could confide in.

He liked Zeb's apartment. He felt comfortable there because he knew what he was doing when he was cleaning. He didn't feel quite so relaxed on the Friday night they both skipped the pub in order to make up for the fact he would be cleaning Brigid's place on Saturday in time for her party. It was different cleaning Zeb's on a Friday night. Zeb was home for one. That was a very big difference. Vinnie preferred to be left alone when he was working but he couldn't expect Zeb to leave his own home at night unless he went out on the prowl. Vinnie couldn't work out which was the worse of the two: Zeb hovering while he worked or Zeb bringing home trade while he was there. The upside of the latter was that maybe he'd find out about Zeb's kink.

"Can I help?" Zeb asked, careful to keep his voice quiet and soothing.

"This was a stupid idea. I never should have agreed to it. I'm a screw-up." Vinnie's shoulders sagged in defeat. Zeb approached warily and dragged the despondent Vinnie into his arms. "It's okay, Vinnie. "You're not a loser. You're a smart young guy who just hasn't found his niche in life yet. But you will and then: Look out world, here comes Vinnie."

Vinnie snickered at the very idea. "You think so?"

"It stands to reason, doesn't it?" Zeb asked brightly. "I'm a successful businessman so you'd expect I know other successful people when I see them. And when I look at you, Vinnie, I see a guy who's trying so bloody hard that, of course, one day he'll be more successful than all of us."

It was a nice fantasy but Vinnie knew bullshit when he heard it. Platitudes were all very well, as were self-help CDs, but they were no substitute for real life. That's what Vinnie had real trouble with.

"You don't have to clean Brigid's place, Vinnie," Zeb added. "I can ring and tell her you got a full-time job. She'll be happy for you. I'll get one of the cleaners from my office to go in your place; she'll be just as happy with that."

Vinnie took a deep breath. "But I won't be. I'd be letting Brigid down after she showed faith in me. I'd be letting you down. I'd be letting myself down." Reluctantly, Vinnie pulled away from Zeb's warm touch, hitched up his attitude as if it were a loose pair of trousers, and got to work. Zeb gave him a mental high five.

Vinnie was surprised when Zeb asked again, "Anything I can do to help?" but gave him the task of clearing surfaces of rubbish and sorting it for recycling. Zeb could do that. Vinnie had his routine and he didn't like it disturbed. He gave Zeb just enough to keep him occupied and out of Vinnie's way. Occasionally they bumped in their clumsy attempts to avoid each other, their hands might touch as they went to put rubbish in the bin, but Vinnie visibly relaxed and began to enjoy himself. With Zeb's permission, he even put on some music and began to bop around the flat as he worked. In fact, he enjoyed it a little too much. It was rather nice sharing an experience with another person. It happened so rarely for Vinnie. In fact, even sex with another person seemed more like two separate solo acts to Vinnie. He did wonder sometimes, in the face of other people's obvious enjoyment of the sexual act, whether he was doing it right. He'd had no complaints but then most of his partners never lined up for a return bout, leaving straight after the Big O. The few that did hang around lasted a matter of weeks until they grew tired of Vinnie and moved on to greener pastures.

In fact, Vinnie's comfortable working relationship – if that was the right word – with Zeb had lasted longer than any of his amorous relationships. And it was far more enjoyable. Considering the public animosity they felt for each other, it was strange they should get on so well in private.

Zeb looked a little uncomfortable by the time Vinnie finished his cleaning. Zeb had kept out of his way as much as possible, sitting in the living area attempting to read some of the paperwork he'd brought home from the office. "Look, Vinnie, there's something I need to tell you." The serious look on his face gave Vinnie a bad feeling. If Zeb fired him he'd be back to loserville, just as things were looking up. Damn. At least Zeb had waited until he'd finished cleaning otherwise there'd be no money coming in that week.

"I get it," Vinnie said sadly. "I knew it was too good to last."

"What? Too good to last? What are you…" Lightbulb moment. "God, Vinnie, no, I'm not firing you. Just the opposite."

"You're not?" Vinnie's relief was palpable.

Zeb, however, still had on his serious demeanor. "I hope I haven't overstepped the mark here, Vinnie. You did say I was your manager and I was glad to help out at the time–"

"And I'm really grateful, Zeb. I am. I'm no good at that sort of thing. I always sell myself short. Not that I'm any great shakes at anything but, you know." Vinnie shrugged.

"Yes, I do know you undervalue yourself. This is a bit different. I've done something without asking you and I'm truly sorry if it's not what you want. My only excuse is that Brigid got me thinking and, well, why don't I just show you? But before I do, nothing might come of any of this but, then again, it might."

Vinnie listened patiently but hadn't a clue what Zeb was going on about.

Then Zeb changed the subject. "Have you thought about how you're going to transport the cleaning gear to Brigid's in the morning?"

"Oh, shit. I assumed she'd have the necessaries." He was such a…

"Don't even go there in your head, Vinnie," Zeb warned, obviously reading the concern written all over his face. "Anticipating is the manager's job. Okay?"

Vinnie nodded mutely, secretly hating he wasn't as organized as Zeb.

"Sort out the stuff from my cleaning closet that you need and I'll be back in a moment. I have something to show you," Zeb directed. "I can drive you to Brigid's, so don't worry."

For one disloyal moment Vinnie wondered what Zeb's take would be from Brigid's payment. He hoped there would be enough left to pay his rent for another few weeks. Did that sound mean?

Zeb returned with a small box about twice the size of a box of matches. He handed it to Vinnie. "Here we go."

Vinnie flipped the lid on the small packet and it was full of tiny cards in the most edible creamy color. He had no idea of the significance and looked to Zeb who nodded that he should take one out to look at it. One side of the card was blank, the other, Vinnie's heart skipped a beat, was emblazoned with a striking burgundy raised type, *Vinnie's Clean Start*, next to a cute caricature of Vinnie in jeans and T-shirt holding a mop and a bucket.

Vinnie's mouth gaped, he looked at Zeb then back at the business card, then at Zeb again who was on tenterhooks. "What do you think, Vinnie? Do you like it?"

Vinnie's head was about to explode. Why would Zeb do such a thing? Did he want to humiliate him?

"Is that supposed to be me?" Vinnie pointed to the little comic figure.

Zeb deflated. "You don't like it." It was a statement rather than a question.

"Why, Zeb? I don't understand."

"I thought…well, maybe I didn't think it through enough. But I thought you might pick up some extra work from the people at Brigid's party. The guests are bound to notice how nice the place scrubs up and I've done a deal that Brigid will hand out your business card if anyone comments. She's not the tidiest of women and people will notice the difference. And you can, you know, set up a little cottage cleaning industry. Nothing too grand. Just enough that you don't have to worry about where your next dollar is coming from."

"You did this for me?"

Zeb nodded. "I got the art department at the agency to work on them. I hope it's not too much."

Vinnie burst into tears.

"Oh, god, Vinnie. I'm so sorry if I upset you." Zeb pulled him into a hug.

"No one's ever done anything like this for me before," Vinnie sobbed.

Vinnie wiped his eyes on his sleeve and stared wide-eyed at the man he once thought of as his mortal enemy. Zeb shrugged. "It pays to advertise."

IT WAS late by the time Zeb had filled Vinnie in on what he hoped would come of the cleaning at Brigid's. "What do you think, Vinnie?"

"It's all a bit overwhelming."

"You don't hate it?"

"I'm just a bit numb." In case Zeb got the wrong idea, he added, "Good numb, not bad. You really think people might want my cleaning services?"

"Definitely. Most people don't like cleaning up after themselves or before some big party they're throwing to impress others. And lots of people have busy schedules and simply don't have the time. We'll use Brigid's as a test run, see how it goes. I hope you won't be disappointed if it doesn't work this time, but there will be other chances. Are you on board?"

"I'd be my own boss?"

"Of course," Zeb replied. "And I'll bow out if you don't want my help."

Vinnie almost shouted, "No. Of course I want your help. I've got a lot to think about. My head is all confused. It's late, I better get going."

"Stay the night, Vinnie. That way we can get up early and ferry the cleaning gear over to Brigid. It's a waste of time you going home and then coming back here." Zeb held his hands up. "No ulterior motive."

Vinnie snorted. "As if someone like you would ever fancy someone like me."

"You don't realize how easy you'd be to love," Zeb sighed.

After a little to-ing and fro-ing, Vinnie relented. It made sense to spend the night rather than travel back to his own place only to return early the following day. He was exhausted what with the work he'd just completed on the apartment and the emotional high of what Zeb had done for him secretly. He had no words to express his gratitude so, after a restful night's sleep in Zeb's spare bedroom where he luxuriated in a bed so large he needed a map to find the pillows, and sheets so silken he was afraid he'd slip out of them during the night, he decided to thank Zeb the only way he knew how.

The smell of breakfast sizzling woke Zeb who wandered into the kitchen looking as handsome disheveled as he did when he was wearing his business suit. "God, Vinnie, what's that smell?"

Vinnie had already set the kitchen counter for two. "Take a seat and you'll find out shortly."

Zeb did as instructed and Vinnie placed a tall glass of green sludge before him. He screwed up his nose. "What's this? A shake made from toxic river algae or something? It looks disgustingly healthy?"

"Oh, ye of little faith. That is an avocado smoothie."

Zeb felt his stomach lurch. "I don't think so."

"Do I have to hold you down and spoon it into your mouth?" Vinnie closed in on Zeb wielding a lethal bread knife.

"Okay," Zeb laughed. "Though I'd like to see you try and pin me down."

"That would be too easy," Vinnie boasted.

A sudden image of Vinnie pinning him to the floor sent a signal straight to Zeb's cock. In an effort to get himself under control before Vinnie sussed him out, Zeb picked up the drink and sipped. He hoped that would be enough to get Vinnie off his back. No, brain, don't go there either.

"Oh my god, this is wonderful." Zeb took a more substantial sip. And another. And one more.

"Good boy," Vinnie said, then patted Zeb on the head running his fingers through his thick black hair. He withdrew as if burned. He'd forgotten his place and hoped Zeb wasn't offended. "Now you get your reward."

Zeb was hoping for a very different reward to the one he received – a delicious full breakfast that would see him through the busy morning ahead – but it was a more than satisfactory substitute.

"You sleep okay?" Zeb asked.

"Dead to the world. Best night's sleep in ages," Vinnie said. He neglected to add that he'd locked his bedroom door as a precaution. Against what he wasn't sure. He didn't really think Zeb would try anything. The lock wouldn't have prevented Vinnie from an after-dark excursion to Zeb's bed – not that he'd been invited.

He was confused. There was definite sexual tension in the air every time he and Zeb were together in private. Even out at the bar on Friday nights he felt a little of it seep into their faux animosity. He found it hard to believe, however, that Zeb would be interested in him regardless of his increasing support and friendship. Vinnie feared an ulterior motive but couldn't pinpoint one in his mind.

"You ready to go once we finish breakfast?" Vinnie asked.

"Let me just have a quick freshen up and change my clothes and I'll be right with you." Zeb finished his smoothie and headed to his bedroom while Vinnie kept busy doing the dishes and stacking them back in their new location on the shelves. He smiled in satisfaction at the order he had installed in Zeb's unruly life.

Zeb looked just as hot in casual wear as he did in his business attire and Vinnie's heart gave a little dance at the sight of the man he was beginning to think of as a friend. There was still an element of caution because he'd been there done that been heartbroken too many times before. He might fantasize Zeb as the object of his lust while taking himself in hand for relief in the privacy of his own dreams but he was acutely aware of the reality. Zeb was a player – with an undisclosed kink. Still, Vinnie could dream, couldn't he? No harm there, especially if no one knew about it.

"HOW long have you and Zeb been going out together?" Brigid asked nosily as Vinnie finished up the downstairs bathroom which had been quarantined for party guests. It smelled like a field of lavender and was so hygienic you could eat off the tiles. She'd been crowding Vinnie while he worked, asking questions that were so far from the truth he wanted to scream at her to go away and let him do his job. Zeb had left him at her mercy in order to slip back to his office to catch up on important client work. She'd been asking impertinent questions ever since he'd disappeared.

"We're not going out together, Brigid. He's so far out of my league I might as well be on Mars."

"Come on, Vinnie. Don't play coy with me. I've seen the way he looks at you when he thinks you're not looking. And you watch him like he's the top meal in a restaurant."

"In that case, I'm a greasy takeaway. And never the two shall meet. Not like that anyway," Vinnie said, flushing the toilet one last time to disinfect it.

"Okay, have it your way, but I've never seen him so smitten," Brigid persisted.

"He must have someone else because it sure ain't me. I'm definitely not getting any bedroom action with Zeb."

"But you'd like to? Right?" She wasn't going to give up.

"It turns out he's a nice guy. That's all I'm saying." Vinnie attempted to end the conversation that was making him uncomfortable. He didn't want to talk about his boss behind his back no matter how perceptive Brigid was about his feelings for Zeb. He hadn't realized he was so obvious. Strange that she thought Zeb had the same feelings for him. Nah, if there was anything to the sexual tension between them, it was that Zeb was after a quick fumble and an even quicker 'so long and thanks, don't slam the door on your way out.'

Brigid let the subject drop. "The place looks amazing Vinnie. I'm sure I won't be the only one impressed with your work. Don't be surprised if you get a couple of calls next week."

"Why are you doing this, Brigid?"

"Because Zeb tells me you're a good man. I trust his judgment. And you do a bloody good job. I have a team of cleaners come in and they play havoc with my schedule and don't do half the quality that you've just done and they charge four times the price. Don't undervalue yourself Vinnie. You're good. Very good. And you're in a highly competitive market, so don't be modest either."

Vinnie could get used to having his ego stroked.

Just then the front door bell chimed.

"That'll be Zeb come to pick you up." Brigid went to the front door to let him in.

"All finished?" Zeb asked.

"You timed it perfectly. I was just telling Vinnie he shouldn't sell himself short. The place is immaculate. So much better than the lazy bludgers I normally use. Vinnie's a treasure. Hope he sticks around." Brigid retrieved an envelope from a side table and handed it to Vinnie. What was it with wealthy people? Didn't they like to handle actual cash? They always seemed to hide payment in an envelope as if the actual bank notes embarrassed them.

"Thanks, Brigid. I appreciate it."

She pecked him on the cheek.

Zeb helped Vinnie carry the cleaning gear to the car while Brigid called, "I hope to see you again real soon, Vinnie. And not just with a bucket and mop. You know what I mean." She laughed as she closed the front door.

Zeb was puzzled. "What does she mean by that?"

"Don't know," he lied. "She says some strange things sometimes."

They finished packing the gear, Vinnie careful, afraid he might damage the interior of Zeb's splendid car. The leather seats alone cost more than Vinnie could earn in a year. God knows how he'd pay for any clumsiness on his part although Zeb appeared totally unconcerned.

"Hop in, Vinnie."

Vinnie got into the car and buckled up. In no time Zeb had them speeding away from the wealthy enclave where Brigid and her husband resided and toward…

"You're going the wrong way," Vinnie pointed out.

"I have a surprise for you," Zeb said, a smirk of satisfaction on his face.

Vinnie loved surprises although there had been scant few in his life. He always found the anticipation was as exciting as the actual surprise itself, so he sat restlessly, his mind awhirl with speculation. Zeb merely looked self-satisfied that he'd been responsible for Vinnie's excitement although that paled significantly when they eventually reached their destination on the outskirts of the city in a rather rundown and ominous area that shuffled warehouses, abandoned houses commandeered by squatters and vagrants, and gas station mechanics like old well-thumbed playing cards.

"Here we are," Zeb said proudly as he pulled into the front apron of one such unprepossessing car repair shop. The sound of buzzing machinery and gruff voices shouting over the racket filtered from behind the closed front entrance. Zeb got out of the car and banged his fist on the shutter door as Vinnie joined him. The sounds subsided and a rough voice called "Who is it?" as if they might have been expecting a raid and were ready to make a bolt for it.

"It's Zeb. Open up."

The screeching clatter of a chain raising the rusty shutter made Vinnie wince. Soon enough the garage was open and he could see a handful of workers spray painting vehicles or making adjustments to motors, the usual sort of activity he associated with mechanics. What wasn't so usual was the woman who strode out and enveloped Zeb in a bear hug. "How are you, ya bastard?" she hollered. "Long time no see."

Zeb laughed. "Don't ever change, Vic."

"Not bloody likely at my age," she retorted.

Vinnie attempted to judge her years but was baffled by the shock of red hair that waved about her head like Medusa's snakes, her face painted with oil and grease and dirt, her figure hidden is sloppy paint-spattered overalls, and…

"This him then?" she said striding up to Vinnie, examining him like he was a specimen in a jar. He was intimidated by her even though she barely came up to his shoulder.

"That's him."

"He's a looker, I'll give you that." She walked behind him. "Great ass." Back to confront him face-to-face. "Seems like he's packin'." She grabbed his arm and squeezed his biceps. "Not bad. He'll do."

Zeb laughed. "Vinnie, this is Vicki, though no one calls her anything but Vic. Let me tell you, not many people get Vic's seal of approval. She must like you."

Vic was still sizing up Vinnie. "Don't believe everything he tells ya. He's a born bullshit artist. Anyone in advertising is. That's their business. But Zeb's more genuine than most. Ya can trust him."

"A recommendation like that is worth more than I can say. Thanks, Vic." Zeb was more sincere than Vinnie had ever heard before. "Is it ready?"

"Whadda ya think? If I say something will be ready it better be fuckin' ready or someone is gonna pay with their neck," she spat. "Hey, Rube, that van ready?"

"Yeah, Vic." A voice answered from deep in the building. "You want I should bring her out?"

"If ya would be so kind, princess. Owner's waitin'."

Zeb whispered to Vinnie. "Ruby is Vic's girlfriend. Been together over thirty years."

"More like thirty-five now," Vic shot back having heard every word. "Hearing like a bat." Proud as a peacock she still had her faculties.

With a sputter and a belch of acrid smoke, a van shuddered its way to the parking apron outside the building. Rube was a matching bookend to Vic. If owners eventually end up looking like their pets then the same rule applied to Rube and Vic. They could have passed as sisters.

Introductions complete, Rube went back to the job she was working on at the back of the garage.

"She's shy," Vic confessed. "Not really a people person. Prefers vehicles, especially trucks, to humans. I think she'd rather snuggle up to an eighteen-wheeler than me sometimes."

"Especially when you go telling lies about me like that," Rube shouted from the back of the work space.

"And her hearing's better than mine, curse it. I can't get away with nothing." Vic slapped the van. "Whadda ya think?" She looked to Vinnie for an opinion.

"It looks like a nice enough van," Vinnie ventured. He knew nothing about cars, trucks or anything on more than one wheel.

"No, dummy. The side, look at the side," she remonstrated.

Zeb was no help. He stood watching, scarcely containing his laughter.

She dragged Vinnie around to the side of the van. He gazed in awe, then checked it was real by looking over to Zeb who nodded in acknowledgment. "Is this for me?"

"Well I'd look pretty silly driving it, wouldn't I? I don't have your skills," Zeb said.

"Can I…may I touch it?" Vinnie asked.

"Go for it," Vic said.

Vinnie traced his fingers along the lettering. *Vinnie's Clean Start*. And his cartoon self beside it.

"It really does look like you," Vic said examining both Vinnie and his likeness.

"You've done an amazing job, Vic. Thanks, Rube. You're a true artist."

"Stop with the bullshit," Rube shouted. "It's me job."

While Zeb went back to the office with Vic, Vinnie examined the van more closely. Both sides advertised his cleaning service with his phone number large enough to be seen from a distance. He opened the rear door. Plenty of space for cleaning products and his buckets, brooms, mops and squeegees. He was gobsmacked it had already been kitted out.

The driver's cabin was comfortable. It seated two, three at squeeze, and Vinnie felt the pride of ownership as he sat behind the wheel. Then it hit him and he scrambled out, barely able to breathe. "I can't afford this, Zeb. It's too much," he said sadly as Zeb reappeared carrying a swag of papers. The shutter was lowered with the same accompanying squeal as when it opened.

"Do you like it, Vinnie?"

"Zeb, it's the best thing I've ever seen. But…but it's more than I can afford."

"Nonsense," Zeb replied. "It's all yours, Vinnie. And I've worked out a plan whereby you can pay it off over time."

"Zeb, let's be real. I don't have a job."

"What do you call working for me, if it's not a job."

"Okay, but that doesn't feel like a job."

"And you just did your first independent cleaning job for Brigid."

"Which you got for me," Vinnie protested.

Zeb brushed that aside. "Plus there'll be more jobs coming in all the time once Brigid's friends come on board. You'll pay it off in no time."

"Something will go wrong, Zeb. It always does." Vinnie was in pain just thinking about losing everything he'd gained since Zeb started helping him out.

"Not this time, Vinnie," Zeb said. "Not while you've got me at your back. It's all shooting for the stars now. So, how about we go celebrate?"

Did Vinnie dare to dream so big? Maybe just this once. Just for the evening. Tucking away his natural skepticism, he hopped into the van and followed Zeb back to his apartment. The van handled like a dream, but all he wanted was to stand and look at his name in big letters on the side with the cartoon version of himself that made him look so confident, so competent, so not-a-loser.

Vinnie was so emotional he couldn't bring himself to sit still in a fancy restaurant in celebration, so Zeb ordered in and they ate pizza and drank beer until Vinnie could no longer contain his gratitude. Launching himself at Zeb, the man he thought he hated, he had his mouth pasted on his, attempting to push his tongue inside Zeb's soft lips when he was pushed back.

Vinnie was utterly humiliated. He stood up to run from Zeb's apartment and never look back. But Zeb anticipated the move and grabbed Vinnie's arm, refusing to release it. "I'm sorry. I thought you liked me," Vinnie stuttered. "Brigid thought so too. Sorry."

"Nothing to be sorry for, Vinnie." Zeb was all kindness which broke Vinnie's heart even more. "I do like you which is why I would never take advantage of you in a situation like this. If we sleep together tonight I'll never know if it's real or if it's just gratitude for the help I've given you getting the van. You understand?"

Yes, Vinnie did. And much as he appreciated the thought and the kindness, it didn't make it any the less frustrating. He nodded his head.

Zeb patted Vinnie's shoulder affectionately. "And, Vinnie, I'm not the man you think I am."

THE NIGHT was getting on so Vinnie had only to subject himself to Zeb's pity, at least that's the way he saw it, for a short while before he could yawn theatrically and say his farewells. He again thanked Zeb profusely for the van which they'd discussed into the ground earlier that evening. Zeb ran rings around Vinnie explaining finances but even so, Vinnie believed he was getting much the better deal and that Zeb was carrying more than his share. Tonight wasn't the night to push it.

Once back in his van, Vinnie's spirits lifted and he almost believed it was the start of a wonderful new career. That was reinforced the following day when he received a phone call from one of Brigid's partygoers. Zeb had set a new ringtone for *Vinnie's Clean Start* on Vinnie's cell phone so he'd know to answer it professionally. It was a mixture of pride and embarrassment when he said the name of his business. He wondered how stupid it sounded to the caller.

"Oh, good," the female voice said, "I was hoping to catch you. I know it's Sunday and you're probably frightfully busy but I have an emergency. Are you available this afternoon by any chance? I'm happy to pay weekend rates as long as they're not exorbitant. I checked with Brigid and she said your Sunday rate is…" She quoted a fee that had Vinnie choking back a gasp of surprise. "Is that figure correct?" When Vinnie neither confirmed nor denied it – he was too flabbergasted to speak – she continued. "That's reasonable for three hours. That's all I need. Would you be able to squeeze me in?" She rattled off an address which Vinnie wrote down and they negotiated a time suitable to both of them. When he hung up he punched the air in excitement. He needed to tell someone but the only someone who would care would be Zeb.

Did he dare? Perhaps Zeb's confidence in him was not misplaced after all. Yes, he dared. The phone rang until it was picked up by Zeb's voicemail. Sure, he was disappointed not to speak to his mentor personally but he left a message into which he poured all his enthusiasm and gratitude.

Sometimes the gods were looking out for him.

At the appointed time he pulled up in his van – *his* van, he still had trouble believing it – outside the palatial residence of Mrs. Sarah Goodall, a woman of exquisite, if expensive, taste if the outside of her mansion was anything to go by. Once he'd rung the doorbell and had been ushered inside by a frazzled woman in her fifties, he discovered her taste was as outrageously costly inside as out.

It was easy money. Mrs. Goodall had a child whose ninth birthday party she'd hosted that morning and children being children there was a certain amount of foodstuffs adhering to the walls of the 'playroom', which was larger than Vinnie's entire apartment, and some small children's stomachs are just not accustomed to so much red soft drink or sugary sweets and that, too, marked the walls and spattered the floor. Mrs. Goodall seemed to approach the results of high spirits in the same manner a hiker does a venomous reptile. That meant she left Vinnie to his task and he could have completed it in next to no time but he realized he would be doing himself and his van repayments a disservice. Even so, after two hours of stretching out a one-hour job, he called it quits.

Mrs. Sarah Goodall, in a fever of disbelief that he'd completed the task to her satisfaction was even more staggered to find the playroom in better condition than it had been even before the party and that it was not going to cost her three hours even though she had agreed to that, but only two. Her astonishment was such that after Vinnie took his leave, she couldn't wait to get on the phone to Brigid first of all to thank her most kindly for the recommendation for 'such a polite young man and just the best cleaner she had ever come across', but also to boast to closer friends about the fabulous cleaning agency she herself had discovered and recommended most highly to their attention.

So it was that, even though Zeb did not return his call all week, and even though Vinnie dreamed about and used just about every waking moment to fantasize about Zeb, he was kept moderately busy fielding calls. After the first two enquiries he'd gone out to a stationary store to buy himself an invoice book, a day-to-day diary, and an accounts ledger. He needed to be methodical if he was going to make his business flourish and he was starting to think it just might.

Making some swift calculations from what he'd earned from Brigid, what Mrs. Goodall had quoted, and his enquiries at professional cleaning agencies, he drew up a rather comprehensive chart of his fees and charges taking into account transport costs, overheads, van repayments. etc. etc. etc. and then doubled it. Quite satisfied with the results he entered it into his computer and printed out a dozen copies. He'd keep the original for himself until he could memorize it.

Was it too soon for a website? – he didn't want the expense if the business tanked. He checked his finances because the first payment on the van was due shortly, plus he needed to ensure he had enough stock of cleaning agents for his new jobs. He felt good about himself. He would have felt even better had Zeb called. He'd kept him updated on the strides he'd made in the business via voicemail, careful to ask Zeb's opinion on a few matters that could wait. He kept Friday night free. Vinnie would be at the pub no matter what. He hoped Zeb would be too.

It was a long five days but eventually Vinnie arrived at the pub. He was early but all his mates were already there. Lenny was in fine form. "Look what the cat dragged in. Our company not good enough for you anymore, Vinnie?"

"Ignore him," Maurie said. "He's just a sad bastard. Been ingesting too many of his drug company's free samples."

"What happened to you last week?" Glenn asked.

"Zeb here?" Vinnie asked, glancing around the pub to see if he'd arrived.

"Getting our drinks. I'll tell him to get you one as well." Maurie wandered over to the bar to speak to Zeb who looked up and, on seeing Vinnie, nodded his head and smiled.

"You still haven't answered the question, Vinnie. What happened last week?" Glenn persisted.

"I had a job."

Lenny almost choked on his beer. "One-night wonder was it?" he asked sarcastically.

"Nope. I've had it for almost two months now. Usually a Saturday job but because I had a new job Saturday I had to do the regular on the Friday night." Vinnie spoke proudly, something his mates weren't used to. It seemed to rankle, particularly with Lenny.

"How come you never told us about this job before?" Lenny asked. "Or does it only exist in that head of yours?"

Before Vinnie could give back as good as he got, Maurie and Zeb returned with jugs of beer and a tray of glasses.

Suddenly Vinnie felt shy in Zeb's company. He watched him as he distributed the glasses and put the jugs of beer within reach of everyone at the table. Zeb looked up and met Vinnie's eyes. "I hear congratulations are in order, Vinnie. Didn't I tell you it would all work out?"

Vinnie was bursting. With joy, with pride, with… fuck it…with love. He was overwhelmed. "I couldn't have done it without you."

Their mates misinterpreted the mood. "Oh, no. You gonna start early on the snarky remarks?" Adrian moaned. "Can't you two just call a truce?"

"Why don't you do us all a favor, just kiss and make up already." Glenn pleaded.

Zeb and Vinnie stared at each other as if a bolt of some unseen force had zapped them both in that instant. They both stood and moved purposefully toward each other.

"Hey, guys, no violence. You'll get us banned," Adrian begged.

Zeb stopped and waited. When Vinnie reached him it did look remarkably like a violent outburst as he grabbed Zeb's head and pulled it to him so they locked lips with enough passion it would have stripped paint from the walls had they been able to harness it. They tussled for supremacy for a few moments before Zeb let him in, the frantic hunger turning to gentler longing.

They broke in order to breathe. "Wow, Vinnie. You sure know how to kiss." Zeb was panting.

"You're no slouch yourself." Vinnie hoped Zeb didn't twig he was adjusting himself because his hard-on was pushing against his tight jeans.

"What the fuck?" Lenny exploded.

"What was that we just witnessed?" Glenn asked while Adrian's mouth just hung open in surprise.

Vinnie turned to the group, his arm around Zeb's waist not only for comfort but for support because his legs were shaking. "Oh, didn't you just say we should kiss and make up."

"It's an expression, dummy." Lenny was determined to take no prisoners.

Zeb's arm shot out and grabbed Lenny by the shirtfront. "Perhaps you'd like to rephrase what you just said. You know, make it less insulting. Less, I don't know, less miserable bastard Lenny."

"Fuck you," Lenny spat.

"So spill. What's with you two?" Maurie asked.

"We found out we like each other," Vinnie said.

"Like each other or *really* like each other" Glenn asked.

Zeb and Vinnie looked at each other. Neither wanted to be the first to say it.

Glenn called it. "Okay, we get it. You really really like each other."

"I always knew you had your eye on his hot ass, Zeb. You tried to play it cool but I know competition when I see it. You wanted to be first to snag his cherry. Not that he's a virgin but he might as well be from what I've heard." Lenny was pissed as well as pissed off.

"Lenny, I think you should call it a night," Adrian suggested.

"Who gives a fuck what you think, dickhead." Lenny was loud in his belligerence. "If it hadn't been for you nelly queens and your sickening ideas of proper behavior we could have been fucking Vinnie's cute ass months ago. Coulda made him our bitch. Nah, you fuckers wanted to play fair. Now look who got in first. Mr. High and Mighty with a kink no one has been able to guess at it's so fuckin' horrible. If we'd followed through that time I put the Rohypnol in Vinnie's drink when he was depressed over yet another crappy job he lost we could have all been riding that ass of his. No, you wanted to put him in a cab and send him home. You don't understand, you gotta grab the opportunity when it presents itself. You're all a bunch of losers."

"You put a date rape drug in my drink?" Vinnie was magnificent in his fury. Even Zeb stood back to watch the fireworks.

"So what?" Lenny snarled. "From what I hear, conscious or unconscious, it's all the same when people fuck you."

Lenny didn't see it coming until it was too late. He staggered backwards and fell on his ass after Vinnie's fist connected with his nose, blood spurting everywhere, covering Lenny's shirt and trousers.

"You've broken my nose, you fuckin' little cunt." He attempted to stand but couldn't manage to get to his feet. Zeb was standing at the ready and security had already been called. After a quick consultation with the barman, the two swarthy bouncers dragged Lenny to his feet, escorting him to the door. "Time to go, mate. You might want to rethink about setting foot in this bar again for a very long time. Enough folk heard you say you spiked someone's drink. Doesn't go down too well with management here. Consider yourself lucky the cops weren't called."

Lenny's yelling and cursing could be heard as the doors to the bar closed behind him.

"That was some punch," Zeb said admiringly.

Vinnie had put his badly injured hand under his armpit in an attempt to stem the pain. Who knew fisting someone in the nose hurt so bad?

"You want to come back to my place," Zeb asked.

Vinnie smiled. "What do you think?"

Maurie, Glenn and Adrian were too stunned by the evening's escapades they just stared open-mouthed as Zeb and Vinnie headed to the car park.

"I didn't bring my car tonight because I was hoping a certain someone might turn up and offer me a lift," Zeb said.

"Oh, yeah. Anyone I know?"

"The cutest young guy you're ever likely to meet. He's smart, good-looking, built, seems to be hung like a horse, sweet ass, successful, has his own business. Sound familiar?"

Vinnie opened the passenger side of the van. "Get in before I do something stupid – I can't control myself when you're around."

Once Zeb was safely inside, Vinnie closed the door and went round to the driver's side. He couldn't believe his luck. His life had turned around in large part by the actions of the man who was in his van. He sent out a special thanks to whatever deity had smiled kindly on him as he started up and headed toward Zeb's apartment.

"I'm so proud of you, Vinnie," Zeb said once the journey was underway. "You stood up to Lenny, but most of all I'm proud of the way you handled yourself this week. I tried to keep away, didn't want to interfere, but all I could think about was how sweet you are. How much I missed you. How much I wanted to be with you." Zeb put his hand on Vinnie's leg and Vinnie covered it with his own hand.

The journey was both the longest and the shortest either of them had ever taken. They were keen to reach the privacy of Zeb's apartment but they also wanted to wallow in the feeling that their future was possible, that everything would lead to their happy ever after.

But once inside the front door, they both turned shy.

"You, um, want a coffee? A beer? A glass of wine?" Zeb offered as if he was going for Host of the Year.

"While those offers sound like a lot of fun, there's only one thing I want," Vinnie replied.

"What's that?"

"Your bedroom," Vinnie said.

Zeb needed no further invitation, grabbing Vinnie's hand he dragged him along the hallway to the bedroom. He turned on a bedside lamp which shed enough light to see but was dim enough to be lovingly atmospheric. Briefly,

Vinnie wondered how many men Zeb's bed had seen but he didn't want to know. This was now, not then.

Vinnie almost froze with anxiety. "What do we do now?"

Zeb tried humor. "People usually remove their clothes and get into bed."

"And after that?" Vinnie was close to freaking out.

"We let nature take its course." Zeb spoke soothingly and ran his hand over Vinnie's chest before slowly unbuttoning his shirt, shucking it off his shoulders to reveal Vinnie's impressive pecs. Zeb couldn't resist and licked the pert hard nipples, nipping them with his teeth until Vinnie's breath hissed in arousal.

Zeb sank to his knees and unzipped Vinnie, dragging his jeans down to reveal snug briefs that tented dangerously. Zeb ran his lips along the ridges of Vinnie's cock through the cotton until a small wet patch appeared where the pre-cum began to ooze. Vinnie kicked off his shoes and Zeb peeled the jeans off until Vinnie stood naked except for his tighty whities.

Zeb stood to undress slowly, Vinnie's pupils dilating as he watched each item removed until Zeb was totally naked, stroking his already hard cock in invitation. Vinnie quickly discarded his underwear as Zeb fumbled through the nightstand for condoms and lube before joining him under the sheet.

Zeb ran his hand seductively across Vinnie's chest, tweaking his nipples, working his way down his taut belly to the *pièce de résistance*, his thick hard cock. He went in for the kill, licking Vinnie's balls before working his way to the prick that barely fitted his mouth. But Zeb was experienced and knew how to suck a man's brain out through his cock. He would have but after a bit of perfunctory oral and a finger or two at the doorway to Vinnie's ass, Zeb asked for what he wanted.

"Suck me, Vinnie. Please."

Vinnie did his best but he was far from the jaded man-whore of Zeb's reputation. What he lacked in experience he made up for with enthusiasm. He loved sucking cock though he tended to gag if his partner was too aggressive, too forceful. Zeb held back as Vinnie tried valiantly. It was now or never. He grabbed Vinnie's hand and placed it as near as he could to his ass. He was grateful Vinnie was a fast learner and was soon prodding not one, but two fingers at his sphincter. "Hold on, Vinnie." Zeb grabbed the lube and squirted some onto Vinnie's fingers while, with his own hand, he massaged more lubrication into his hole.

"Now try it," Zeb said.

Vinnie concentrated on pleasuring Zeb, fascinated to watch as his fingers disappeared into Zeb's hot ass. He loved the feeling and wondered what it would be like to feel his cock gripped by such tight hot muscle. He'd never topped in his limited experience. Men looked at him as if he had Bottom tattooed on his forehead.

"That's it, Vinnie. Now add another finger. Oh, fuck, that feels so good." Zeb's body bucked as Vinnie picked up the pace thrusting in and out of Zeb's inviting ass. What was he waiting for? An invitation? Zeb's moaning was surely all he needed. For once, he'd take a chance. He kept up the penetration of Zeb's hot ass while leaning across to the nightstand to retrieve a condom, ripping open the foil pack with his teeth, and with more dexterity than he believed was possible managed to sheath his cock with one hand.

He withdrew his fingers wiping the excess lube on his condom-coated cock, gently lifted Zeb's legs, positioning them on his shoulders to give him direct access to Zeb's lube-shiny butthole. Vinnie positioned his cock at the entrance and pushed. There was little resistance, just a sigh of satisfaction from Zeb. Vinnie slid in with minimum effort and no apparent pain on Zeb's part. So, that was the secret. Sexual man-whore, Zeb, was actually an experienced power bottom in bed while to all outward appearance he was an aggressive top.

Vinnie could live with that. As he sank his cock into Zeb's ass he shivered that this felt so right. It was meant to be. He started slow, increased the speed and severity of the thrust until Zeb was begging for more. He leaned forward, prodding his tongue into Zeb's eager mouth as he slowed his thrusts because he was in danger of coming too soon. That would not have been a good move.

For a solid twenty minutes he pounded Zeb's willing ass until Zeb cried out that he needed to come. Vinnie had been there so many times but he was saving himself for the moment Zeb blew his load. Vinnie increased the friction careful to penetrate at the angle that had Zeb whimpering. With a mighty bellow Zeb spewed his spunk all over his chest without anyone touching his cock. The grip of clenching muscle around his own cock, had Vinnie grunting as he thrust wildly inside Zeb, filling the condom with his cum till he thought he would never stop.

Holding the end of the condom, Vinnie pulled out. He unsheathed, dropping the rubber beside the bed after tying off the end. "Fuck," he breathed heavily.

"That was amazing," Zeb sighed. "Your bad reputation is thoroughly undeserved. I'll make sure everyone knows."

"That's because guys always fuck me. They never let me top."

"You're a natural, Vinnie. And tops are in great demand."

"I don't want to be in great demand. Except by you." Vinnie admitted.

"Aw, Vinnie, what am I going to do with you?" Zeb asked wistfully.

Vinnie's response was enthusiastic. "Anything you want. Especially if you feel you might like to put my ass to good use later."

Blissfully exhausted, Vinnie spooned Zeb, a totally surprising position. "So, um, is your great secret that you're a power bottom not a top?" Vinnie asked.

"Yes, I am a power bottom, Vinnie, although I can flip flop as required. But that's not a secret although I doubt you've met many people who have boasted of sex with me."

"No one. You're quite mysterious. But you must have guys lining up to date you." Vinnie hated the twinge of jealousy he felt as he said it,

"Lining up, yes. To date me, no." Zeb turned to face Vinnie. "I guess you'll always wonder unless I tell you the great secret which is really not all that interesting but it does sort out the kind of guys I go for. Guys like you, Vinnie. I've liked you from the moment I first saw you and I just developed stronger feelings the more I got to know you."

"Why? I'm such a loser."

"You are no such thing, Vinnie. I never called you that. Not like the others. But you never took any notice of me so I started being sarcastic to you. It was a sort of defense mechanism. At least it meant you noticed me. It was a very unhealthy way to a relationship. I watched as you dated a series of assholes who treated you badly. I never expected you'd see me as a possibility until the perfect opportunity arose and I could offer you a job to clean my apartment. Full disclosure. I'm not nearly the untidy slob you think I am. I exaggerated so you wouldn't suspect I had an ulterior motive."

Vinnie pretended he was shocked. "So the secret is that you're really a neat freak. I can live with that."

"Afraid not. The fact is, Vinnie, I'm demisexual."

All sorts of weird and wonderful images passed through Vinnie's mind. Best get it out in the open. "I don't know what that is but I really like you and I want to help you work through it."

"Oh, Vinnie, you're such a breath of fresh air. A demisexual is someone who needs to care for someone, needs to love someone, before they can have sex with them."

"You mean…"

"Yes, Vinnie. I grew to love you. Even more so when we became good friends."

"Wow. Cause you know what? The more I got to know the real you, the more I liked you. Until, one day, I knew I was falling for you too. Is it okay if I'm a bit demisexual myself?"

"Okay, Vinnie, just this once. And Vinnie?"

"Zeb?"

"It's a good idea if you stay over on weekends when you clean my place, that way you save wear and tear on the van. Get an early start in case you have other jobs on a Saturday. What do you think?"

"I'd like that."

"Maybe, later, we could make it a more permanent arrangement. Or, you could just use the spare room."

"Nah," Vinnie said. "This bed is comfy. Besides, if I share your room you won't have the extra expense of another room for me to clean. Saves my time and your money."

"Makes sense. Good economics. And just maybe I can learn where you've put all my pots, pans, bowls, and spoons. I can't find a bloody thing anymore."

"That was my cunning plan. Make myself indispensable."

"Well it worked a treat." Zeb snuggled up against Vinnie. It felt so good.

"Um…Zeb?"

"Yes, Vinnie?"

"So, if you're demisexual, do you still like slamming your cock in some tight ass?"

"Yes, Vinnie. Why do you ask?"

"Cause a willing ass is a terrible thing to waste." Vinnie relaxed and handed Zeb a condom.

For the first time in his life, he wasn't worried about the future.

ABOUT THE AUTHOR

Naughty or nice? Sugar or Spice? Whatever way you like it, Barry Lowe writes M/M Romance and Erotica that's as addictive and satisfying as your morning cup of coffee. If you like it short and sweet with a happy ending then saucy romance is for you. But if you like a stronger brew with fetish, cuckold relationships, taboo, and all things steamy then try the Erotica – but watch out for the heat!

Go to https://www.facebook.com/barry.lowe.3591

ROMANCE BY BARRY LOWE

PLAYS

Available in eBook and Print

THE DEATH OF PETER PAN: Gay Historical Romance

NOVELS & ANTHOLOGIES

Available in eBook and Print

THE MAJOR AND THE MINER: Historical Gay Romance

ROMANCING THE BONE: Gay Romance Erotica

COCK-EYED OPTIMISTS: Gay Romance Erotica

BACHELOR BOY: Gay Romance

EVERYTHING'S COMING UP ROSES: Gay Romance

THE BI-WORD: Bi Romance

SELECTED SHORT FICTION

Available as eBooks

GEORGE AND THE CHRISTMAS DRAGON

HOMO FOR THE HOLIDAYS

LOVE WITH A SIDE ORDER OF PELICANS

CHRISTMAS IN JULY

HOW MUCH IS THAT DOGGIE IN THE WINDOW?

THE DAY OF THE CLIFFORDS

HE WON'T SEND ROSES

HARD ON HIS HEELS

THE NEW DAD'S CLUB

For all Barry's titles please visit his page at: lydianpress.com

Lydian Press is dedicated to bringing you the finest GLBTQ erotic
literature on the web.

Visit us on the web at:
http://lydianpress.com